KU-515-775

BLUES
FOR THE
PRINCE

Bart Spicer

NO EXIT PRESS

1989

No Exit Press
18 Coleswood Road
Harpenden, Herts AL5 1EQ

Copyright © 1950 Bart Spicer, renewed 1977

First published in U.K. 1951

British Library Cataloguing in Publication Data

Spicer, Bart 1918–
    Blues for the Prince – (No Exit Press Vintage Crime)
    I. Title
    813'.52[F]

ISBN 0 948353 47 3

9 8 7 6 5 4 3 2 1

Printed by William Collins, Glasgow

To

NANCY

CHAPTER ONE

MY TELEPHONE was making an angry clatter that I could hear from the hallway outside. Somehow I didn't much care whether I made it in time or not. I fumbled for my key, fishing it out of a pocketful of change, and coaxed the stiff lock open. The phone made one last nose-thumbing peal and then stopped. That was fine with me.

I stripped off my heavy overcoat and dropped it on a chair. The three letters lying on the floor under the mail drop looked like things that might call for some effort. I left them there and eased my battered body into my swivel seat. The room smelled dusty and too warm with the badger's den smell it gets when it has been closed for a long week end. I touched my fingers gently to the purple bruise under my left eye. It didn't feel very puffy now, but I knew it still had a lurid color.

In my day I've had my fair share of mouses, possibly even more than a fair cut. I never bragged about getting any of them. But the current shiner was a little embarrassing, even for me. I got it from the up-turned point of a ski. It takes a lot of doing to bang your skull on the tip of a ski when your feet are strapped to the center. Running into a tree is the best way to manage.

1

At least, that's how I managed. It had been a fair week end up to that moment, which came in the twilight on Friday afternoon. You might logically expect that a crack-up like that would dampen the sport, but it worked out fine for me. I had my bruises cooed over and I got the big chair by the fireplace and the first beaker of hot buttered rum. While a pack of healthy athletes were hi-yo-ing down the slopes, there was Wilde curled up with a long adoring blonde and a short hot noggin of grog to keep the fire going. It was the best week end I'd had in years and I was looking forward to more like it. A little experience like that makes a man appreciate winter sports. But such a week end is no preparation for sitting in a dusty office wondering whether a job would walk in and offer itself.

I looked around and my bruises began to ache more every minute. The office wasn't as bad as it had been when I first started out in this business after the war. Then I had been happy to have some furniture the building superintendent had salvaged and peddled to me for five bucks. I had some fairly respectable stuff now, but it wasn't anything special. I'd kept my old swivel chair, not from sentiment but to save the price of a new one. I had a pair of slightly peeling leather armchairs that wouldn't chase a customer away—if I could get a customer. My new desk was veneered wal-nut and it was nice and shiny, with seven drawers in good working order. Even as short a time as a year ago, the office would have seemed fine to me. But now I looked at it and thought of long low slopes of glittery snow with ski tracks criss crossing the whiteness, a chattery little fire, a pot of hot buttered rum and a blonde who said I was wonderful. The sight of the office made my head ache.

I pushed gingerly up from my chair and turned to crack open a window. A week end load of soot on the window sill blew through the room with a heavy blast of icy air. I let it blow for a moment and then slammed the window shut again.

I hung up my coat neatly on a new metal clothes rack and stooped slowly for the envelopes on the floor. I snagged the morning paper from my coat pocket on the return trip and made it safely back to my squeaky chair.

I watched the shadows of people pass my ground-glass door. A cut-rate law factory at the far end of the corridor did a lot of business with cheap divorces. The traffic was heavy sometimes, and Monday was always pretty good for them. I could understand that, if many people felt as grim as I did. I liked the lettering on my door panel. It still looked just as good as I thought it would. There was a little discreet "Investigations" about halfway down on the right side and my name above it in nice bold characters. From the other side, you could see the gold leaf on the letters, but from the inside, they were just black. My name was curved along the top, reading from inside, EDLIW YENRAC. For nearly a week after it was painted I saluted myself soberly as Ed Yenrac and I still plan to use it if I ever get a chance to pass a phony name.

I took one fast look at the envelopes and dropped them unopened into my top drawer. I don't particularly like getting bills and I especially don't like seeing them on Monday. I swung my legs up on the desk and spread

3

the morning paper across my knees. I read the first headline on the right side of the page and I felt worse right away.

The Prince was dead. He had been found in his studio with a bullet in his chest last Friday. He was murdered and the cops had his killer, a man I had never heard of, a guy named Magee who worked as arranger for him. It was sewed up and that was that. The Prince was dead.

It's hard to explain why the death of some men hits you so hard. Men you don't know, I mean. Just men who did their jobs well enough to make you feel that they had something in them that made the business of being a man a thing to be proud about, if that makes sense. Like when Roosevelt died. I was on a hot little island in the South Pacific then, a place called Morotai, and we were pretty busy, but somehow everyone went around quieter and sadder that day. The base newspaper printed a smudgy picture of him with a gray-black border around it and I've still got that picture somewhere. The Prince was like that. He was practically a legend and it would have been easy enough to accept the fact that he wasn't alive these days, but it didn't seem possible that he was suddenly dead.

The newspaper had a carry-over to page six, and page six was all The Prince. There was a four-column cut of him sitting in front of a white piano, big stocky body spilling over the bench and a wide, happy, cock-eyed grin that was just as gay and bright as his clothes. Drooping slightly from a corner of his mouth was one of his tan cigarettes. You may remember his cigarettes. The Prince was a chain smoker, and he was never seen without one of those extra-length, tan-paper cigarettes shoved in his mouth. He had them custom made originally, but about ten years ago a tobacco company put a brand on the market much like his. They were the same unusual length and the company called them "Prince-size" and wrapped them in the same shade of tan paper. He wouldn't be The Prince without that cigarette.

It was a good story the paper had. Chronologically, it traced him from his Western High School days in Chicago, when he was one of the first young hot men, and it carried him through to the end. It outlined his career from his first song; his first and, for my money, his best, *Red Devil Blues*, and wound up with a sketchy outline of his folk operetta, *Sunset in Harlem.* It probably left out a lot that the editor didn't think fitted in, or maybe just didn't know; but you got the flavor of the man and you got a quick glimpse of what it was that made him The Prince.

Harold Morton Prince he was born. In south-side Chicago after the first war, people began to find out how to make a kind of music that was more American than corn whisky or a covered wagon. A gang of high school kids seemed to lead the pack. They had a lot to learn and they worked hard, but most of all they had the feel, the instinctive beat of hot musicians. They and the people who played with them are legends now like Daniel Boone and Kit Carson. More real to me, because I could remember a little bit of it. I was just getting my first teeth when they hit their stride, but I'd seen some of it and I'd heard The Prince's music in my cradle.

There was a big bubbling in the melting pot in those days and in jazz music it was stewing at its fastest pace. About the time that King Oliver and Louis Armstrong and Jimmy Noone and Sidney Bechet came up from New Orleans to point the way with the Dixieland touch, there built up a keen rivalry. The Chicago kids, like Bix, McPartland, Long, Mezzrow, Teschmacher and The Prince developed a hard fast drive that brought them up with the Storyville musicians and when it all came to a peak, there was The Prince, sitting on top of the heap, wearing his crown cocked over one ear, puffing huge billows of tobacco smoke and flashing the broadest, happiest grin you ever saw.

I sat there looking at the picture of The Prince with his big brown hands poised lightly on the keyboard. He'd been cock of the walk for a long time in his racket. Long enough to graduate from cheap gin mills to Carnegie Hall with an American folk opera. He was really big time and he looked the part. He was The Prince.

The phone rang while I was reading and the sudden noise was startling in the quietness. I let the paper drop on my lap and caught the receiver just in time to keep it from ringing again. It was a woman's voice, a brisk, competent secretarial voice. She asked for Mr. Carney Wilde and I made the usual answer.

"You are a private investigator?" she asked crisply.

I looked up at the framed license bond hanging on the wall. "That's right," I said.

"I am calling for Doctor Lawrence Owens," she went on. "He would like to discuss a problem with you."

"Fine," I said. "What kind of a problem?"

6

"He didn't say," she answered firmly. "Will it be convenient for you to see him at eleven o'clock this morning?"

I delayed my answer just long enough to give the impression that I might be checking through my engagement calendar. But the answer was a clear, definite yes.

She gave me an address on South Gilmore Drive and I copied it down as carefully as if it were the password to Fort Knox. It had been just a little too long between jobs.

I assured her I would be there and she was willing to take my word for it. We said good-by and hung up.

The Prince's picture was staring up at me and I took another look before I dropped the paper. I remembered the first time I had seen him. It was in 1935, when I was eighteen. I had a brand-new roadster and a pair of white flannels that still smelled of Bailey's Department Store. I had six bucks, which bought me two tickets to the Lakeside Casino and left two dollars for feeding and pampering a girl I was mad for. I can't recall the girl and I don't remember much about the evening. I remember the feel of the chilly breeze on the veranda when we had worked up a heavy steam on the dance floor and I won't ever forget the way my new flannels hung ropily in the wind or the freezing feel of a starched collar that had gone limp and wet. But mostly I remember The Prince. He led his band from the piano and I wouldn't know if he was good or not. I mean, intellectually I wouldn't know. Maybe his kind of rightness makes a bubble in your brain that lets you know. I think it was mostly what he played, the songs you have whistled off key for the past twenty years, the

7

songs that made a big happy brown boy from South Chicago The Prince to every American with a sense of rhythm.

I pitched the paper onto the desk and swung my legs to the floor. The paper fell edgewise and split at the sports section. And there was The Prince again. It was a cartoon done by the fellow who specializes in spraddle-legged football players and worn-out horses. I guessed that all the syndicated weeping willies would have a piece on The Prince in that paper, but I let them go. I didn't need anyone to tell me about him. He was a great guy and he made a lot of sense to me. None of the great thinkers on the editorial page could change that.

I rammed the paper into the wastebasket and lifted down my overcoat. I had a date with Doctor Owens about a little matter and I meant to be on time. Or maybe a little early.

CHAPTER TWO

SOUTH GILMORE DRIVE is in the Walnut Hill section. Economically, it's hard to define. Once Walnut Hill had been a place to bring up children and there were still a lot of big handsome houses that had meant big handsome incomes. Now the district was spotty. Most of the large old houses were for sale. An electrical assembly plant had sprung up, and a dye works, a lumber yard and a streetcar marshaling yard. The sort of thing that reduced property values without really hurting anything much.

I took it easy driving out. The snow was still fairly heavy and banked against the sidewalks in dirty mounds. The asphalt streets looked safe until you dug through to the ice layer and then you were in trouble. I drove cautiously and promised myself I'd put on the chains damned soon.

I turned slowly into Gilmore Drive and spotted the number I wanted near the corner, a few doors from a white-tiled chain cafeteria. Number 1269 was a large frame house with a wide driveway along the side that led to a covered port. The entrance was marked "Ambulances Only" so I parked in the street and walked up the path to the door. From the street I could see a connecting passage that ran from the rear of the frame house to a large red brick building behind it. Over the brass-bound door was a sign that read CLINIC and beside the knob was another placard announcing the hours the clinic was open for trade. I noticed that eleven was the dead-line for the morning rush, so I expected I wouldn't have to wait to see Doctor Owens. I pushed open the door and went in.

The clinic was empty. The usual hard wooden benches were arranged in immovable rows, facing forward toward a desk where a brown-skinned woman sat stiffly in a nurse's uniform. The high mass of tidy gray hair under her white cap looked as rigid and formal as sculpture. Her high-bridged aquiline nose seemed to dare the world and wise brown eyes measured me carefully as I worked my way through the waiting room.

She raised her eyes and focused them tensely on my hat and waited for my manners to come back. I peeled the hat back with one hand and fished for a business card with the other.

"Is this Doctor Owens' place?" I asked.

She took the card from me and read it carefully. She nodded once and flipped a button on an annunciator box beside her. "Doctor Owens is expecting you," she said to me in the same competent voice I had heard earlier on the telephone. She spoke my name into the box and got an okay. She flipped the switch to "Off" and turned to point to the door behind her. "Through there, Mr. Wilde. It's the third door on the left."

I said thank you and went through. A white-painted hallway ran the length of the building and then curved off to the right to meet with that covered areaway I had noticed from outside. The doors leading from the hall were varnished wood swinging doors such as an old-fashioned saloon might have. They reached from eye level to within two feet of the floor. I found the third one on left and went in.

It was an examining room of some sort. It had the padded table, the strong fluorescent light, the rack of weird medieval medical devices that would frighten the healthiest man on earth. The usual smell of worn-out antiseptics and medications hung heavily in the air. A deep voice from an inner room called out, "Just one moment, Mr. Wilde."

I said okay and padded around the room, looking at the racks of bottles. A small sterilizer the size of a generous humidor was bubbling on a side table and I burned my finger testing it. After that I left the gadgets alone and looked out the window until my man was ready for me.

Doctor Owens was young, in his early thirties, tall enough, with soft black hair that hugged his head, and a handsome thin-lipped face. He was Negro and I wasn't expecting that. He held out a long-fingered hand that had the rounded spatulate tips that doctors are supposed to have and seldom do. We shook and he led me into his office.

He sat in a stiff chair facing his desk and waved me to the one beside him. I dropped my hat on the desk and started the conference.

"You have a chore for me, Doctor?"

He looked at me soberly and then slowly his mouth spread to a smile. I was sitting opposite the window and the light caught my face just right. "That's quite an eye, Mr. Wilde," he said.

I grinned back. "It'll teach me to stay away from skis, maybe," I said.

He laughed softly, a deep pleasant rumbling. "You have a novel alibi, at any rate, Mr. Wilde."

The laughter didn't stay with him. There was trouble in his eyes and it moved out and settled on his face. He reached down beside the desk and brought up the morning paper. "Have you seen this?" he asked. He pointed to the story on The Prince.

I said I had glanced at it. There was a little silence and then I said that it was hard news to take. He seemed to perk up then. He folded his long hands tightly and leaned toward me.

"I do have a problem, Mr. Wilde. And I think you might be able to help me. Do you know anything about

11

Mr. Prince?"

"Not really," I said. "Just his music."

He went into his shell again. He made a double fist with both long hands and stared down at it. I looked around the room and waited for him to go on. He had a nice office, rather small but I don't imagine a doctor needs much of an office. It held his desk, a few hard business chairs and a filing cabinet. And on the other side of the room toward the window was a butt-sprung easy chair with a reading lamp handy, a smoking stand and a cheap wooden bookcase crammed with those learned-looking pamphlets that all medics love to collect. He had the usual diplomas and citations hanging in frames against the plain white wall. I stared across the room at one that seemed familiar.

Owens coughed. "You can imagine what a blow this is to his family," he said vaguely. He eyed the newspaper again.

"Sure," I said. "It's a blow to me and I didn't even know him."

He cracked a thin smile at that. He took a deep breath and spoke rapidly. "I am engaged . . . or rather, I was engaged to Miss Martha Prince, his daughter." He ran into a full stop again.

He rubbed his hand over his face and I could see big veins standing out from the pressure. "Mr. Wilde," he said after a moment, "I'm not very knowledgeable about this sort of thing. I imagine a private investigator respects a confidence? I mean, even if he doesn't accept the assignment?"

"Yeah," I said. "Some of them, anyway. I guess it's pretty much the same with doctors. Every racket has its

12

bastards." I pulled out my cigarettes and offered one to him. I grinned over the match flame. "Anything this side of a murder confession, Doc. Anything else stays secret."

The tension eased gradually from his face and he relaxed. He took a deep drag at the cigarette and let the smoke dribble out slowly as he talked. "It's a difficult problem, Mr. Wilde. It's really a delicate matter. Lieutenant Grodnik recommended you to me when I spoke to him Saturday."

I nearly choked on that. I managed to hold it back. Cops don't make a point of throwing business to private men. You might say they don't care for what little competition they have. If Grodnik tossed me a bone, it wouldn't be strictly from love.

"It's like this," Owens went on. "The man who shot Mr. Prince, 'Stuff' Magee, was Mr. Prince's arranger and he also served as his secretary. But he claims he was more than that. When the police caught him, they found he had a brief case full of legal documents, affidavits and that sort of thing. All of them designed to prove that Magee and not Mr. Prince had written all that music."

I blew out smoke in a thin stream and felt a growing sickness. If The Prince was a phony, a lot of things would look sour. There would be the kind of stink that would build up a lot of newspaper circulation and tear down a lot of respect. I cleared my throat and tried to think of something to say. "This evidence," I mumbled. "What do you think? Is it solid?"

"No! Absolutely not! I don't believe a word of it. I think it's a fraud and a very clumsy one, too. But that isn't exactly why I called you. Now here is the situation:

"Magee and Mr. Prince had an argument and probably a fight in Mr. Prince's studio on Friday afternoon. Something must have alarmed Mr. Prince's father just about that time. He had been resting and he got up, knocked over his bedside table in his hurry and rushed into the studio. He collapsed when he saw his son lying there. The cook found them later and called me. It was a terrible shock for the old man. Not just because he saw his son lying dead, but when Magee left the house, he didn't bother closing the french windows. It was a freezing cold day and the old man was lying on those cold tiles for at least fifteen minutes. I got him to bed as soon as I could. He's been my patient for some years now, but his son's death has nearly killed him, too. He used to be very active for a man over seventy, but after he found Mr. Prince, he went into shock and I've felt impelled to keep him under constant sedation ever since. I mention this merely so you will understand why we have not yet been able to ask him what happened last Friday. Not that we can be sure he knows anything useful, but I still won't let the police question him for another day or so.

"However, the police have questioned the other people in the house and Lily, that's the cook, told them about the argument between Magee and Mr. Prince. She heard things crashing around and shortly after that, she saw Magee leave the house by the studio entrance. She didn't pay much attention to the noise, since Mr. Prince was rather a . . . volatile man. In fact, the servants seldom went into the studio when Mr. Prince was there. He didn't like to be disturbed. Only Lily would have dared to break the standing orders.

"Anyway, when the police heard about the fight, they went for Magee. I suppose Magee lost his head completely. In any event, he tried to get away and he very nearly made it. A policeman just barely saw him in time. Magee wouldn't stop when the officer shouted, so the officer threw his club at him. It was a lucky shot, I guess, but it works out rather badly for us. The club caught Magee behind the ear and he has a multiple concussion that may kill him.

"So, you see, no one can explain those papers Magee had. The police have them now and they can guess what they mean. We have kept the matter entirely secret. No one but Miss Prince and I and the police know about those papers in Magee's brief case. Except you, now."

Doctor Owens seemed to run out of steam after that. He fiddled with his cigarette and knocked off a spray of ash. I waited.

"Miss Prince believes it, I'm afraid," he said softly. "I think she really does." His voice sounded a little unbelieving, as if he would be able to change a fact if he just doubted it hard enough.

"You said you used to be engaged to her," I broke in. "Is that why she broke it off?"

He nodded silently. We smoked without speaking.

"She never approved of him very much," he said later. "She used to get a little stiff with me sometimes, because he was . . . well, he was a hero to me, I guess. When I was a boy, there weren't a great many Negroes who had made big successes. Just a few then." His eyes were looking far beyond the top of his desk toward a dark country I didn't know. I waited for him to come back. "He was rather flamboyant, you know. Large appetites for everything. A huge, vital sort of man. He wouldn't be easy to live with. He would be especially hard on his children, probably. At any rate, Martha said she wouldn't marry me. I think she feels she has been disgraced. She probably won't even take her scholarship . . ." His voice dwindled off again.

After a silent moment, I primed the pump. "Scholarship?"

Owens stirred himself with a brief shake. He looked up sharply. "Oh, uh, Martha won a scholarship to a music school in New York. She's supposed to enroll pretty soon now. She's a very fine pianist, too. People say she has a sure career if she doesn't let it slip away from her. In a way, the piano is something of a symbol to Martha. It was the instrument her father used most. I think she focused on it largely in order to compete with him. At first, I mean. Now it seems she has a very real talent."

"Okay," I said, just to be saying something. I didn't need all the extra personality bits and it looked as though I had all the facts that Owens knew. "I don't know whether I can do anything at all, Doctor. As I see it, knocking over the evidence that Magee has would be largely a legal problem and, too, it probably calls for more musical knowledge than I have. If the police suggested that you get a private man, that probably indicates that they just wanted to soothe you, or that they see some trouble ahead and don't want any part of it. I can certainly understand that. It'll be one hell of a smear when it comes out."

We eyed each other solemnly. He didn't say anything.

"I'm just one man," I said. "I can't actually do anything the police can't do. And usually they can do it better and faster, if they want to. I'm not turning it down, Doctor. I just want to make sure you know what you're up against. Hiring me comes a little steep and you probably won't want to go in for it unless you have a good idea what you're paying for."

"Thank you, Mr. Wilde," he said. "I appreciate your frankness. As you said earlier, it's something like medicine. We can't guarantee a cure, either. We just do the best we can with what we have, which in this case," he waved a hand to include the clinic, "is pitifully little. If you will undertake the job, Mr. Wilde, I'll be satisfied with what you are able to accomplish."

"It's a deal," I said readily. I shoved out my hand and we shook on it. He smiled suddenly.

"Good man," he said.

The annunciator came on abruptly with a snap. The receptionist's voice crackled thinly and stated that a Ward Three patient was doing something I didn't catch. But Owens caught it. He snapped, "Okay," into the box, bounced out of his seat like a high-board diver and threw a "Back in a minute," over his shoulder to me. He whipped out of the room and down the hall. I heard his feet drumming through the areaway in a fast sprint toward the hospital.

There wasn't going to be anything more for me until the patient in Ward Three stopped doing whatever he was doing.

I got up and wandered over to the window and stared down at the soiled snow lying along the street. It was dirty the way everything gets dirty in my town.

A familiar insigne on top of one of Owens' framed items near the window caught my eye and I bent over to read it. The top line was enough. It was the thank-you note that Ike had signed by the thousands for officers assigned to his headquarters units. I never thought I would ever get so far away from the war that I would just stare at that blue shield with the rainbow edging on top and wonder what was so familiar about it. The citation said good-by to First Lieutenant Lawrence E. Owens, Medical Corps and thanks for coming along, well done and cheerio. It made a nice decoration but hanging under it, almost hidden by a chair, was an item you don't see quite so often. It was a framed General Order citing the same lieutenant for valor and awarding him the Distinguished Service Cross. I didn't need to read through the citation to figure out whether he earned it. No First Lieutenant ever got a bauble that good without earning it the hardest way there is.

Owens returned a little more sedately, but still moving at a fast clip. He smiled briefly. "Sorry to run out like that, Mr. Wilde. It's my first patient in the hospital. I guess I'm a little nervous."

I grinned. "First patient? Haven't you had . . ."

His face went stiff again and he sat down at the desk without looking at me. "No, not my first patient, Mr. Wilde," he said in a flat tone. "I've been in practice for seven years now. I've had my share of patients." He waited for me to sit down. I sat and tried to guess what was bothering him. "It's all right, Mr. Wilde," he said softly. "The hospital doesn't take Negro patients. The clinic is for Negroes, but no more. Very few of the white patients in the hospital care to call upon a Negro doctor. This is my first one. I'm afraid I get a little . . . tense about it sometimes."

There wasn't anything for me to say. It's the kind of brick wall you come up against everywhere and my town is no exception. It's a hard thing to accept and it must be a damned sight worse to be on the receiving end. I cleared my throat and had a drag from my cigarette that tasted like alkali.

"Why the clinic?" I asked.

He shrugged. "Conscience, maybe," he said dully. "It's a good distance from the hospital. But let's get back to the subject. You say you will take the job. What are your fees?" His voice was brittle and businesslike. He didn't want any more hospital talk.

"Here again, it's a lot like medicine, Doctor," I said. "You can get the work done for almost any price you want to pay. This job looks like something that might run into money. I'll bill you for fifty dollars a day for myself and we'll argue about the expenses later."

"Well," he said hesitantly. "I suppose I could cover that. Could you give me any idea of what the expenses might be?"

I shook my head. "I don't know any way to anticipate, but just for myself, without hiring anyone to help me and not greasing any palms, I'd say it probably wouldn't go over ten a day. I'll check with you before I let you in for any unusual expenses."

He nodded thoughtfully. He pulled out the center drawer in his desk and brought up a flat checkbook. "I suppose you will want to see the documents the police are holding. Lieutenant Grodnik said he would let you

19

inspect them. If you can just prove they are fraudulent . . ." He scrawled across the face of a check blank, tore it from the book and handed the check to me.

"Let's leave the documents for a while," I said. I took the check from his hand and looked at it. He had made it out for one hundred and fifty dollars. "I may not need all this," I said, not believing it myself. I folded the check and tucked it down behind the handkerchief in my breast pocket. "I'm more interested in seeing The Prince's daughter. How old is she anyway?"

"Why . . . why, she's twenty, I think. Yes, that's right. Twenty. But what difference does it make?" he asked slowly.

"Look, Doctor," I said earnestly. "I don't want you to think I'm pointing the finger at her for anything. Just look at it like this: The Prince has been the biggest jazz composer in the country for twenty years. No one ever poked at that reputation before, so far as I know. Now all we have that tears it down is a mass of paper that might possibly be evidence. Even I find that hard to accept. And I never knew The Prince. When you tell me his daughter thinks he was a phony and she breaks off her normal life and goes all broody about it . . ." I spread my hands. "I want to see the girl, Doctor. First."

Owens rubbed his chin thoughtfully. "I never thought of it in that light," he said softly. "But she won't see us, I'm afraid. I'm not at all sure she will even let us in, but . . . yes, maybe she will. I'm still the old man's doctor. At least no one has told me I'm relieved. I would have to see him anyway. You could come with me and maybe we can find Martha then."

"That'll do," I said.

We stood and he lifted his overcoat from a rack and shrugged into it. "You have a car, Mr. Wilde?"

I nodded.

"That'll save a little time," he said. "If you'll give me a lift?"

"Glad to," I said. We went down the hall toward the reception room. Owens was wearing a heavy blue overcoat that had seen a good bit of wear but he carried it like a dancer with a long cape. He had a talent for clothes you don't see very often. Like Barrymore had. A flour sack and a piece of horse blanket and they look better than you and I would in Billy Foxx's best.

"Want to grab a sandwich first?" I asked. "I missed my breakfast this morning."

"Nothing around here, Mr. Wilde," he said gently. "I'll have Mr. Prince's cook get us some lunch."

"But there's a cafeteria . . ." And then I got it. Restaurants have the same sickness that hospitals have. "You call it, Doc," I said.

CHAPTER THREE

THE Prince's house wasn't what I expected. I was looking for something on the order of a duplex apartment, and the low sprawling fieldstone house Owens directed me to was more the thing you would build to raise a large family, rather than a place to write hot music. The house was on the edge of Seneca Park where we have our best homes, but it was discreetly on the edge. I was beginning to develop an eye for that sort of thing now.

A semicircular driveway curled from the street to the front door and continued to the street again. A spur took off around the side of the house, probably toward the garage. I pulled into the drive and up the spur, far enough along to keep from blocking traffic. The entire side of the house was one window with narrow fieldstone supports to hold it together. Heavy sea-green drapes shaded the windows I could see, a foam-green like the sea off Cape Cod in December. Owens and I crawled out of the car and walked to the front door. He leaned his thumb against the bell push and we waited.

The bell made a lonesome sound somewhere in the quiet house and then there was stillness again. Owens touched it lightly once more and said, "I'm glad to see the newspapers have let up on them. Reporters were living in the trees most of the week end. Two of the maids quit and the handyman hasn't been sober since. I guess old Lily is all by herself today."

The door opened silently and a round, well-fed woman with gray-black skin and tightly matted hair peered out cautiously. Her eyes widened at my livid black eye, but Owens reassured her.

"Hello, Lily," he said. "I've come to see Mr. Prince. How is he today?"

The woman widened the opening but she blocked the way diffidently. "Well, now I don't know, Doctor," she muttered.

"It's all right, Lily," he said soothingly. "I'm his doctor,

22

you know. He needs me."

"Yessir," she said. She smiled timidly. "That's right, Doctor. And he really ain't very good today."

She let us in then, closing the door softly behind us. "Miss Martha, she say not to let nobody in till she get home," Lily said, "but I don't 'magine she meant you." She beamed at the doctor.

He patted her wide shoulder. "I'm sure she didn't, Lily," he agreed. "Where did Miss Martha go?"

"I don't rightly know, Doctor. But she'll be back for lunch."

"That's good," Owens said heartily. "Now I want to see old Mr. Prince." He peeled off his coat and gave it to her. He held mine while I slid out of it. Lily staggered into a hall closet with the load. Owens headed toward a white double door and paused with his hand on the knob. "Oh, Lily, can you give us a sandwich or something in a few minutes?"

She grinned at him from the closet, made cupped hands and whispered, "We got fried chicken."

Owens winked soberly and turned the doorknob. He stood with the door open, waiting for me and said softly as I passed, "Better not smoke in here, Mr. Wilde. Old Mr. Prince has a toxic reaction to it." I nodded and we entered a high-ceilinged room, nearly bare except for an enormous bed.

The walls were covered with a pale gray silk, pasted flat. The far side of the room had a glass door that opened into what appeared to be a solarium that ran the length of the house. The same changeable green drapes hung over the door and windows, holding the room in deep shadow except for a tiny pink night light that glowed on a bedside table. The bed was the thing that caught your eye.

It was a four-poster tester bed made of heavy carved ebony. Ebony cherubim held up the corners and an unknown thing that was obviously female romped along the foot. The tester was a thick crimson satin, stretched taut to the snapping point toward each corner and held at the center by a gold medallion that was delicate and graceful enough to be a Cellini. It was a bed for Hollywood, a dainty, sneering dandy of a bed that looked just a trifle silly for the dignified figure that lay in it.

Owens walked softly to the bed and searched under the crimson spread for a wrist. The man in the bed lay perfectly motionless. He was nearly bald, with a few pale silver strands clinging vaguely to a domed golden skull. He was just that, a golden color. You got the idea that his teeth would be a good grade of ivory and he would very likely bleed rubies. The bed probably built the illusion. The bed and the dim pink light. The man's face was deeply lined and looked rather fragile, as though all the flesh had been fined down to the bare essential. His cheekbones were sharp and the golden skin stretched tightly to his jaw line and held deep erosions of age.

Owens straightened after a moment and whispered to me, "He's been under constant sedation since Friday, but I think he's coming along." He nodded toward the glass door and motioned me toward it.

We had made about two steps when the old man's eyes opened wide and he looked at me. The eyes stared closely and the pupils widened gradually to bring me into focus. They were large eyes, slightly protruding, with a luminous shine from the sedative. The old man didn't move. Owens froze still in place and I stayed where I was. The old man closed his eyes again and his mouth opened slightly. "Why didn't you duck?" he asked in a dim rumbling voice. His breath picked up the slow easy rhythm of sleep again. Owens tugged my sleeve and pulled me through the glass door into the long solarium.

"It works that way sometimes," he said softly. "Just a sort of flash consciousness now and again." He grinned at me. "You really best get that eye fixed, Mr. Wilde."

Then it dawned on me what the old man had meant. We choked over it for a moment, with Owens holding up a warning finger at his lips and making weird gobbling noises. We moved away from the bedroom, still gurgling.

Owens waved a hand widely when we were near the center of the studio. "Mr. Prince did most of his work here," he said simply.

I looked more closely then. The studio was about fifteen feet wide and it ran the length of the house, about sixty feet. Pale gray tiles covered the floor with a misty tone. There were three pianos spread around, all grand and all fancy. One made of the routine mahogany, with pearl inlays, another of a polished honey-colored wood and the other of redwood that glowed like a faraway fire in a dark forest.

Along the wall were racks of music reaching up about five feet from the floor and above them was a solid mass of pictures, theater programs, caricatures of The Prince and the usual sort of junk a man will collect during a busy life. Probably no more than thirty people could have been seated in the available chairs and couches, but if there were more present, there was plenty of room to sprawl on the tiled floor.

Every flat surface in the room had its ashtrays. The pianos were covered, the bookcases, the music racks. Some of them were simple crystal, but most were contorted and fanciful designs in ceramics and metals. From where I stood I could see more than thirty and among them were half a dozen cigarette boxes. It was the workroom of a chain smoker and you had no doubt about it.

The room was a roar of color. The bare Mexican colors of a woolen serape were there, the thin civilized tones of a Chinese shawl, the rich decadent smoothness of a Persian prayer rug and the too daring, too clever messes of a latter-day American decorator.

At the far end was a Capehart console with a few thousand records heaped around it. An enormous breakfront in dark oiled walnut was serving as a liquor cabinet. I could see at least twenty bottles behind the glass-fronted doors. All the bottles sported unbroken revenue stamps. The wide desk space in the center of the breakfront held a silver ice bucket and probably fifty assorted pieces of glassware. The studio looked like a hell of a fine place to throw a party and, from all reports, The Prince was a guy who could organize a wonderful binge.

I looked at Owens. He nodded morosely and his face was a sad and solemn mask. "He was one of the great men."

Owens leaned against the door leading to the dining room. He ushered me through and closed it. We skirted

26

around an elegant refectory table long enough for a bowling alley. He pushed back swinging doors and we went into the kitchen. Lily, the cook, was hunkered down in front of a black iron hotel range, peering into the oven. She straightened and wiped her forehead with the back of her hand.

"How is he, Doctor?" she asked anxiously.

"Looks fine," Owens said readily. "Has he been getting his medicine on schedule?"

Lily bobbed her head earnestly. "Yes, indeed, Doctor. Miss Martha give it to him just like you say."

"Good," he nodded. "I knew I could depend on you, Lily." He bent closer to her round dark face and squinted closely. "You don't look very fit today, Lily. Is your back acting up again?"

"Oh, nossir," she giggled. "I just got wore out fixing up everything. The house was a mess, I can tell you that, what with those policemens and all the reporter people and feeding everybody. The big studio was all cluttery with about a thousand cigarette butts where The Prince and that Magee rascal was fightin' and even the old master's room was messed up with that broken liquor bottle and all the medicine and the glasses and things broken, and then the shif'less, no-account servants all gabbin' round, not 'tending to they jobs." She shook her head angrily. "Makes a sight of work."

The telephone interrupted just as she was warming up. It rang distantly from the front of the house. Lily turned quickly and ran toward it.

After a long moment, I heard her call softly for Doctor Owens. He shrugged at me and followed Lily's trail along the central hall. For the time the door stood wide

I could see Lily standing in a recessed area in the hall, holding the telephone toward Owens. From the brisk tone of his voice, I guessed the hospital had tracked him down. That patient in Ward Three was probably up to something again. I walked out to the hall.

Owens said crisply, "I'll be there in fifteen minutes," and hung up. He snatched the phone up again and dialed a number, a simple number with lots of zeros that turned out to be the cab company. He gave his name and The Prince's address and told them to hurry. He put the phone down and turned to me.

"I'm sorry, Mr. Wilde. Apparently it's a busy day for me." He smiled at Lily and cancelled the lunch. "I have to get back right away," he said, "but you will probably want to go on into town to check with Mr. Grodnik on that matter. That's why I called the cab."

He was a little vague, but I gathered that he didn't feel Lily should know about my job. She was probably the house gossip. I said I did want to see Mr. Grodnik and agreed I'd best get going.

Lily hauled our hats and coats out of the closet and we bundled up. She said good-by to us at the door and went back toward the kitchen.

Outside, Owens said, "I'm sorry our idea didn't work, Mr. Wilde. Maybe we can arrange to see Martha later on today."

I started to say that I'd leave it to him when a long cream-colored Cadillac convertible swept up the drive and around to us. The driver passed the front door in a smooth rush and brought the car to a halt when the hood was even with Owens. The frosted window rolled down and a young girl shoved her head out. Anyone who had ever seen The Prince would have known who she was.

She had the same broad forehead, the same wide, deep jaw that seemed to hold more and bigger and whiter teeth than anyone else ever had. But in her glance there was little of The Prince's gaiety and certainly no warmth for us. She looked at Owens and waited for him to speak. He tried a smile that died without drawing a breath. Then he said, "Hello, Martha. This is Mr. Wilde."

His hand turned palm up in my direction and the girl's eyes followed it. She flicked a stiff glance at the mouse under my eye and looked quickly back at Owens with question marks in her eyebrows. "Yes?" she asked, as if surely there must be more than that to it.

Owens moved closer to her and bent down on a level with the car window. "May we speak to you for a moment, Martha? It's very important."

Her eyes regarded him blankly and she didn't answer. The door clicked open and Owens moved back to let her climb out. "No," she said with no expression. "No, I think not, Larry."

The far door of the Cadillac swung out and a man began to unwind from the seat. The unfolding process continued until about six-and-a-half feet of man was glowering at me over the roof of the car. One look at me was enough for him, too. That black eye was doing me a lot of no good.

Owens said, "Hello, Randolph," in a voice as chilly as the weather. He turned earnestly to the girl and began to speak when a taxi pulled into the driveway and stopped near the sidewalk. "That's my cab," Owens said hurriedly. "I have to get back to the hospital right away. Please talk to Mr. Wilde, Martha. Please."

He waited a moment and got no answer. His face broke into a warm smile at her indecision and he touched her cheek once, gently, with a long bare finger and whispered, "Bless you." Then he was gone in a flurry of snow and running legs toward the cab.

CHAPTER FOUR

THE girl and I were left facing each other. She stared at me with very little interest. The tall young man brought a dark and ugly face around the car and moved beside the girl. He stood a foot taller than the girl and a good three inches better then I could reach. His face was thin and strained, with a deep crease that ran to the jaw line from a point near his nose. The broad flattened nose gave his face an ominous cast and his eyes watched me warily. His face was young but his eyes were full of an ancient bitterness.

"Come in for a moment, Mr. Wilde," the girl said. "It's too cold to stand out here." Her voice was a little shaky, but that could have been from the coldness. She spun on her heel and walked ahead of me into the house. The tall young man kept pace carefully on my flank.

We went through the coat routine again with Lily, without anyone saying a word. Lily's fat old face was sorrowing and worried and she watched her mistress.

The drawing-room was a more standard affair than the studio. A pair of pebbly gray couches faced each other across the fireplace with a fancy custom-made coffee table between them. The room was a pleasant blur of cool gray and silver with an occasional flash of color. The girl went straight to the fireplace, stared into it for a moment and then turned, holding her chin high and proud with a fierce young pride.

"What did you want to see me about, Mr. Wilde?" she asked briskly.

I shrugged and fumbled for my cigarettes. I hung one in my mouth and fished out a light. I fanned the flame under my cigarette slowly, looking toward the tall young man who stood protectingly near the girl. She followed my eyes.

"This is Mr. Randolph Greene," she said. "You may speak in front of him."

I nodded to him. "I've heard of you," I said, in what I thought was a pleasant enough tone. I had heard of him. Most people in town had. He was a student editor on the newspaper at State College. About a month ago an association of newspaper publishers had offered him an award for college editorials and he had turned it down. He turned it down and wrote a piece of bombastic tripe accusing the publishers of cynicism, bad faith, poor race relations, and probably barratry, simony and not washing behind the ears. I hadn't read it all. The papers ran his picture and most of them printed his blast. Then for a few days, the good people said good things and the nasty people said nasty things and most people said nothing and felt he needed a kick in the pants. I agreed with most people.

Greene eyed me disdainfully for a silent moment. He permitted his tightly clamped mouth to open just a crack. "I've never heard of you," he said stiffly.

"Maybe that's because I don't shoot off my yap so much," I suggested.

The crease deepened in his thin cheek and his voice lost its light airy tone. "You think I should bow and say 'Sir' when you speak to me, Mister Wilde?" He made the "Mister" sound like a dirty word. He had the kind of voice and the expression that made you want to slam him merely for saying "Hello."

I moved my feet slowly and came toward him. The girl broke her tight composure. She stepped swiftly to his side and swept an arm in front of Greene. I guessed that was to keep me from making a scene.

"Please wait for me in the library, Randolph," she said in a wavering voice. She kept one eye on me. "Please," she insisted.

There was stillness for a few minutes. Greene stirred. He needed a little time to get his biting phrases well in mind. "You needn't put up with him, you know, Martha. I can throw him out for you."

The girl wasn't impressed with the offer. If anything, she became more worried. I leaned my hip against a radio cabinet and looked at him. He was tall, with a long reach, but he wouldn't weigh much more than one-fifty with his overcoat on. His temper was giving him delusions.

I grinned at him. "You don't have meat enough to make it stick, sonny."

His eyes glared hotly and the girl grabbed his arm tightly. Her mouth quivered and she blinked rapidly to keep the tears back. "Please, Randolph," she pleaded.

He drilled hot holes in me with his eyes. Any minute now I would melt and run out through the cracks in the floor. "The great white god speaks," he sneered.

"Run along, sonny," I said. "As soon as the grownups are finished you can come in and recite your piece." I'd had about all of Mr. Greene I wanted. I felt sorry for the Prince girl. A happy companion like him would hardly be restful. But I have a notion that any guy who looks for a fight should find it fast. It makes for a peaceful world that way.

Greene didn't care for my language, but he couldn't seem to decide what to do about it. He leaned against the girl's pressure and stood rooted. I tried to help him decide. "You don't have to work this hard for a fight, Greene. Just hang around till we're through here and I'll see what I can do for you."

The girl grabbed him hard then. She threw all her weight on his arm and pulled him off balance toward a side door. She kept up a soothing patter as she opened the library door and pushed him through it. He didn't offer much of a tussle. Just about the amount a tough talker makes when he finds he can get away without a fight. She closed the library door and leaned against it briefly, putting her forehead lightly against the cool enamel as though it relieved some pain. She turned and took up her staunch pose on the hearth again, struggling for poise and making a good job of it.

"I'm sorry, Miss Prince," I said quietly.

She tried to shrug but it didn't come off very well. She sat in the corner of the gray couch and folded her hands tensely in her lap. Her fingers were long and broad, rather large-knuckled and strong. They trembled slightly. "Randolph is a little . . ."

"Yes," I agreed. I sat in the couch opposite her and leaned forward, holding out my cigarettes. She shook her head.

She smiled wanly and asked. "Now what is it all about, Mr. Wilde? What did Larry want you to do?"

I settled back in the couch. She sat squarely with her shoulders straining tensely against her locked hands. I spoke to her gently.

"It's about your father's death, Miss Prince," I said. "Doctor Owens feels that you might need help."

She looked puzzled. Her pale forehead wrinkled slightly and she cocked one eyebrow at me. "Oh?" she asked absently. "Just what are you, Mr. Wilde? A lawyer?"

"Licensed private investigator, Miss Prince," I said.

She nodded. "And how could you help me?" There was no note of challenge in her voice. It wasn't a dare. She wanted merely to know what good I could possibly be to her.

I leaned forward again. "When your father was killed last Friday, the police found some documents on his killer. That's what Doctor Owens told me. Those documents have not been authenticated. As I get it, Owens thinks that finding those papers, on top of your father's death, has been a sizable shock for you to stand up under. He thought you might feel a little better if I could find out the truth about those documents."

She looked down at her clenched hands and murmured softly, almost to herself, "I think I do know the truth about them."

34

Her meaning was obvious, even to me, but I wanted to hear her say it. "You really believe The Prince was a phony?"

Her eyes sharpened at that and her body tensed. Then she broke the tension and her eyes went blank with the blankness of self-doubt. Her long fingers swept back hair from her temples and she pressed them against her head in a movement that was painful to watch.

"I . . . I don't know . . ." she said hoarsely. "I . . ."

The tears came then. The racking sobs that take the edge from fear and pain. Her head lay hard against the back of the couch and tears rolled down her face through her fingers. I made an elaborate ceremony of snuffing out my cigarette and lighting another. I kept my eyes on the coffee table.

She brought herself back under control in a few minutes. It was a nice thing to watch. She let the tears run themselves out, the way a really fine horseman will exercise a young horse. But when the first storm was over, she put on a touch of pressure, just enough to show who was in command. Another brief moment and her handkerchief was removing the stains. Only her breathing was still wobbly.

"I'm sorry about this exhibition, Mr. Wilde," she gulped. "It's been nightmarish lately."

I nodded my head in case she was watching. I sat quietly and waited.

"I'll have one of your cigarettes now, if I may," she said crisply.

The handkerchief was out of sight as I stretched forward with my pack. Her eyes glistened sharply in the brief light from the match, but her lips were firm as they closed around the cigarette and inhaled deeply.

"Since Larry has told you of Magee's papers, I suppose he also told you that our engagement has been broken?" She watched me carefully, as if my answer would mean something important to her.

"Only to explain his interest in The Prince's death," I said casually. "I guess he is considerably more concerned about you than he is about the papers."

"He needn't be," she said stiffly. "This news about my father is hardly the shock he thinks it is."

"What?" I choked on cigarette smoke. "You mean it's true?"

She looked up at me with heavy young scorn. "Apparently you think my father was an outstanding man of character and ability, as so many people do. He wasn't. He wasn't anything like that." Her voice rose higher and it took on a shrill tone.

"My father was a cheap loud man with bad taste. He had a glib superficial ability with popular jingles that people seemed to like. He was a primitive in his music, just as he was in his life. And his primitive, intemperate habits made my mother leave him and probably caused her death." She ground out her cigarette viciously and glared at me. "I don't know whether Magee's claim is true or not. And I don't care. I wouldn't lift a finger to protect my father's reputation. I don't care. I . . . just . . . don't care."

The tears rolled again. Hot bitter tears that had their meaning in ancient sorrows I couldn't even guess at. I got up and walked around the room for a moment. I stopped near a glassed-in cabinet set in the wall behind her. She was bent forward, shading her face.

I made my voice come softly, normally. "This is a little out of my line, Miss Prince, but the man was your father . . ."

"Don't try to tell me about him," she broke in angrily. "He was cheap. He wrote cheap music. Little slave songs about a slave's sorrows. He didn't have any feeling for his race and he didn't have any feeling for his music. If it was his music." Her words fell quickly, thoroughly mixed with tears.

"I can't argue music, Miss Prince," I said. "Not in your league, anyway. I don't know that much about it. I'm one of the people who thought The Prince was great. The world's full of people who still think so." I took a deep drag at my cigarette and blew smoke at the glass panels hard enough to smash them.

She raised her head and stared bitterly at me. She shrugged silently and in the movement, I could notice how very young she was, and how bewildered. "It doesn't matter, Mr. Wilde," she said dully. "It doesn't matter. I know he was a lecher, a drunkard. He might have been a fraud as well. It doesn't matter."

"Will you defend a suit if Magee brings one?"

She blinked. Her mind turned away the ready acceptance of her father's fraud. Thoughts moved slowly and strongly behind her eyes. "Yes," she said after a quiet moment. "Yes, I suppose so. Grandfather and I need the money, so . . ."

"Yeah, sure," I said sourly. I had a lot of questions I wanted to ask, but I didn't think she would tell me the answers, even if she knew them. There could be sound reasons for the juvenile hysteria, but just then I didn't like Miss Martha Prince enough to give a damn what the reasons were.

"Thank you, Miss Prince," I said tightly. "If I find out anything you can use, I'll let you know." I walked to the coffee table and punched my cigarette at the ashtray. I looked at her. Her face was a hard, composed mask, a pale amber decoration you could hang on the wall, stiff and formalized.

"Then you are going ahead . . ." she began.

It was my turn to curl a lip. "You'd like to win that suit, wouldn't you?" I asked nastily. I turned and pointed a thumb toward the library door. "I don't imagine Laughing Boy wanted to do anything but talk, do you?"

Her composure didn't break. We let the silence build up and neither of us seemed to have anything more to say. I moved over to the hall door and muttered, "Good-by."

The room was still as I closed the door and the house was still as I got my hat and coat from the hall closet. I looked toward the bedroom while I struggled with my coat. Just a few feet away an old man lay, barely breathing, just waiting for death. I was willing to bet that he had more life and warmth than his grand-daughter just then and neither of them seemed to have much of The Prince's quality, not that I could see. The door to the old man's room opened softly while I looked at it. Randolph Greene backed out quietly with an empty water glass in one large fist.

His face was bland, composed, until he saw me. Then the familiar sneer leaped to his mouth and eyes. It was probably habitual by now.

"Don't bother to come back," he said briskly. "Just close the door silently—behind you."

38

"I'll be back, sonny, but don't wait up for me." I pulled on my hat just in case I should want both hands free.

"There will be no further interference from you," Greene said haughtily. "You're through."

I grinned at him. "Better check with the grownups first, sonny. You may find some changes."

Greene's long fingers tensed on the glass and he glared hotly at me as I pulled the outer door open and went through.

CHAPTER FIVE

I PARKED my car in the usual slot near my office building. From there, it's a few short blocks to City Hall. I decided to walk and I regretted my decision as soon as I crossed the street. The average city will get the snow banked up and cleared away within a few days after it falls. Ours had been lying around for the past week and there were still narrow pedestrian lanes carved through the snowbanks at the corners and gutters running over with filthy slush that refroze every night. I waded through a six-inch-deep pool in front of City Hall and cussed the City Fathers and their fathers before them.

I climbed the high steps into the Hall and turned right just before I reached the grimy statue of blind Justice standing huge under the smirched glass of the rotunda.

Detective-Lieutenant Grodnik had a roomy outside office with a fine view of the square. Some time ago I had thought the Annex office came to him because he had a bright young partner whose father made brick for the city. That was in the days when I was fooled by Grodnik's appearance and behavior. He cultivated his placid pose of an indolent fat man, I thought, with little interest beyond the next meal and the day he could retire. The state penitentiary had a club of long-term inmates who had once believed it, too.

Grodnik's room was 236, between the Assistant Fire Commissioner and a room marked only PRIVATE. I knocked twice and went in.

Nothing had changed since my last visit. The furniture was just city furniture. Nothing special. Dark wood desks with cigarette burns scalloping the marred tops, a clothes rack, several nondescript chairs, a police radio fastened to the wall above the windows. Grodnik was alone in the office, balanced precariously back in his swivel chair, with his large shoes on the window sill, his heavy, round, dew-lapped face brooding out the window toward the public square. He didn't turn when I let the door close behind me.

On my way to the desk, I slid a chair toward him and sat. I dropped my hat over his telephone and unbuttoned my heavy coat. Grodnik could see my feet within his circle of vision, but he was in no hurry to investigate.

His tweed trousers were shoved halfway up his thick calves displaying black wool socks, Yukon weight, and a pair of black half-boots that any ex-mailman would respect. A pair of black metal-buckled northwoods overshoes lay carelessly in one corner with a thick woolen muffler coiled around them.

Grodnik swiveled his head placidly just far enough to see me. "Hello, Wilde," he said slowly. "You take the job?" He let his shoes slide back to the floor with a light plop and turned to face the desk. He leaned back again with elaborate ease. From the front he seemed to have no hair at all. What there was lay curled in a tight ring between his huge ears. His eyes were the point you always remembered. They were a soft tan with little dark flecks in them. They were serene and restful, the eyes of a man at peace with himself, a man of sedate intentions. The eyes were liars, but the placid appearance was useful to Grodnik.

I smiled thinly at him. "Maybe," I said. "Owens tells me you'll let me go over those documents Magee had with him."

Grodnik nodded. His gaze focused on my black eye and his button mouth twitched. "Swinging door, I suppose?" he asked mildly. He pushed a pack of cigarettes toward me.

"Or a swinging blonde," I said. "I forget which." I held out a match for his cigarette and then lit my own. I looked across the room at the empty desk next to Grodnik's. It was completely bare with a faint sifting of dust evenly across the top. I blew a streamer of smoke toward it. "Lost your partner?" I asked.

Grodnik stared blandly. His voice became very, very gentle. That was a bad sign, I knew. "Something clever in mind, Mr. Wilde?" he purred.

I spread my hands in wide innocence. "So help me, Lieutenant," I said, "I was merely curious about Henley.

Cute little fellow."

"He went back to the Air Force for a rest," Grodnik said sourly. "I thought you were slipping me the business because of Barton." His kindly eyes were still thoughtful.

"Never heard of him," I insisted. "He your new partner?"

"Just let it go, Wilde," Grodnik said. "Barton's suspended for a little trouble with the Commissioner. I draw all the dogs. Let's talk about The Prince instead."

"That's why I'm here."

"Okay. You get filled in on it?" he asked mildly.

I grinned at him. "Not when you ask it like that," I said. "I know a little. Not much. Maybe you better tell me the story."

Grodnik offered me the thin edge of a smile. He brought his thick arms up and locked them behind his bald head. "It's really ticklish," he said. "I nearly stopped breathing till we got that Magee. It took us just about thirty minutes to find him, but I got gray hairs waiting."

"How come?"

He lifted his shoulders lightly. "Just that he was The Prince, that's all. He was big league. If we didn't have his killer, the newspapers would get some scalps. Mine first."

I grinned silently.

"The Prince was too big. He meant a lot to the public. We really needed that boy Magee."

"No doubt he did it, I suppose?"

Grodnik eyed me grimly. Just for that moment his spurious gentleness left him. He looked all cop and all tough. "You aren't getting another clever idea, are you?"

42

he asked tightly.

"Relax, Lieutenant. Just an honest question."

His eyes were still full of fight, but he let it ride. "Get it straight right now, Wilde. Magee is the one. You can't play with it and don't even try. Get that?"

"Sure," I said agreeably. "He still in that coma?"

Grodnik grunted. "Okay. You're a smart boy, Wilde. I see what you mean. I don't mind saying I'll feel a lot happier when I get a statement from him."

He brought his arms down and reached for the telephone. When the operator came on the line, Grodnik said, "Sergeant Goldstein." He waited for his connection. "Lieutenant Grodnik. Get me Number 73, Goldstein. It's a sealed package. Send it up." He returned the receiver to its cradle and looked up at me. "You can do a job with those papers, if you want to," he said firmly. "That's all though. The murder is closed."

"You don't have to drive it down my throat," I complained. "It's your baby. But I need some information about it. Especially about Magee."

Grodnik bobbed his head. "Sure," he said. "You'll get it. Magee is out of the coma, but the medics won't let us in yet. He's still dopey and they're afraid he might kick off if we try to put the question to him. Be another day or so before we get the full story."

"He must have got an awful wallop."

Grodnik smiled faintly. "Damned good throw. Might say it kept my job for me. If Magee had made it down that alley, I'd be in a real jam. As it is, I got plenty of trouble from the do-gooders."

"Huh?"

"Oh, just the usual howls. Every time you bring in

a prisoner who got a little roughed up, somebody yells about police brutality. And then there was the racial angle." Grodnik waved an expressive hand. "Good thing for us Connolly is a Negro."

"He the cop that tagged Magee?"

"Yeah. Used to be a semi-pro pitcher." Grodnik's round face split in a wide happy grin. "He really burned that baton down the groove. Like to split Magee's skull. Was he a white man, we'd probably have to bust him down and send him out to guard the drinking fountains in Fairview Park. As it is, we give him a commendation, maybe even a promotion, and everybody's happy."

The door behind me opened. A slim young uniformed policeman waited for Grodnik's permission to enter. He put a bulky package wrapped in brown paper on Grodnik's desk. He left without speaking. Grodnik shoved the package toward me and lifted a thin sheaf of clipped together flimsies from his desk. "Go ahead," he said. "You can't take them out, but I'll get you some photostats if you need them."

I broke the police seal from the package and stripped off the paper. Most of the bulk was a thin leather brief case. The hasp had been broken loose and I turned back the flap and pulled out the documents.

It took me about twenty minutes to skim through them. Sixteen sheets of laid-finish bond held the story. Magee based his claim of ownership on two songs especially. According to an outline attached, he rested his claim on those two, because he could get more solid proof that he had written them. He insisted, however, that he had written almost all The Prince's songs. The list was long and impressive. It included *Red Devil*

44

Blues, Man With a Whip, Forty Days Till I Go Home, Pedigreed Poodle, Cross-My-Heart Blues, Early Morning Blues, Glory Land, Recitation In a County Jail, Still Water Blues, Beginner-Brown Blues, The Star Pointing North and quite a stack of others I wasn't so familiar with.

The first song Magee claimed was *Red Devil Blues*. That one Magee said he had composed in 1916 and he claimed he had let The Prince pose as author because The Prince had enough local influence in Chicago to get it published. The song had been published first in 1917 under The Prince's name. Magee offered brittle yellow sheets which he claimed were first drafts of the song and clipped to them was an affidavit from a woman named Arabella Joslin, living at a Chicago address. The Joslin woman stated that she had heard the song early in 1916 and that she had been living with Magee when he was working on it.

The second song Magee claimed was *Glory Land,* that wonderful job that brings down the second act curtain in The Prince's opera, *Sunset In Harlem.* I'll never forget that high winding trumpet introduction that starts it off. Every note is played full and true in big rich tones with a powerful drive. Magee had the same setup for that one. The same Arabella Joslin affirmed and duly stated that she had been present when Magee wrote it, that it was written for her and that she had the original draft which she had kept as a souvenir. The original was attached and Magee had added a note explaining where he had made a few changes before using it in *Sunset In Harlem.*

The documents added up to a fairly sensible claim.

The language looked legal enough. The story was fairly clear. As Magee explained it, he and The Prince had set up the fraudulent arrangement because The Prince was a fine front man and a fair musician, while Magee did not have a personality for show business and did not play very well. Magee claimed that he had always worked for The Prince as his arranger, just as a cover-up while he actually did all the work. He also said that he was making his claim now, not because of any disagreement, but because he knew The Prince was seriously ill and might die any time and then the deal would be off and Magee would be out in the cold with nothing but his talent to keep him warm. If you believed it, Magee had a sorrowful tale to tell.

The last page was a notarized declaration by William L. Magee, sometimes known as "Stuff," in which he stated that he was the sole composer of some fifty-six songs that had been published under The Prince's name. He listed the songs by title and they were all the best things The Prince had ever done. Magee swore they were his own work, but he based his entire claim for compensation on the basis of *Red Devil Blues* and *Glory Land*, because he could furnish an independent, disinterested witness to substantiate his claim.

I folded the papers together in their proper order and slid them into a manila folder. I put the folder back in the brief case and dropped it on Grodnik's desk. He looked up with one bushy eyebrow cocked.

"What do you think?" he asked.

I shrugged. "Just what you think, Lieutenant. Magee's got a case that means practically nothing, except that he has just barely enough to get into court. I don't think it would be thrown out, but any good lawyer should be able to knock it over without too much trouble. It all stinks, for my money."

Grodnik nodded. "Probably," he said easily. "Got nuisance value, I guess. Some of the dirt would stick probably. Can't see much more to it."

"It could be a hell of a mess for The Prince's family."

"Maybe." Grodnik tapped a broad fleshy finger on the package. "Let's say everything in here is just as honest as a six-dollar bill. It wouldn't be hard for Magee to get this stuff. It all hinges on that one woman. And, anyway, maybe Magee was the first one who actually wrote them down. Nothing there proves to me that The Prince didn't do the composing. So let's say this Magee gets his stuff together and he gets this woman to come in with him for a split of the take. Then he goes over to The Prince and makes his pitch. A few grand and The Prince gets the papers. Otherwise . . ." Grodnik watched me for a reaction.

I nodded. "Maybe."

"Maybe, hell," he said placidly. "Don't go cute on it, Wilde. That explains the papers. Pretty crude blackmail. That explains the papers and it explains the fight and it explains why Magee killed The Prince. It also solves the problem that seems to be bothering your client."

"You're right there," I agreed. I sat silently and thought about it. I looked toward Grodnik. "You haven't any doubts about that fight between Magee and The Prince? You're sure it happened?"

"That part's okay," Grodnik said. "That cook out at The Prince's house heard most of it. No talking, but a lot of noise. The Prince probably jumped Magee when he saw those papers and Magee had to kill him to get away. The Prince was a pretty impulsive guy, you know."

"So is his daughter," I said absently. "I think she has convinced herself The Prince was a hard-working phony."

Grodnik rubbed his chin thoughtfully. "That's a hard one to figure, all right," he admitted. "But then, from what I gather, she was pretty well down on her old man all the way. I guess she would believe anything, provided it was bad enough."

"What's the background on that?" I asked. "What kind of a beef would she have? From where I sit, the setup looks pretty soft."

Grodnik shrugged heavily. "Neither of us can judge how cozy it would be for her. She's a lot like her father. It might have been a little tough to sit back and take a free ride. Apparently she's got the makings herself. And nobody knows how hard it would be to put up with The Prince on a rampage."

"What does that mean?"

"Well, I guess there's no secret about it. We've tried to give him the breaks and we've had to stretch quite a few regulations to make it. Nothing bad, I don't mean. Just drunken scrapes. He was a hard man on a bottle. The downtown boys all knew him and they would try to ease him toward his house. I don't guess he was any better there though. His local precinct has a list of calls a foot long. All from his daughter. They've had to go out and quiet him down pretty often. Tough job, too. Took a heavy sedative to do the job. They usually just

48

called his doctor and took him along."

I whistled softly. "The things I don't know. I always thought he was a very quiet guy except when he got in front of a band."

"Well, dammit, he was," Grodnik insisted. "Never met a nicer fellow. He always came to play at the Policemen's Ball. For free, too. Just once in a while he'd go on a bat and he went pretty queer then. Yelling around and banging his fist against the wall. Watching him probably put the girl on the wagon. Nobody else in the house drinks. Come to think of it, he was loaded with liquor when he was killed, the medic says. Probably explains the fight with Magee. But he damned seldom got in a fight." Grodnik's sleepy tan eyes were sharp and keen now. He nodded forcefully at me. "He was a damned nuisance sometimes, but I always liked him."

"I can see how the girl might get sour with that sort of thing," I said slowly. "What about this illness Magee mentions? Do you know what that was?"

Grodnik rubbed out his cigarette in the wastebasket. "Hell, I don't know," he said. "The man's got a hole in his chest. That's illness enough for me."

I held up an open palm peacefully. "All right, Lieutenant. I'll check that with Owens. Now, what about the weapon? Where did that come from?"

"It was The Prince's," Grodnik said. "It was always there on a shelf behind some books. Magee would know about it though. He was there often enough."

"He left it behind?"

"Yeah, right by the body. And don't ask about fingerprints. There weren't any at all. And there's no mystery about it. Magee came in through the studio windows from the driveway. They're french windows and it was a habit with The Prince to use them. Magee was in the studio for maybe half an hour and I guess he never took off his coat or his gloves. He was still wearing gloves when we got him."

I almost said something about circumstantial evidence, but I saw the look in Grodnik's eye and I saved it for my memoirs. I shook my head. "It makes a messy problem," I said ambiguously. "Unless it's just blackmail, like you say."

Grodnik grinned widely at me. "That ain't all. Magee leaves the window open. It's freezing cold and we can't fix time of death. Not that we need to, with the cook's evidence, but if you want to wrestle with the real weighty problems, you solve that one, too."

"Sure," I said easily. "I can see why you're so happy. You are all set. You have Magee and these documents of his don't matter a damn to you. If they are phony, they give Magee a good motive for fighting with The Prince and killing him. If they're the real goods, they give him an even better motive. Either way, you're set."

Grodnik beamed rosily.

"What did the place look like when you got there?" I asked.

"Just a room." Grodnik shrugged. "Big studio. Lotsa music, pianos, that kinda stuff. The Prince was lying on his side facing the open windows. A helluva stack of cigarette butts on the floor, but not much blood. I guess The Prince put up quite a tussle."

I nodded. "Do you think the old man might know anything?"

"The Prince's father? I don't expect much from him."

50

Grodnik yawned widely. "He just found the body. Damned near stopped his heart, lying there in that cold studio after he keeled over. Maybe he did hear something. He was in his room, just off the studio, having a nap. He certainly got up in a hurry. At least, he came up full of steam. He knocked over his bed table getting up. Busted a bottle of brandy doing it, too. Room smelled like a gin mill when I saw it. But the old man just managed to get to the studio, see the body and then he fell over. Maybe he heard something, maybe not. His doctor was there when we came in and the old man had a skin full of sleeping dope so we couldn't talk to him. Won't matter much to our case, either way, but we'll ask him just as soon as Owens lets us in to see him."

I grunted sourly. "Now, about those documents," I said. "Will you mention them in your statement for the papers?"

Grodnik shook his head. "I told Owens I'd give the family a break there. We'll sit on it. They go in with my report, but I won't be ready to send it in until I see Magee. Gives you a couple of days to work, maybe. It's a cinch Magee will spill it whenever he starts talking, but it will give you a start."

"It will that," I said fervently. "Thanks. Now about this woman, Arabella Joslin. What's your plan there?"

Grodnik smiled contentedly. "You just told me the plan a minute ago," he said blandly. "If those papers are good, that's fine with me. If they're phony, that's fine, too. Either way, the Department won't split a gut trying to find Joslin, just because she might be able to back Magee's claim. We wired Chicago and asked them to

51

check that address she uses in those papers. No reply yet."

"Makes sense from your angle, I guess," I grumbled. "Well, thanks, Grodnik. Appreciate your help." I shoved myself to my feet. "Who would know most about The Prince and the people he worked with? Background, music, general character, that kind of thing? Somebody here in town."

Grodnik stood. "That's probably Manny Brenner, I suppose," he said. "You ought to know Manny. He runs the HOT BOX. He went to school with The Prince back in Chicago. Used to play in his band way back in the days when I was courting."

"Sure I know him. Every kid who ever grew up here knows Manny. You might even say we're old pals. I'll have a talk with him. You'll probably have me on your neck again as soon as I run into something."

"You know why I suggested your name to Owens?" he asked with sly cunning.

"Sure. Sure." I gave him the heavy-lidded stare. "You want first crack at any changes in the script, huh?"

Grodnik smiled rosily. "See?" he asked the room. "Didn't I say he was a brainy kid?"

I thumbed my nose at him and picked my hat off the desk. I waved it at him.

"Get a piece of steak for that eye, Wilde, and keep it out of keyholes from now on."

I said, "Go to hell," mechanically, and went out.

Grodnik had made a good deal. I knew just enough now to start turning over dead logs to see what I could find. If I got anything, Grodnik had the inside track. If I merely collected a few days' pay, he didn't lose a thing. Every time I was close to thinking disrespectful thoughts about Detective-Lieutenant Grodnik, he sat winking his pale tan eyes at me, while his slow dependable brain built a booby trap for me. I had run a lot of errands for him, because he had a way of making my business his business. He was a placid old man, bald and fat with very little real interest any more, but he was patient and methodical, and routine was what he did best. Grodnik would be a good man any place, but he was made to be a cop. He was a hell of a good cop.

CHAPTER SIX

It was nearly four o'clock when I left City Hall and headed south toward the Lazarus Department Store for my semiweekly check-up on their house men. For the long haul, the store is my best client. Their retainer keeps me fed and pays my rent while I wait around for the good jobs. I pick off another retainer regularly, too, from the Johnson Insurance outfit, but it doesn't amount to much unless they have a job for me at day rates.

I prowled the fur department and the jewelry display and wandered through the main showroom for a while. All the operatives braced me politely. One of them was a new hand and we had a speck of trouble getting straightened around. That's the best part of the Lazarus job though. They do the hiring. I just supervise, which is a job I am very happy doing. I took the elevator to the executive offices on the top floor and left a routine report on the boss's desk. Old Eli Lazarus was sunning his navel at Palm Beach and writing snorty postcards to his friends while his store ran like clockwork. His desk was uncluttered. I shoved my report in the second drawer, worked up a tired leer for his scrawny secretary and sloshed my way up the street to my office.

I didn't bother hauling off my hat and coat, as I had hopes of getting home for an early nap and didn't want any unnecessary delays. Sitting at the desk, I hooked the telephone toward me. I had the receiver off the standard and sat staring stupidly at the dial. Then I put it back and started fresh with the directory. Doctor Owens was listed at a home number in the South Side and at a Leave-a-Message number that doctors use. I dialed the service number, got the combination for his clinic and called him there.

"Hello, Mr. Wilde," he said cheerfully. "Anything for me?"

"Not yet, Doc," I said. "I've just had a session with Lieutenant Grodnik. I have enough to start with, but there is something I need. Grodnik didn't know what was wrong with The Prince. Magee made a reference in his affidavit to a serious illness that might knock him off any time. Do you know anything about it?"

"Well . . ." he hesitated. "I suppose I can give you a very general idea, but it isn't my field and he wasn't my patient. I'm a heart man, you know, and Mr. Prince was being treated for severe headaches, I believe."

"Uh-huh," I grunted. "Is that bad?"

"It's a little hard to say, Mr. Wilde. I just don't know."

"All right, Doc. You get an 'A' in ethics. Now make

a guess for me. I'm not going to quote you."

"Yes." He coughed. "Yes, of course, Mr. Wilde. I really meant it when I said I didn't know. Headaches can mean so very many things. Migraine, from nervous strain, for example. It could mean a growth, malignant or otherwise. It might mean cancer and then again it might mean nothing serious at all." He cleared his throat and chuckled into the phone. "So you see, Mr. Wilde, I just don't know. I could ask his doctor, if you think it important."

"I see," I said vaguely. "How did he act about it? Did it worry him particularly?"

Owens laughed easily at that. "I never saw him worry about a thing, Mr. Wilde. However, he was rather close-mouthed about it. All I know is what Martha has told me and she did say that her father had refused to discuss it with her. She overheard him talking to his doctor on the telephone some time ago. But that probably means nothing. Martha and her father were not very close lately."

"Yeah," I said. "I noticed. What's the score there, anyway?"

"Well," he stumbled. "I mentioned the feeling of competition that was strong between them. I suppose the police told you all about Mr. Prince's habits. I should have told you myself, possibly, but somehow I just didn't want to talk about it. Mr. Prince was under a great strain of some kind, I think. His behavior wasn't as bad as Martha seems to feel it was, but it certainly was erratic. I often wanted to speak to him, just in case I could help, but Martha made such a point of her antagonism that, well . . ."

"Yeah, sure," I mumbled. "Just give me a yes or no to this: Do you think he was a psycho?"

"Absolutely not," he said firmly; a little too promptly, I thought, but still he was very firm about it. "Mr. Prince was a creative artist, remember. Sound motives in him might be neurosis in another man. His periods of elation and depression were quite normal, I should say. They were just more noticeable simply because he himself was so noticeable."

That seemed to cover that. I listened to the empty noise in the receiver for a moment and then said, "Thanks, Doc. If you will check with his doctor, that covers it, I guess. That's all for now. I'm going to talk to a few people later on today and then I want to check back with you."

"Any time, Mr. Wilde. I'll see if I can get the information for you sometime this afternoon. By the way, how did you get along with Martha?"

"I didn't."

He made an indefinite sound. "Yes. Well . . . she's still upset, I suppose," he said lamely.

"If she is, it doesn't stop her much," I said.

"You . . . you just don't understand, Mr. Wilde. It's a very complicated relationship."

"No," I agreed. "No, I don't understand. She's a new one to me. And that guy Greene, too. How does he keep from getting his ears knocked off?"

"He doesn't," Owens snorted bitterly. "I've had to tell him off myself. But he's not a bad fellow actually. Just a little tense about things. And a little bitter. Old Mr. Prince is very fond of him. That's why he's around the house so much. He's doing some research for the old man."

I let it go. "Okay, Doc." I stood up and stretched my back muscles. "I'll get in touch with you tomorrow. I may have something then."

"Do that, Mr. Wilde. I'll be here at the clinic all day if you want me."

I turned off the lights in the office and snapped the door lock. I walked back to the parking lot, ransomed my car and drove to my apartment. At the corner, I parked and lifted my two-suiter out of the trunk compartment.

The switchboard girl waved cheerily as I came into my apartment building. I managed a sleepy leer and choked back a yawn. The trip down the lobby and up to the third floor in our halting elevator seemed as long as a trip around the Horn.

I opened my door, threw my bag on the couch and dropped my hat and overcoat beside it. At the coffee table I poured a stiff jolt of brandy and carried it into the bedroom with me. I walked just as far as the bed and stripped off my clothes. I threw down the brandy in a swift gulp, shuddered and crawled into bed for a fast nap. I had a vague memory of having slept somewhere during the week end just past, but I had a dead taste in my mouth and hazy little pinwheels in my head that told me I hadn't had much sleep for quite a time.

I set the alarm for nine o'clock, fell asleep with the clock still in my hand and dreamed a long complicated dream about going to the White House to see the President. As I walked up the drive to the executive wing, the White House changed color and grew slowly black and when I saw the President, he began to change color, too. And then I was running down the long corridor to the central house and screaming. Then I woke abruptly with a hot tension in my throat, my hands gripping the alarm clock which was blaring a shrill noise.

I stumbled into the bathroom, set the taps running for a hot tub and went back to the sitting room for my bag. I opened it and dumped everything on the bed in a loose pile. The bag went up on a high closet shelf and another rumpled suit joined the one on the floor for a date with the cleaner. The dark blue suit still looked fairly well and I left it on the bed with a fresh shirt and went into the bathroom to soak my bruises.

After I parked my car I stopped at Sam's, had a brief beef-on-rye dinner and hung around, trying to pick a possible winner at Hialeah. I backed a long shot with two bucks and took my slip from the wizened little ex-jockey who lives in the first booth on the right. Once he was one of the country's top riders and he made and spent a fortune. Now he was making a second one a lot easier just picking up horse bets for the Syndicate.

I wasn't in any hurry about getting to Manny Brenner's place. He stays open all night usually and, while he unlocks the door in time for the cocktail mob, nothing much begins to stir until eleven o'clock. We have a two o'clock bar curfew here and Manny observes it scrupulously by locking the door. After that, you can't get in unless you walk upstairs and climb down the fire escape, which quite a few people do. No one was ever asked to leave Manny's. If anyone wants to stay, Manny is always right with him.

When I turned into the alley, I could see Manny's

sign cutting through the darkness. Until the war, he had managed without one, but the big profit years got him finally and he gave in. The sign was eight feet tall and half that wide. It read MANNY'S HOT BOX in startling pink neon. The sign didn't have any relation to the entrance which was several feet beyond. When you shoved the door in, you found yourself in the entrance hall of an old house. A staircase went up from the hall in front of you and a blank door to the right was the one you wanted. The door was heavy steel-bound oak with more solidity than the walls and it still had the little Judas window that was left over from the bad old days. I leaned against the door and went in.

There wasn't much to the HOT BOX. Just a room about fifteen feet wide and possibly fifty feet long with a tiny bandstand at the far end and tables jammed in tightly. Near the door was a bar with room for five stools and wedged in beside it was a juke box for the moments when Manny and his band were tired. A tight knot of well-scrubbed young people was huddled around a pinball game Manny had installed for the early customers. The room was quiet and the barflies were speaking in hushed tones. A slow night so far.

I hung my hat and coat on a rack near the door and ordered a rye from the bar man. The walls had been bare on my last visit, but since then Manny had put up four large busy murals in crudely accented colors. That was probably an improvement but I didn't see it. A wide-bottomed Negro was playing the piano lacka-daisically and a slim, slick-haired boy who tried hard to look like Eddie Condon sat near him with a guitar in his lap, striking soft chords. A tall girl in a pale gray dress leaned over the piano, thumbing slowly through a stack of sheet music. The room was quiet and an occasional good roll on the pin-ball machine set up a rhythmic clamor.

I leaned across the bar. "Manny around?" I asked.

The bartender looked up wearily. "Be fifty cents," he said and held out his hand for the money. He took my dollar, dropped the usual four coins in change and pointed a thick finger toward the bandstand. "Inna corner, but he ain't feelin' good, Mac. Don't bother him."

"You rather I bothered you?" I asked softly.

He stared at my discolored eye and shrugged tired shoulders. "I only work here, Mac. Go bother Manny."

"Thanks," I said. I downed the short jigger and slid off the stool. I picked up the quarter from the wet bar, leaving the rest for the bartender. I could see a man sitting alone at a table far down the room and I worked my way through the tables toward him.

Manny was facing the wall, sitting with his back to the bar. I moved around the table, pulled out a chair with my toe and sat down. Manny was hunched over the table, holding a clarinet loosely and just barely blowing into it. I could hear it faintly from where I sat. Three feet away it wouldn't have been audible. He looked at me unwinkingly, without interrupting his soft blowing.

"Long time, Manny," I said.

He lifted his shoulders and let them drop. He held the mouthpiece lightly between his lips and spoke around it. "Ain't seen you for a while, kid. Still gumshoeing?" His lazy eyes flicked at my tailoring, checked my haircut and counted the money in my wallet. He wasn't impressed by any of it.

Manny was a short man, built like a solid statue made of hard rubber balls. He had a round pink face that didn't show much beard even at fifty. His light brown hair was thinning and he brushed it economically to get the maximum mileage out of what was left. He dressed just the way he had wanted to when he was a kid and wore his brother's castoffs. It might be a little loud for some people, but it seemed just right for Manny.

I gave him my light gay grin and helped myself to the bottle of Canadian Club on the table. He drank it straight, as most musicians drink, not bothering with water.

I noticed a thin wide book lying face down in front of Manny. It was spread open and the spine was brittle and cracked deeply.

"Business?" he asked.

"Not much," I said ambiguously. I drank my rye and then Manny poured himself a short one and knocked it off. "Too bad about The Prince," I said.

"Uh-huh, I thought so." Manny's eyes were red-rimmed and they glared at me intently. "What's the pitch?"

"Whoa, Manny. I'm not selling anything. I've just got a little job to do for Doctor Owens."

"Owens?" Manny's eyebrows went up. "Oh . . . that's the kid who's going to marry Martha?"

"Was," I said.

He shook his head sadly. "She kicked that one, too?" He pursed his lips about the mouthpiece and blew a plaintive note. "Rocks in her head," he muttered.

"Hear she's good on the piano," I suggested.

He brightened and lifted his head up from the clarinet. "Good? My gawd, she's got a tone you could eat with a spoon. Too bad she don't give a damn for the hot and blue. She makes her old man sound like Three-Finger Fred."

I grinned. "I always thought The Prince was pretty fine," I said.

"Sure," Manny agreed easily. "He had the beat to steady down a little combination, just like a good drummer. He really kept two hands full of piano. It's in the harmonic pattern, though, where you want a piano. And that's why The Prince was on top. But a really fine top piano comes on with a steady four-four rhythm you can build a house on. The Prince wasn't really so strong there. His bass was always a little honky." Manny wasn't talking to me any more. He was outlining something important about The Prince, but he was talking for history. His eyes lifted and seeing me broke the spell.

"Well, anyway," he said. "The Prince wasn't the kind of piano that would worry Jelly Roll or Fats Waller none. I'd say he was close to being as good as Teddy Weatherford though. At least, some days. Sort of like Tony Jackson or Lil Armstrong, maybe. He ain't so much a musician in the playing sense, anyway, you understand. He's a composer. It's like being an inventor. You got a million ideas. You can't hardly stop one long enough to get it down on paper. But man, how he could build a song. He could take a little ballad, like some sloppy *I-Love-You-Truly* number and work out a head arrangement in half an hour that had wide-open chords you could really work on. Same for his own stuff. Fine big stuff, too. See what I mean?"

"Only if you say so, Manny," I said. "But what about that girl? What makes her teeth so sharp?"

Manny closed his mouth around the reed and breathed a fragile series. He stopped and sat unmoving with his tongue licking out occasionally at the mouthpiece. After a long moment he looked up. "You know who her mother was?"

I shook my head. I poured a drink and pushed it over to him.

Manny stared down at the glass with somber intensity. "She was Billie Jones," he said heavily.

I grunted. That explained a lot. "I'm sorry, Manny. I didn't know that." I didn't need any help to figure that one out. "They had split up, I guess?"

Manny nodded morosely. "Yeah, Billie was goin' home with the kid, when . . ."

He didn't have to finish it. It's a story that everyone has heard about. Quite often one of the slick magazines does a piece about it, trying to prove something. It doesn't prove anything, except that the world is full of sick people. In her day, Billie Jones was a giant. She sang. She sang anything; blues, jazz, lullabies, opera. She was tall and smoothly brown with a deep chest and the sort of singing equipment that a few people are born with every generation. Not very many people these days remember what she sounded like. She made a lot of records and all of them are collectors' items now, but back then records weren't very good and the ones you hear are mostly thin and reedy, without much tone. Billie Jones was a great singer. She had a ringing vibration that was made of vitality and a deep sadness. Hardly anyone remembers how she sang, but almost everyone knows how she died.

It's a short and nasty story about a drunken driver, a runover woman who bled to death because she was in the wrong part of the world. There is a hospital in the Murder and Old Magnolia Belt that probably has the usual bronze plaques to back-wash celebrities and gold stars for dear departed employes. It wouldn't have a plaque to Billie Jones. She was carried there after the accident, but her skin wasn't light enough to get her in. She died before she reached a sane hospital.

There wasn't much stink about it at the time. I don't know where I first heard about it. I hadn't even known she and The Prince were married.

I looked at Manny. He had his eyes fixed vacantly, staring at nothing. "I remember about Billie," I said. "But The Prince wasn't there, was he?"

Manny blinked. His round pink face looked suddenly gray and haggard. He shook his head. "No," he said huskily. "Just that the kid maybe figures it was his fault, sorta, because Billie left him. I guess she feels The Prince shouldn't have let her go. I don't know." He looked glumly at the bottle on the table. There was a little twitch of muscle at the corner of his mouth that jerked in slow rhythm. "It's tough, boy. Both of them gone now. Two people like that don't happen often."

I made a sympathetic noise and sat silently.

In the thick silence, the guitar player came suddenly to life. He ignored the fumbling from the piano and slammed into a deFalla flamenco that crackled like a forest fire in the still room. I swiveled around to watch. Even Manny was caught by it. He gestured toward the stand.

"Watch that hand, Carney," he said softly. "The kid's good."

The kid was very good. He had most of Segovia's tricks, even the little finger that operated independently of the pick and rattled out a staccato counterpoint that laced together with the pick work. It was fine stuff. Even I knew it was fine and it seemed to snap Manny out of his glum daze.

"There's always some young ones comin' along," he said. He tossed off a snort of rye and lifted the thin book from the table and turned it over. "Look here, boy," he said. "That was me and The Prince. Way back then." He shoved the book across to me.

A clumsy paste-up montage made a double spread in the book. It was the yearbook for Western High School in Chicago for 1915. Grinning up from a rickety upright piano was The Prince, younger, but obviously The Prince, already large and solid. He was flanked by two thin young clarinetists who held their instruments stiffly and had frozen smiles plastered on their faces. One of the white blurs would be Manny's face, I supposed. Six other dim photos made up the spread and the whole layout was mounted on a piece of sheet music that was headed, *Riot Squad A'Comin'*. I could faintly see the first lines. Done well by a good technician, it might have been a telling composition, but the pictures were bad to start with and poor reproduction made the spread look like a portrait drawn in a bucket of mud. I pushed it back to Manny.

"I like you better without the hair," I said.

Manny smiled thinly. "Boy, that was a time we had then." He stabbed a finger at the page and banged at it. "That was The Prince's first show. 'Western Ragtime Stomp.' Boy, we were really hot then." He waggled his head sadly at the memory.

I leaned across the table and spoke softly. "I want to ask you something, Manny. You're not going to like it, but I need the answer." I paused a moment to get his attention off the book. "What would you say if you heard that somebody else claimed he had written all The Prince's music?"

Manny's face grew hard and cold. His mouth pulled down drunkenly in a grim thin line and he glared at me. He puckered his mouth and spat, turning his head just in time to miss me.

"That's a good answer," I said. Manny wasn't sober enough to talk to about it. Just then the guitar player subsided in a leaping run of glittering chords and a woman's voice, light and pleasant, spoke over my head to Manny.

"Throwing spitballs, boss?"

Manny looked up quickly and his face lost its heavy lines. He leaned back in his chair and forced a smile. "Hiyuh, Nancy, baby." He kicked out a chair beside him and gestured at it widely. "Siddown, kid. Wantcha to meet one of my old boys." His eyes turned briefly to me, as if to warn me I was on probation, but Manny wouldn't push it.

As soon as the girl cleared the back of my chair, I shoved it out and rose. She was the same girl I had seen leaning over the piano when I came in. She wore a gray dress, a wide-skirted affair that was probably a "crea- tion." At least she wore it that way and there were changing tones in it that did happy things for pale blond hair and bounced silver lights from her blue eyes. She waited easily while I made a fast inspection. Her eyes were clear and appraising, in the way a horseman might examine a possible starter in the paddock.

Manny said, "This is Carney Wilde, Nancy. Time was he usedta hang around in here and slop up some beer and try to learn some sense, but it sure didn't take. He's a lousy gumshoe now." Manny's smile was wide and relaxed now, but I suspected that he would bounce the bottle off my skull if I asked any more questions about The Prince's music. Manny patted the girl's arm happily.

"This is Nancy Lucas, Carney. Remember the name. One of these days you'll see it in lights. In the big time. She sings anything." He looked toward me quickly and his eyes moved back to the girl. "Sorta like Billie some ways," he said softly.

We muttered the usual things and sat down. Nancy held up a finger and a waiter came on the run. Nancy's order was a tall glass of something that I guessed was plain seltzer, or maybe Perrier. She looked as if she might know about such things.

"Goin' to stick around for some music, Carney?" Manny asked.

I shook my head. I had a lot of things to ask Manny, but I needed to get to him while he was fairly sober. I didn't want a brawl with him if I could help it.

"Not tonight, Manny," I said. "I need some sleep. I got a basketful of bruises to cure." I touched my inflamed eye gently and they both laughed at me. "I'll be back though, Miss Lucas. I didn't know about you before."

Manny leered. "Carney's mad for hot music, Nancy. Was it some old goat that chewed tobacco, he'd still come around to listen."

I got up then, hoping to get away before Manny told her too much about me. "I'll be back," I said firmly.

"Please do," she said softly. Her thin delicate face held a light smile as though it had been made for the purpose. There was a quiet content deep behind her eyes that I wanted to learn more about.

I reached for my hat and stopped beside Manny. "Do you know a woman named Arabella Joslin, Manny? She comes from Chicago. I think she was a friend of Stuff Magee's."

Manny chased it around in his memory, working a deep frown across his brow. He shook his head slowly. "Can't place her," he said thoughtfully. "I never had much to do with Stuff, even then. We never hit it off so good." He watched me keenly and I could almost see his mind trying to guess what it had to do with the question about The Prince's music.

I smiled. "Well, keep it in mind, Manny. See if you can come up with something. I have to find her. And fast."

I left then, giving Manny a flip of my hat and Miss Lucas a cheerful grin that was supposed to make her remember me until I got back. Just thinking about her made the trip to my apartment a pleasant jaunt and I went to sleep trying to guess how that light, controlled voice would handle a low blues note. It gave me something to look forward to for tomorrow.

CHAPTER
SEVEN

I woke in the morning with a numb ache in my head from too much sleep.

My routine took more than the usual fifteen minutes, due to my athlete's bruises. From the mirror I could tell that I was well along with recovery, but I was still having some trouble in the back muscles.

The percolator was chugging steadily by the time I had finished dressing. I picked up the morning paper from the hallway and halted at the sitting room mirror for another look. After-shaving powder fairly well covered the discoloration, but I was due for another two or three green-and-purple days before I was finished with the mouse under my eye.

The morning paper had another long story on The Prince. Nothing new, except for a picture of Magee. A dried-up nasty face with a tight prunes-and-prisms mouth and hardly any chin. Not a particularly vicious face, but it was easy to see why he didn't have the personality to lead a band. He would need a front man all his life.

Three cups of coffee and half an hour later I threw back the lock of my office door and went through the daily round of picking up mail, airing the room and wondering what the day would bring.

Disposing of my mail took the customary five minutes.

The offers today were nothing new: a chance to subscribe to a racing tip sheet, a bulky selection of elegant letterheads in case I wanted to pick something that went with my complexion, an opportunity to share in the proceeds of a new meat packing business for a minimal investment. All but the letterheads went into the wastebasket. I propped my feet up on my desk in my best thinking posture and busied myself with manufacturing a series of paper darts from the heavy letterheads, getting my mind nice and blank in the hope that an idea might come in to visit.

For my money, Arabella Joslin was the key. She knew the real answer to the claim Magee had made. Without her, I was fumbling. Magee would have to produce her if he hoped to make his claim stick, but Magee was going to be rather busy with a murder charge. One thing I was sure of: The Prince's reputation was likely to wobble unless Magee's claim could be solidly disproved.

I sailed my first paper dart across the room, aiming at my license bond on the wall. It went off to the right and dropped short by a foot. It was too flimsy, like my thinking. No weight and no direction. I was fiddling with another sheet when the hall door opened quietly. The tall, shadow-thin figure of Randolph Greene stood framed in the entrance, sneering lightly at my childish games.

I went on with the problem of manufacturing, trying two sheets together this time and figuring the wingspread to be a touch wider. Greene moved across the room in long strides, like a pair of calipers measuring off the distance. He sat in the leather chair beside the desk while I finished the engineering. This one was better. I put more steam behind the pitch and raised my sights to allow for trajectory. It was perfect. It smacked the license right over the Great Seal of the Commonwealth and fell lazily to the floor.

Greene applauded slowly, dull heavy claps sounding as obviously insulting as his expression. "Now you can quit for the day," he said, keeping his lip well curled.

I leaned back in my squeaky chair and looked at him. He was dazzling in a hard-finish gray worsted suit that had been cut with some devotion, a cream-colored shirt with lots of cuff and a broad tie that sported cavorting dogs in the kind of exotic pattern that Countess Mara specializes in. He crossed his legs negligently and displayed glossy cordovan shoes and something casually splendid in lisle socks. I nodded my appreciation.

"All right," I said. "I'm impressed. Now what?"

He balanced both elbows on the chair arms and made a steeple of his long dark fingers. Both index fingers pinched together on the point of his chin and that posture he held. It was the sort of pose you see on the backs of books written by daring young poets. He was just young enough to strike such poses.

"Despite the fact that Miss Martha Prince advised you yesterday that she did not want your interference in her personal affairs," he began portentously, "you refused to comply with her request."

I nodded agreeably.

"You are representing Miss Prince, I take it?" I asked.

"I am coming to that," he said stiffly. "To continue: You further annoyed Miss Prince by demanding explanations of her actions and finally threatened interference when she asked you to leave. Miss Prince plans

71

to institute civil action against you unless this ridiculous investigation is discontinued immediately. My visit here today is your official notification of intent. Your future behavior will determine whether the suit is to be filed."

I beamed at him. "You memorized your piece fairly well, sonny. You get a big, fat 'A.'"

Greene's sneer disappeared in a deep scowl. His steepled fingers trembled slightly, as if with inner rage but he controlled himself with a visible effort. He was impressive and sure, in the manner that calls for long hours before a rehearsal mirror. "Is that all you have to say?" he asked tightly.

"No, stick around," I said. "We'll have a little paper dart tournament and you can tell me who buys your clothes for you." I moved my feet to a point where I could kick back from the desk and come up standing if I had to. There wasn't any need. Mr. Greene was still noticeably in control of himself. He made his voice chill and stern.

"Do you understand the warning I have delivered for Miss Prince?"

I nodded again. "I get it all," I said. "Now tell me just where in hell you come into the Prince family. What's it to you?"

"I don't come in the family," he said tightly. "Mr. Prince has helped me through college. He is employing me now on a research project. I owe him a debt of gratitude."

"That's nice," I said nastily. "You owe him a debt, but not enough to want to see his reputation cleared."

"I don't mean the man you call The Prince. I was referring to Martha's grandfather," Greene sneered. "I owe her father nothing. He is, he was, a useless, caterwauling Uncle Tom. His father, though, is a great Negro, a man of his people. His son was a nothingness."

I pulled my feet under the chair. "Sure, that makes sense," I said. "The Prince was a big man. You little punks have to hate him for that, don't you?"

Young Mr. Greene ignored me. He fixed an unforgiving stare above my head.

"It's been a pleasant chat, sonny," I said. "Now tell me what you're trying to cover up. Just why do you really want me to quit? Did you kill The Prince? Or was it Martha?"

That did it. He took too long to get at me, but he tried hard. I think he intended to slap me. It was a good enough idea, except that I wasn't there when he swung.

I had plenty of time to stand and get my head away from his hand. He put a lot of muscle into his swing and it nearly turned him around when he missed. I snatched at his wrist as it went by and helped him on his way with a quick pull. Under his own momentum and my help, he twirled across the room like a drunken dancer and banged against the wall with his back, facing me and snarling darkly from a mad young face.

I pressed his shoulder to the wall again with my left hand and held him there for a moment. "That's all, Buster," I grunted. "Once is all you get. Just blink an eye and I'll crack you." I let him see my right fist cocked and ready.

He moved both hands cautiously and placed them flat against the wall. His breath was coming heavily and his wide full mouth was pressed tensely closed under flaring nostrils. The angry redness in his eyes cleared gradually as he glared at me, just inches away. I held him there until he quieted and then stepped back.

I went over to my chair and sat down. Greene didn't stir. "Any time you're ready," I said lightly, "you can tell me what's really bothering Miss Prince. That legal double talk you tried may impress you, but it's only a laugh to me. Miss Prince doesn't have a case, sonny. Any lawyer would tell her that. And if her lawyer did decide to let her dig her own grave, he wouldn't try a civil suit. He'd make a charge with the licensing board and have me put out of business. So the gag doesn't work. What's more, I don't believe the girl sent you here. I'll bet this was your own brilliant notion."

I spoke without any particular expression, not looking directly at him. Gradually he came erect and moved away from the wall. He walked to his chair and stood there, staring blankly down at the floor, looking lost inside his man-about-town clothes. I kept talking, trying to get a soothing note into my voice.

"It's easy to see why the girl would be upset," I said. "I know a little more about her now and it's pretty obvious that she has had a rough time. But most of it is in her mind. You're not stupid, Greene, except for trying that hard-guy pitch with me, and you know that the girl has manufactured most of her grievances." I saw his head come up and turn slowly toward me. "I don't mean that she doesn't have some emotional basis for the way she feels. But you know as well as I do that she hasn't any logical reason for disliking her father or his work as much as she does."

Suddenly Greene sat down with a weary sigh, folding up and letting his six-and-a-half feet come down to the

74

chair gradually. The habitual sneer was gone for the moment and there was a deep and thoughtful frown wrinkling his forehead. He cleared his throat with a clumsy sound.

"Then . . . then why did you accuse her . . ." he began hoarsely. He coughed again and tried to find his voice.

"Oh, hell." I waved it away. "I haven't accused anyone of anything. In my own clumsy fashion, I'm trying to find out what's behind those documents Magee had when he was arrested."

"What . . . what do you want then?"

I took it slowly and easily, hoping he wouldn't duck into his protective shell before I got some answers. "I'm working for Doctor Owens," I said. "I don't want to bother Miss Prince and I don't think it's necessary. That isn't part of my job, at any rate. The cops have the killer and I have to find out what kind of a fraud he was ringing in. I imagine you know all about his papers?"

Greene indicated that he did know about them. "Then . . . then why . . ." Greene's face tightened as he heard his tongue stumbling. He started again. "What's all that to do with Martha?" he demanded.

"There you got me," I admitted. "At first, I would have said she didn't have a damned thing to do with it. And even now, I'm damned if I can guess where she comes in. But you were there when I talked with her and I'll bet you listened to everything we said. Just put yourself in my place. What I'm trying to do would help her more than any other one person. But instead of trying to help me, she just doesn't give a damn about it. That's a little peculiar, don't you think?"

Greene tried his sneer on again, but it wasn't as sure and easy as it had been. "Only if you don't know the background," he said testily. "Her behavior is perfectly understandable when you consider her relationship with her father."

"Unh-uh," I shook my head. "You're whistling in the wind, Greene, and you know it. Just forget The Prince for the moment and let's talk about her relationship with money. Let's say just for the sake of argument that all Magee's claim would mean to her is the loss of money. Now, do you think it's logical for her to pitch The Prince's dough out the window, just because she didn't like me or my black eye?" I watched him think about it.

"I'm still working for Owens . . ." I began.

Greene jumped suddenly to his feet. "That sniveling pup," he snarled. "He's behind all this."

I laughed at him. "Where did you pick up that 'East Lynne' language? Owens is a doctor. He wants to help Martha Prince and he doesn't try to lie to me. All of which makes him about eight times bigger than you."

Greene wheeled toward the door after that. He stopped with his hand on the knob and spoke over his shoulder. "You've been warned," he said in an infuriated tone.

"All right, sonny," I laughed. "Tell Martha I'll be out to see her soon."

I don't know whether he heard me. The elevator door crashed then and Greene slammed my door almost in unison with it. My door opened again after a light knock. Two visitors in one day was my best record to date. I got to my feet in case it should be a customer.

CHAPTER EIGHT

GRAY was for Miss Lucas. She wore a pale, soft-textured gray dress in a tone that had no accents. She held a gray suède handbag in wrist-length white gloves that were startling against her dark gray fur coat. No hat for Miss Lucas. She knew the effect of that pale blond hair and she held its length in place with a flat silver bar low on the nape of her neck.

"Did I just miss the big dramatic scene?" she asked, smiling gently at the paper darts on the floor.

"Only the first act." I grinned and scooped up the darts and rammed them in the wastebasket before they lost me all my prestige.

"This isn't quite what I expected," she said, looking around my bleak office. "No gay Paris prints. No violin. No hypodermic. Not even a small but complete kitchen." She shook her head in mock dismay and her clear bright singer's tones almost covered her slight embarrassment.

"Try the customer's chair," I said quickly. "I'll get out my jug of cheap rye while I give you the real low-down on Etruscan pottery or slip you a fine recipe for oysters Suzette. All dicks get a once-over-lightly course in such concerns, but I never had a chance to use mine till now."

"You've never met the right people," she said. She accepted a cigarette and bent forward to reach my lighter.

"I have now," I said with my best leer. "You stick around and I'll even remember all the choruses to *Christofer Columbo*. There's no limit when the audience cheers." I perched on the edge of the desk and offered a smile, the young engaging one that proves I'm the boy who knows the road to adventure is just over yon hill.

She cocked an eyebrow at me and blew smoke out quickly before she choked. "I'm really here on business, Mr. Wilde. I have a message from Manny. He was going to call you, but I did want to see what a private detective looks like in his native habitat."

"You don't get a good look unless you see one at feeding time. Just like the seals at the zoo. No good till you throw a fish. Come to lunch and we'll get to Manny's problem later."

Her laugh was high and silvery. It dropped around the room like a spray of ocean foam.

"It's just eleven o'clock, Mr. Wilde," she laughed. "That's barely breakfast time for me. And far too early for lunch."

"Tut-tut," I insisted. "We'll have Sam make a whacking big omelette and you can carve off a breakfast portion while I have the lunch section."

"An amiable compromise," she agreed. "But what about Manny's message?"

Faint dimples jumped in her cheeks while she tried not to laugh.

I held up a lordly hand. "Manny's message has served its purpose, my good girl. It brought you here. Now let it take care of itself for a while. As soon as I've heard

78

it, you'll begin to think you should leave." I turned flat palms shoulder high to point up my implacable logic. "We'll save the message, huh?"

She pouted slightly around the cigarette and considered it. It was a nice piece of timing. Just the right pause before she nodded.

"I'd like that," she said softly. "Though maybe I should tell you that Manny thinks he may know something about the woman you mentioned. What was her name?"

I got back into my chair then and wiped the smirk off my face. "The name was Arabella Joslin," I said. "What does Manny know about her?" I pulled over a long yellow pad and found a pencil.

"My, you do get stern and businesslike all of a sudden, don't you?" She made a small hurt-pride pout just for the record. "I don't think it's especially flattering for you to forget about lunch so easily, but if the invitation still stands, I'll tell you the message." She took my nod as a commitment, which it definitely was, and continued. "Manny says it came to him when we were doing a number last night. He remembered a singer who used to come around to the HOT BOX occasionally with Stuff Magee. Her name was Bella Joe as he recalled it. But he said he never saw her in Chicago. He thinks it might be the same woman."

I wrote it down. "Maybe," I said.

Her eyebrows moved up an inch and she said, "And?"

I grinned. "And thank you and yours to the tenth generation, dear Miss Lucas. I love you all, but how in hell do I find this woman now that I know her alias?"

"You interrupted," she said with bogus severity. "I was going to tell you. Manny said if she is the woman, you can get the information you need from Al Gilman. Gilman is a booking agent and he handles almost all the bands and singers in this part of the country."

I scribbled the name on my pad and hooked the phone book over with my elbow. "I'm sorry you can't see me in one of my brilliant deductive moods, dear Miss Lucas. Today was a dull and turgid mess until you came in." Albert Y. Gilman, Theatrical Agent, was listed in the classified section. I made a note of the address and phone number. The Washington Trust Building, State Street at Channing.

Miss Lucas sat fingering her cigarette, looking wise and serene while I got the phone and dialed Gilman's number. The phone conversation was over in a few seconds. Gilman was out, would be in and free at two o'clock, and would see me on a matter of extreme urgency that would take no more than ten minutes. The secretary warned me that credentials would be expected and if I thought I had a good gag for getting in to see Gilman about a new dog act, I could forget it. I offered reassurances that didn't interest her at all. We hung up in an atmosphere of measured suspicion.

"Mabel is really a lovely girl," Miss Lucas said lightly. "But she has a terrible time with gate-crashers."

"I can see that," I said. "I'll use your name when I go up there. I'll even call you Nancy and pretend we went to school together."

"You could call me Nancy now," she offered gently. "Just to get used to it, I mean."

"Natcherly," I agreed. "No other reason. Maybe you'd better call me Carney, just to remind me."

We bowed in solemn agreement. I lifted my coat from

the rack while she doused her cigarette in the oversize clam shell I use for a customer's ashtray. One puff had been enough for her. Either it was the wrong brand or she was protecting a singer's throat from smoke.

Sam spread himself when he made the omelette. He conveyed it to our table on his big silver platter. He fatigued the salad precisely in a polished birch bowl and fluttered around afterward with a silver pot of coffee, refilling our cups and doing his best impersonation of Caesar of the Ritz. It didn't do him a bit of good. I identified him for my guest, but all he heard was "Nancy" and I kept the conversation on jazz, which is not one of Sam's subjects. Anything other than fine cookery, race horses or foreign policy is a subject that makes a reluctant listener out of Sam.

Nancy aimed her career at hot music. That alone caught me. Far too many singers and musicians ape the primary school critics who sneer at jazz. They like to pretend that they work with a hot combo only as a springboard to better things. All of which is a fine indication of a lousy workman. Nancy had none of their minute fears. The requirement for rich melodic invention, the spirited teamwork and weaving counterpoint of a hard-working hot crew were a keen challenge to her. The requirements are frightening to people who can work only from a written score. Building a full harmonic background for an extemporaneous solo is a job for experts. No better instrumentalists have lived than America's hot men. And few have even been recognized as they deserve. It's a safe bet that there isn't a symphonic clarinet in the world that could beat Jimmy Noone. Good hot singers come even less often. The glides and skidding elisions are tough enough on a voice, but put on top of that the fact that hot music demands a sweet and lyrical invention with no brutality and you have a series of first requirements that would eliminate half the singers in the country before they could start. I still didn't know how well Nancy sang, but she had the feeling for hot music and that was enough to make me put down a small wager on her.

It's largely the emotional feeling about hot music that makes the distinction between good workmen and outstanding musicians. The kids playing bop these days don't have the feeling. Some writers in the polished-paper magazines regard the bop lads as something new and fine. They even see a post-war spiritual significance in bop, as they do in existentialism and surrealism. Jazz is unfortunate these days. Too many people understand and appreciate jazz. Jazz is out with advance guard society.

Bop can be fun, I'm told. It's an adventure in dissonance that seems meaningless to me. And I feel a lot better when I see that old Satchmo agrees with me. Bop is a limited language, with practically no vocabulary. It does nicely as long as you are satisfied with the major generalities. As long as you are convinced hunger has no subdivisions, bop has its meaning. Deeper, you need jazz.

I was trying on offers for an afternoon walk or a stop at a matinee, or some such gimmick to keep Nancy around for the afternoon. None of them worked. She was scheduled for a rehearsal and no appeal would be considered. We made a tentative date for walking her home after her stint at Manny's and I sprinted around the streets to find her a taxi.

I got back to my office by twelve-thirty with that strange out-of-rhythm feeling that comes from a too early lunch. Sunlight from my one window made large yellow patterns across the floor and made the office look just that much emptier. Just for company, I dialed Doctor Owens' number at the clinic. I hardly expected to find him in, but after a short delay, the nurse-receptionist found him.

"Carney Wilde, Doc," I said. "Just had a conference with our Mr. Greene."

"I heard about it," he said crisply. "He came here afterward."

"Still breathing fire?"

Owens snorted. "Very nearly. He's just twenty-one, you know. The world is a very serious affair to him."

I grunted at that. The world can seem grim to me, too, but I've had my chip knocked off enough to learn to carry it in my pocket. "He wanted me to lay off, I think," I said. "We had a little discussion about it. I told him I wanted to see Miss Prince again. He didn't care much about the idea."

"No," Owens said. "He wouldn't, I suppose. He seems to feel an investigation is not particularly advisable just now. I'm afraid I didn't give him much chance to develop his thesis. He has a strong protectiveness about Martha and I find that a trifle annoying, as you can probably understand. I'm sure he has no real authority from her though. I've tried to call her, but she won't come to the phone."

"Want to go out there with me today?"

He didn't answer for a moment. Then he spoke decisively. "Yes. Yes, I would. It's time Martha and I had this thing out. Let me see . . ." There was another delay. "I'm free after four-thirty. Is that good for you?"

"Fine," I said. "I'll pick you up."

"Just a minute," he said briskly. "About Mr. Prince's illness. You wanted me to inquire."

"Sure. What did you get?"

"Well, it's rather an odd business, Mr. Wilde. Doctor Warner won't tell me anything. Of course, a lot of doctors won't talk about their patients to anyone, but Warner was one of my instructors at medical school. We've always been friends, but he still wouldn't tell me. I suppose that makes it important to you, doesn't it?"

"Yeah," I muttered. "The brush-off always bothers me. We'll have to dig into that. Probably Lieutenant Grodnik can get the doctor to tell him without too much trouble. Thanks, Doc. I hope you didn't get blown down for asking."

"No." Owens laughed. "Warner is really a fine man. He just likes to mix a little drama with his medicine."

"Okay," I said. "I'll catch you up on things when I see you. I think I have a lead on the Joslin woman. I'll tell you about it later."

"All right, Mr. Wilde," he said. "Four-thirty."

I puttered around the office until one-thirty. I lined up my first-of-the-month bills and wrote a stack of checks, with envelopes to match. There's always a large virtuous expansion that comes over me when the bills are paid. I dropped the checks down the mail slot and rang for the elevator. I had plenty of time to get over to Gilman's office on State Street, have my brawl with his secretary and get in by two o'clock.

CHAPTER NINE

IN MY town, the Washington Trust Building is still a "good" address. New businesses like to start out in the building, but they seldom stay for long. The dank air of the corridors, the inferior lighting and sparse rest rooms chase most of them. I found Gilman's name on the bronze call board and took the elevator to the twelfth floor.

The open door of the agency was just opposite the elevator. The walls inside were covered with playbills for ancient attractions. On my trip toward the secretary's desk, I noticed one for Maurice Barrymore in *As You Like It*. The room had benches against all the walls, but none of the twenty-odd people there bothered with them. They were postured alluringly about the room, looking lithe and young and very vigorous. Their chins were high and gay and their clothes were beyond reproach. I slunk through them, attracting no more attention than a waiter in a college hangout, and elbowed my way to the desk.

I had my leather pocket folder in my hand and I offered it to the secretary. One side of it holds a photostat of my license and the other has a deputy sheriff's badge. It makes a useful gadget to flash at unsuspecting tourists and the buzzer is particularly good with law-abiding citizens. Ten dollars to the police fund and an okay from your ward committeeman and you can get one, too. Neither of the items impressed the secretary. She pushed her pencil up into a mat of brittle red hair and shrugged elegantly at my credentials. Her chair pivoted around and she disappeared through a door directly behind her.

It took her about three minutes to make the trip and in that time at least seven newcomers were crowding me away from the desk. Nothing obvious or offensive, just good clean angling for the opportunity. I let them push me closer toward the door where the redhead had vanished and then I took up a firm stand. No one really looked at me and none of them seemed to be talking to anyone in particular, but the room was buzzing with gay tinkling laughter and jolly good fun. Either Gilman was casting a light comedy or I was quietly going nuts.

I did draw attention from the beautiful mob for a moment when the secretary returned. She held the inner door open and crooked a finger for me. The noise stopped for a brief breath and Wilde was the star for the length of time it took to get through the door. The redhead pointed down the hall to a closed door at the end. I played along with the silence gag and nodded mysteriously as I started off.

Gilman's office was a workroom and there was nothing fancy about it, except the chair he had which was a handsome piece of leatherwork that would have made a fine bed. Gilman was short, dark and quick. He jumped up, shook hands, offered a cigarette and got back to his chair before I had my hat off. A nervous energy controlled his short fat hands and his fingers were never still. They prowled his face, tweaking ears and nose.

They moved over the desk, fiddling with pencils and papers. Occasionally he noticed what they were doing and hauled them into his lap, but after a breather they were off again about their restless work.

I told Gilman I was looking for a woman named Arabella Joslin, a singer he might know as Bella Joe. I said it was confidential and important and suggested Manny Brenner and Doctor Owens as sponsors, if he wanted information.

He waved away the thought of credentials. He punched down one of three buttons on the base of an interphone and told someone at the other end to see what they had on either name.

"What makes it important?" he asked sharply. "Don't like to waste time with foolishness."

"It isn't foolishness, Mr. Gilman," I began.

"Call me Al. Call me Al. Everybody does," he snapped irritably. His vocal speed was about twice mine and I noticed that I began to pick up his tempo after a while.

"It still isn't foolishness, Al," I said. "It's a confidential problem right now. I can't tell you about it. But I will be able to give you the whole story later on, I think."

He snorted at the mystery. In two puffs he ruined the best part of a cigarette and flipped it peevishly in the general direction of a majolica urn standing in one corner. There were dozens of cigarette ends lying on a cork matting under the urn. Al's aim was nothing much.

A long arm reached through the door, tossed a letter-size manila envelope on Al's desk and vanished. The method of delivery didn't surprise him. He read the name on the envelope and then held it upside down over the desk, dumping its contents on a welter of glossy photographs, papers and press clippings. He took the photograph that had come from the envelope, turned it over and read something carefully. Then he pitched it over to me and picked up a thin file of papers.

The picture was a stiffly posed studio shot of a large, heavy, dark-skinned woman wearing a white dress spangled with rosettes of black sequins. It had the sort of glamor lighting that makes everyone look like everyone else. But the information on the back was more help. It was routine stuff. Name: Bella Joe (no mention of Joslin). Address: 997 West Willow Lane. Height: five, eight. Weight: 180 pounds. Hair: Black. Eyes: hazel. Singer now with Gene Marigny's Old Dixieland Band, eight men. I copied the facts on the back of an envelope. I had most of it when Gilman snorted again and peered suspiciously at me over his desk.

"Confidential, huh?" His heavy black brows closed in a straight line as he frowned nastily. His voice became deeper and menacing. "What's the gag, Wilde? You trying to get that bastard, Magee, out of jail?"

"Hold it," I said. "There's no gag. I said it was confidential, but I don't mind telling you, I'm not working for Magee."

He wasn't soothed. He folded three papers together and tapped them on the arm of his chair while he glowered at me. He was another one who thought you can spot a liar just by staring hard. I gave him a minute to think about it. Then I asked for the papers.

He shook his head. "Not without I know why," he said firmly. "The Prince was my best friend. I don't give a hand to a guy on Magee's team."

I didn't waste time arguing. A man in Gilman's position probably has half the secrets of the city in his head. He was going to get whatever I had to give him for a look at those papers.

"All right, Al," I said. "My client is Doctor Owens. He is engaged to marry The Prince's daughter. He hired me to check on a racket that Magee and this woman, Bella Joe, had lined up to rook The Prince. My job doesn't have a damned thing to do with Magee, except to prove he was a phony. I don't want to tell you what the racket was, but you can check with Lieutenant Grodnik at the Central Homicide Bureau and he'll confirm everything I've said." I spoke my piece as forcefully as I could and it seemed to do the trick.

Gilman broke the rhythmic tapping with the papers and held them poised for a moment. "That Magee," he said sadly, in a low voice, "he's about as bad as Hitler to kill a man like The Prince. Makes me sick to think about it. I couldn't even read about it. Guy calls me onna phone, says The Prince was knocked off by that no-good and I'm back in bed with my ulcers again. Me, that just got up a day before. I'm right back there again." His thick hands worked gently against his vest and his face was pained. "That was a terrible thing to do," he muttered.

I didn't know which he thought was worse, the murder or his ulcers, and I didn't like to ask. He sat glumly, patting his vest sourly for a moment and then he made up his mind. He threw the thin file across his desk to me. "I get the story later, huh?"

I agreed to that. The papers weren't worth much in trade, but Gilman hadn't got very much for them anyway. The thing that had tipped him off was a recommendation from Magee, written on The Prince's letterhead. Magee wrote that Bella Joe was well known to him, had wowed them in Chicago and was currently at a club on the South Side with Gene Marigny. He suggested that Gilman sign her, if he wanted the hottest thing in jazz singers since Billie Jones.

Another sheet was a scout's report, which, briefly summarized, said she was run-of-the-mine, but might do for fill-ins. The last page was a balance sheet of fees charged for jobs and dates of payment. There were only three, the last being more than a year old.

"Marigny's band looks like the best chance of finding her," I said.

Al interrupted savagely. "Naw. Naw. She left them. Just didn't show up one day. They got somebody else quite a while back."

I nodded. "Okay, I'll try the Willow Lane address then. Now what about Magee's connection with her?"

Al shrugged. "Just the letter is all I know," he said.

"No help there," I muttered. "Do you know whether her name is really Arabella Joslin?"

He shook his head. "Half the people in show business got fancy names. Names don't mean nothing."

"Well, how about Marigny's band? They might have a line on her. Maybe she had some friends who know where she is. Is the band still in town?"

Al grabbed the phone, barked the name into the receiver and waited impatiently, drumming his fingers on the desk. "Marigny's booked at Hollie Gray's," he said. "Down in The Bend. Not much demand for Dixieland any more," he added apologetically.

90

"It may help. Do you mind if I take this picture with me?"

"Go ahead," Al said agreeably. "I won't need it. Nobody tied up with Magee ever works out of here again."

I shoved my loot in my coat pocket and stood. "You knew The Prince for a long time?"

"Well, I wasn't no Chicago boy," Al said. "I been handling his bookings since he came East though. That's some fifteen years, I guess."

"Still going strong?" I asked absently.

"Strong? Hell, yes!" Al snapped. "The day that bastard shot him, I'm talking to him about any one of four big spots that want him. And I mean want him. Single act, play, sing, lead a band, anything he wants. They just want The Prince to come and pay the rent for them. And let me tell you, he always did, too. Drew top dollar any place."

"That's good to hear," I said. Then I caught what he had said. "Wait a minute. You say you talked to him Friday? What time was that?" There hadn't been any mention of that before.

"Huh? Why, about two, two-thirty, thereabouts. What of it?" Al demanded.

"Not a thing," I said quickly. "Just didn't know about it. Helps fix the time of death. He must have been killed right after you talked to him. The police will be glad to know about it."

"If I could fix that Magee, I'm your boy," Al said fiercely. "Ulcers or no ulcers, you tell them to call me if I can do anything."

"I'll do that," I said. "Thanks for the help. I'll probably be back for more pretty soon."

"Sure. Sure," he said briskly. "Any time. Just call me first, huh? I don't get down here very early any more."

"I will. Thanks."

He didn't get up as I left. Before I was out the door, his busy fingers had punched down a phone button and he was deep in a fast-talking conversation with someone. I shut the door behind me and went down the corridor.

The waiting room chatter picked up when I opened the door, but it dwindled when the gay throng saw who it was. Their reception sent me slinking out just the way I had come in. The brisk theatrical world is not for me.

By my watch it lacked some minutes of three-thirty and I decided to spend the time until my date with Doctor Owens by testing the address Gilman had for Bella Joe. I checked the address with the cross-referenced street guide I keep in the glove compartment. West Willow Lane was old-town. All the tree-named streets come from the original settlers who didn't waste any thought on street names until they ran out of botanical choices. Even then, they exhausted all the numbers before they looked around for other names.

According to the guide, number 997 was just beyond Sixth. I parked at the corner and picked my way down the littered street to a sagging brick house. In the muddy foyer was a row of slots holding tenants' names and a sound-powered speaker above with a push-button for each name. It took no wisdom to see that the buttons had been out of order since the troubles in Cuba. I banged on the entrance door, which stood up nobly under the first rap and sprang open with the second. It wasn't unlocked; it merely had the well-warped lintels common in a town that lies in a damp tidal basin.

I pushed the door back and went into a dingy hallway that was saved from total darkness by a feeble twenty-watt bulb high on the ceiling. I tried the first door I came to and waited patiently for an answer.

The first-floor apartment belonged to the owner, a sour-smelling, greasy-haired slattern who could neither read nor write, and hence had no record of previous tenants or their forwarding addresses. She let me thumb through a stack of addresses that her former tenants had forced on her, but there was no Bella Joe or Arabella Joslin.

The landlady had no memory of her. She suggested the local precinct house. Not that she knew anything bad about the woman, but from the kind of tenants she usually had, the police always made a useful reference. I said thank you and got out before the warm stench from her apartment knocked me flat.

It was easy to see why anyone would move from that house and it was just as easy to understand why no one would bother leaving an address. I took a deep breath and the light tinge of smoke and gasoline vapor in the cold air seemed clean and crisp after the apartment house.

Doctor Owens must have been peeking out the window, waiting for me. He was on the porch and down the walk before I came to a full stop.

"Any luck with the Joslin woman, Mr. Wilde?" he asked as he climbed in the seat beside me.

"Not yet, Doc," I said. "I still have a lead though."

He didn't push it any further. During the slow journey to The Prince's house, he sat stiffly quiet with strained lines digging grooves in his cheeks. He held his hands folded tensely together in his lap and stared straight ahead as if he were practicing his part of an unpleasant interview.

When we were still a few blocks from The Prince's address, Owens raised one hand abruptly and said, "Slow down, now. We'll park in the next block."

I eased my foot up from the accelerator and waited for the explanation.

"I'm not taking any chances," Owens said firmly. "Possibly Martha has told the servants not to let me come in. We'll walk up and go in through the studio entrance. Then we'll see what happens."

I followed his lead, parking at the next corner and walking beside him along the slippery sidewalk and up The Prince's driveway. Owens went around the house to the long solarium-studio. At a window just about in the center, he stopped and stepped over a row of low shrubs. The wide door-windows were set a few feet from the ground above the fieldstone supports. Owens put one hand on either side of a center-joint and shoved both hands sharply together and down, forcing open the simple catch with a brittle crack. He turned to me.

"I've seen Mr. Prince do that often. He used to climb right out of his car into the studio sometimes." Owens permitted himself a faint smile and then waved me ahead. "Move quietly," he warned.

I raised one leg over the sill, shoving the sea-green drapes back with my foot and muscling myself up and through the window. I pulled the heavy drapes aside when I got in and turned to give Owens a hand. He unbuttoned his overcoat to give plenty of play to his legs and leaped lightly through. We pushed the windows shut and locked them again.

Owens moved his mouth near my ear and spoke softly. "You wait here until I find Martha. I won't be long."

I nodded and Owens opened the door leading to the dining room, went through and eased it shut behind him.

The studio looked much the same as it had on my first visit. The staggered piles of records had been tidied and all the pianos were closed tightly. The breakfront liquor cabinet still held nothing but unopened bottles. The room was gradually taking on the air of a long-ignored museum. I prowled around quietly, skimming the book titles and reading parts of the playbills and souvenirs that hung on all the free wall space.

I thought I was being moderately careful, but I made one slip. Somehow a button on my coat sleeve caught in the thick fringe of an embroidered shawl thrown across one of the pianos. I felt something slide with the shawl and I pivoted and made a quick grab at a small square silver box that was then just inches from the tiled floor. I stood there stupidly for a moment, feeling the heavy pulse pounding in my head, holding the gaudy little box as if it were a dozen eggs. And then the damned thing went off. It was a music box, geared to start when it was lifted. A tinny version of *Glory Land* made thin sharp tones through the room. I stood there, holding the box tensely and wondering whether I had ruined the Doc's plans. The first eight bars had played before it occurred to me that it might stop if I put it down. I slid it quickly back on the piano and the tinkly notes were cut off abruptly.

In the thick stillness I listened sharply for any sign of response. Only after a long silence did I hear it. A light, high voice, calling querulously from the doorway at the far end of the studio. That would probably be old Mr. Prince's room, I guessed. I moved briskly up the studio, keeping my feet on the rugs and making no noise. I turned the handle on the fragile glass door and shoved my head cautiously through the entrance, squinting into the dim room.

The only other time I had seen The Prince's father, he had been lying flat and still, a shrunken ghostly figure in his ornate ebony bed. Today he was sitting propped high on enormous pillows, with long thin arms in white pajamas of heavy ribbed silk stretched across the crimson counterpane. His deep-set dark eyes focused slowly on my face. They were sharp and clear today, like bright black beetles in the gold leaf of his skin. The luminous shine of the opiate was gone now. He regarded me blankly for a moment and then he smiled, a precarious, old man's smile that stretched already taut skin to the splitting point and traced a fleeting grimace across his face.

"That eye is getting a lot better, son," he whispered.

I grinned widely and stepped through into the room. I sat in the brocaded chair that faced the old man.

"I came with Doctor Owens," I said by way of explanation. "My name is Wilde. Owens asked me to wait in there for him."

He nodded impersonally. At his age he didn't waste any more energy than he had to. I had my first good look at him. It wasn't the sort of face you see very often. The long fined-down jaws were still firmly set and the shrunken temples only emphasized the wide-domed skull above them. There was an immense amused tolerance in that face. It was a face that had seen a lot of the world's fumbling arrogance without becoming bitter or resigned.

The fragile lids raised from the eyes slowly and the old man looked toward an indefinite area above my head. "You startled me at first," he said in a barely audible tone. "We don't have many visitors these days. Harold Morton used to keep the studio filled with people. That's why I moved my bed down here. But it's very quiet now." His voice was sad and tired, with the grief and weariness of an old man who has little time left.

"That was The Prince, you mean?" I asked, just to be saying something.

He nodded with a barely perceptible movement.

97

"That's what they called him," he said proudly. " 'The Prince.' That was my boy."

"He was a great man, Mr. Prince," I said softly. I took out my cigarettes and had one halfway to my mouth when I remembered that the old man couldn't stand tobacco smoke. I put it back and tried to forget about it.

A light smile touched his lips and the high-beaked nose was fiercely proud. "Everyone says that," he said happily. "It's strange how the music was in him from the first. Just like it is in his little girl. None of us had it before Harold Morton."

"He's been one of the great ones since I can remember," I offered.

"Yes," the old man breathed softly. "It was always there. I couldn't see it at first. It took a long time for me to see it. I never did understand it, I suppose." He closed his eyes again for a brief moment and then continued, "His mother and I expected he would go through school and be a teacher then, like I was, and help his people in their troubles. All my days, I've tried to help young boys become teachers. Negro people always need teachers. I've found some good ones, too, like young Randolph Greene. Fine young men," he said happily. "Harold Morton's way was different. And just of late days, I've come to the thought that maybe it was better."

The old man's whispered tones and the faint light built a weird jumpiness in me. A sort of other-worldliness that wasn't particularly pleasant. Mr. Prince's breathing was light and quick, little pulsing inhalations that hardly seemed enough for life. His eyes were closed again. Somehow, with the strange tension and the

98

spontaneous intimacy of his conversation, I thought I could see a past picture of him in his stiff black Sunday clothes, leading a small boy through Chicago's crowded South Side streets, with the boy dancing and eager for the music of church, for the companionship of any group that spoke his language, and the father slow, erect and solemn in a white shirt front as rigid as his inflexible principles.

"I was a little stern with Harold Morton in those days, maybe," the old man murmured in a detached voice. "Too many young colored boys grew up useless. I wasn't going to let Harold Morton forget his Christian duties and drift along with the rest." He took a deep breath. "Maybe I could have done better for him, if I had had the understanding then, the knowing that there was greatness in him. Maybe. But even so, it didn't seem to hurt him much."

"It certainly didn't," I said firmly. "He wasn't the kind of man anybody could disturb much, from what little I knew of him. I don't see how he could have gone much farther, no matter what kind of a start he had."

The old man nodded with calm detachment. His thin bloodless hands fell in a composed pattern on the counterpane and he smiled briefly again.

"It's nice to hear somebody say that," he said. "So many young men these days feel that Harold Morton failed. Failed himself and failed his people. Here lately I've come to think about it and I wonder sometimes . . ." He turned to look directly at me, rolling his head on the pillow. "I used to think that a teacher could best show the way to freedom for my people," he said faintly. "Now it comes to me that a man of music *is* freedom. Even when they have it, too many people don't know what to do with freedom. They give it away to some bad-souled man with a gun, they exchange it for the glitter and forget the value. But a man of music now, why he's free like happiness and birds flying in the sky. Wouldn't you say that was about the way of it?" His dark peaceful eyes searched mine carefully.

"If The Prince were in my family, I'd be a proud man," I said inadequately.

The old man nodded fiercely and then settled back to his reclining position, shifting a slow inch at a time until he was flat again. A thin pulse beat weakly in his temple. "That's a nice thing to say to an old man," he said quietly. I'll remember that—for my time."

Even the dim pink glow seemed to bother him. He shut his eyes firmly, squinting them to keep out the light. He lay as still as he would finally. Mr. Prince was a man waiting for death and he had the special mark of the un-living upon him. He waited for death with no fear and no defiance. He was merely available when it was his turn, as he might wait in a doctor's office. I sat as quietly as I could, wondering where Owens was, wondering whether I should leave the old man.

His eyes opened and stared at the overhanging tester. "That's a silly thing for an old man," he whispered. "Harold Morton bought it for me in France. You know what it is?" He didn't wait for my answer. "There was a French family once, de Lunabiere was the name. Long ago, one of them owned my grandfather. That was in Louisiana. Owned him body and soul. This is their bed where all the children of that fine family were born. Now it's the bed where I'm going to die. Harold Morton thought it was important to get it for me. Harold Morton was a good boy and he became a great man. He didn't get the bed for me out of any bitterness in his soul. It was a big joke to him. He used to call me 'Marquis' sometimes and we'd play games about it. But the bed isn't enough. It doesn't mean anything. It's just a big silly bed." His faint grieved voice dwindled slowly away and his thin gnarled hands relaxed on the bright counterpane.

I sat there listening to his shallow breathing, waiting for him to sleep, knowing there was nothing for me to say or do. There isn't anything you can say to death. And you can't speak of death to a dead man. You save your speculation for the living. You can't tell a blind man about darkness or a mute about silence. Or a Prometheus about bondage. Old Mr. Prince was his own expert on his own past and his own future.

CHAPTER ELEVEN

THE old man's shallow breathing became gradually deeper, more regular in its impulse. I stood watching him for a moment longer. A faint smile drifted over his face. At his age, his dreams probably had as much reality as his waking moments. I rocked up on my toes and eased out into the studio.

Doctor Owens stood at the window we had used for

an entrance holding back the sea-green curtains and looking out toward the street. He heard my footsteps and pivoted quickly.

"There you are," he said with evident relief. "I was afraid you had gone."

I jerked a thumb back over my shoulder. "Talking to the old man. He looks pretty chipper today."

Owens nodded. "He's all right, you know. I think he'll come out of the shock fairly well. He hates to stay in bed, but I'm going to keep him there another week if I can."

"I thought he spent most of his time in bed," I said.

"Oh, no," Owens said quickly. "I don't imagine he has been any less active than you have." He grinned widely. "This is a remarkable family, Mr. Wilde. Full of surprises."

I angled an eyebrow at him. "Your girl give you another quick run around the block?"

He shook his head silently. His lips were pressed tight. He wanted me to guess.

"All right, so she forgives you. Wedding bells tomorrow?"

"That's close," he grinned. "Let's go in and talk to her." He poked a slim thumb in my ribs and winked. His happiness had the infectious quality that makes the world look fine. I grinned back and let him lead the way along the littered studio to the hall door and through the hall to the drawing-room where I had last seen Martha Prince.

From Owens' enthusiasm I had expected bubbling happiness or at least a quiet contentment. Instead, Martha Prince was curled in a lithe catlike knot on one

102

of the gray couches, hugging her knees tightly and staring into a bitter picture she saw somewhere beyond the flame. She started with something like fear when Owens touched her shoulder lightly.

"I've brought Mr. Wilde, my dear," he said softly.

She looked up blankly and gradually I came into her mental focus. She manufactured a wan smile and offered it. She tried to speak then, but she had to clear her throat and make a second try.

"I'm afraid I was rude yesterday, Mr. Wilde. I owe you an apology." The words came out firmly, with some determination, but the voice was thin and shaken.

"You don't owe me anything, Miss Prince," I said as quietly as I could. "It's been a rough shake for you. All round."

The smile came larger now. The voice took on a deeper tone. "Thank you, Mr. Wilde. Let's start again, shall we? I suppose Larry has told you that we—he and I —are engaged again?" A light rosiness colored her amber cheeks. She was just a little embarrassed, but her pride was obvious. She looked at Owens with the sort of look that suggested Carney Wilde had no business in these parts. I got the conversation back on my client's problem.

"Maybe you haven't talked to Doctor Owens about it yet, but what about Magee, Miss Prince?" I looked at Owens.

He sat close to the girl, shoving her feet to the floor to make room. He waved me to the opposite couch and grinned apologetically. "All right, Mr. Wilde. I guess we should talk business. Martha has changed her mind and she wants you to carry on, but before we talk about that, why don't you tell her what you have been able to find out?"

"That's an easy one, Doc." I slid my cigarettes out and offered them around. When we had them going, I got my few facts assembled and started. "I saw the police after I left you yesterday, Miss Prince. I read through the documents that Magee has to support his claim. Now, I haven't any legal advice worth listening to, but I'd say you could beat him in court with one hand behind your back. But if I understood Doctor Owens correctly, a legal decision isn't just what we want. When Magee goes to court, you should be able to present just the right evidence to get his case thrown out before he is able to open his mouth. And that's the angle I've been working on.

"Magee's entire case rests upon his word and upon affidavits from a woman named Arabella Joslin. If we can find that woman and tie her in with the fraud, establish collusion with Magee, then we've done the job.

"Manny Brenner, who runs the HOT BOX, thinks the Joslin woman may be a singer he has seen with Magee. I traced her. She uses the name Bella Joe, which is close enough to look hopeful. So far, I haven't found her, but I still have another lead to try.

"That's about it, so far. I've just been fumbling around with this case because I don't know what I'm trying to do and I don't know who I'm supposed to be working for. If it's all decided now, maybe you would let me in on it." I forced a thin smile to take the sting out of the complaint, but I pinned a questioning eye on Martha Prince and kept it there.

104

She flashed a quick look at Owens and opened her mouth, but he beat her to the draw. "Just a moment, Martha." He turned to me. "What do the police think about Magee, Mr. Wilde? Are they going to charge with him with murder? You were a trifle brief there."

I blew smoke across the coffee table and watched it spill down the far side. "The police don't think anything about Magee, Doc. They are all very happy about him because they can pin a ticklish murder on him. He hasn't been charged yet. That's probably because they want his statement first, just as a precaution. Lieutenant Grodnik has built his case and he will turn it over to the District Attorney as soon as he gets Magee's statement. The gun that was used doesn't figure in this. Grodnik has convinced himself that Magee wore gloves. The motive is good. However you figure the documents, the motive is the same.

"Now, on the matter of Magee's claim, the police just aren't interested. As I said, they don't figure in our problem. If it's an honest claim, Magee might have been threatened by The Prince and so might have something like a self defense plea. If the papers are phony, all the more reason for a fight. So there you are. Maybe the D.A. will decide he needs to know the answer and then he might put some of his men on finding the Joslin woman. The police end is pretty well finished."

Owens nodded soberly. "That's an excellent summation, Mr. Wilde. I can see you have been busy. I'm afraid that is just about what I suspected. Possibly the District Attorney will help, but I'm fairly sure he would search for her with considerable publicity and that isn't what we want. We'll have to do it ourselves. Or rather, you will have to do it for us.

"Now, I want Martha to tell you what she has learned from old Mr. Prince today. It has some bearing on the matter of motivation, possibly, and it certainly means a great deal to me."

We both looked toward Martha. She wasn't pleasant to watch just then. The happy glow went back behind her eyes and her face stiffened. She leaned forward to get rid of her cigarette and she stayed that way, with her head bent forward, one arm stiffly before her, as though she didn't want anyone to see her face.

"I feel so ashamed," she said hoarsely. "Grandfather made me hate myself. Just ten minutes talking with him made me know what a shameful life I have lived."

I fiddled with my cigarette and sat silently. Her head was low and the top of her shiny black hair bounced lights in my eyes. Owens patted her arm once, very gently and she quivered under his touch like a young colt. We waited for her to take it again.

Abruptly she tossed her head back and stared at me with damp eyes. "My father was ill, Mr. Wilde. He was dangerously ill for years and I . . . and I . . . " Her voice broke the way glass breaks, with a brittle harsh jangle. There wouldn't be any more for a while.

I thought it would probably take a few minutes for her to come out of it. I twitched around on the couch, feeling just as useless and uncomfortable as any man feels when a woman cries. I wondered if I should go away and let Owens stay alone with her. I looked toward the hall and was half raised out of my seat when the door opened slowly and a slim dark maid in a frilly uniform slid in cautiously.

She looked at me blankly, knowing I hadn't come in by the usual route. Then she spotted Martha and she moved toward her. "Miss Martha, ma'am, Mr. Greene is here to see you."

Martha Prince fought down her bitter frustrated tears. She poked a lacy handkerchief at her eyes and said shakily, "Tell him . . . "

"Tell him yourself, Martha. He's here." Greene's voice was gay and light.

Owens muttered something irritable and he rose. "Hello, Greene," he said briskly. "We're very busy just now. Would you be good enough to . . . "

"What's wrong?" Greene's long narrow eyes flicked toward me and then to Martha. "What's wrong, Martha?" he persisted. He got no answer. He pushed his dark ugly face toward Owens and snarled, "Have you been bullying her again, you . . ."

Martha Prince took over then. "Oh, sit down, Randolph," she said with jaded patience. "Let's have no drama just now." Her voice was weary and shaken but the casual dismissal shook Greene.

"But, Martha, my dear, I . . ." he stammered.

"Sit down, Randolph," she said. "Sit down and be quiet or go away."

Greene's large mouth dropped open. He stared with no belief. His eyes fell on me again and he sneered, "Has this ofay clodhopper been . . ."

"None of that, Greene," Owens' tone was a crisp snap. His thin controlled face tensed and lines grew deep around his mouth. "You'll mind your manners here, Greene," he said in a voice that was a cold threat. "And you'll show more intelligence if you forget the secret

107

race language."

Greene scowled heavily and he had a face that did full justice to a scowl. I was out of it now. Owens was fighting whatever fight there was, and even if it didn't make much sense to me, I could see he was doing fine.

"So you're selling out your race, too, eh, Owens?" He curled his meaty lip and made a gesture for Martha's attention. "Didn't I tell you there was nothing to this flatulent cut-guts? As soon as a white man talks to him, he curls up like a poodle, with his tongue hanging out."

Owens smiled bleakly. "I'm a citizen, Greene. I try to act like one." His tone was light now. It was almost bantering and yet if he had been talking to me, I think I would have looked around for a handy weapon. Greene didn't notice.

"You talk like a frightened, bent-down field hand," Greene snarled.

Martha Prince rose swiftly. "Randolph," she warned.

"A cringing . . ."

That was all for Greene. It was nice to watch. Owens moved like a fast welterweight. Leading with a right is for patsies, but Greene was a patsy and it was a fine right. It landed square on Greene's underslung chin while Owens' arm still had a small hook at the elbow. Owens followed through with a movement that would have carried him out of the house if he had missed. Greene's head snapped back and his knees locked in a high-toed position like a ballet step. He posed there daintily and then fell backwards, skidding on the deep carpet, landing with a solid clunk. Owens stood above him, breathing hard and rubbing his battered right hand.

"I'm sorry, Martha, but he's had that coming for a long

108

time," he said crisply.

Martha looked at him demurely. "Yes, dear," she said, almost primly.

We stared at her in deep surprise. She flushed faintly and reached for a bell pull beside the fireplace. She tugged it sharply twice and said, "I think we should go into the library, Larry. Mr. Wilde." She walked to the door and held it open for us.

Owens looked at me with blank wonder. We went into the library, admiring Miss Prince each step of the way. She stayed behind to tell the maids what to do with Mr. Greene. I had suggestions, but after the demonstration I had just witnessed, I didn't think Miss Prince would need any of my hints.

Owens nursed his right hand as he sat in one of four soft leather chairs that circled the library fireplace. It was a cheerful room, designed for work or rest. A long wide table in one corner was stacked high with papers and books, looking as if a heavy research program were centered there.

I grinned at Owens. "Break it, Doc?"

He shook his head. "No," he said faintly. He rubbed it again. "You know, that's the first time I ever seriously hit anyone?"

I grinned wider then. "Next time don't lead with the right, Doc. It wouldn't work very often."

That brought him out of the deep wonderment that had caught him. He smiled, faintly at first, but it grew. "Boy, I really belted him, didn't I?"

"You really did," I agreed readily.

"But you will please not make a habit of it, dear," said Martha's voice behind us. "Grandfather likes to have Randolph feel at home here." She patted Owens' head happily as she passed him. She sat in a chair beside me.

"Before all the heavy dramatics," she said calmly, "I was having a quiet little cry because I was trying to tell you about my father. It's always a shock to learn you are a fool. It's even worse to find you have been a fool most of your life, which is what I have just learned. And now let me finish it.

"I haven't lived with father for years, you see. I've been at school or at camp or traveling. I never wanted to come here and I very seldom did. Father let me do as I wished and he said nothing about it.

"I suppose I began trying to hate my father after my mother was killed. I lived with her parents for a while but they were very poor and my father offered to send me to school, which they couldn't afford. I was very lonely and homesick at school. I thought it was his fault. I suppose some of that is normal. Any child hates to have her family broken. But what comes later, there isn't any excuse for."

She chewed her lip for a moment and stared at the empty fireplace. Owens reached over to pat her hand. She shook her head savagely. "No, Larry. I'm all right.

"I used to spend vacations and holidays here at first. My father wasn't here often and I liked being with Grandfather. I woke up one night and saw my father struggling with a policeman out in the yard and screaming like a painted Indian. I thought he was drunk. I was frightened and . . . ashamed. It happened several times. And then once when I came here for Christmas, I heard a woman in his bedroom—my mother's room. She

110

was laughing and telling him not to move around so much. I didn't even let him know I'd come home that time. I went back and spent Christmas at school. I didn't know until today, when Grandfather told me, that the woman was a special nurse.

"For nearly ten years father had a brain tumor that periodically gave him great pain. When he knew he was due for a siege, he canceled all engagements and came home until it had passed. He knew he behaved wildly then, but he preferred people to think he was a drunkard rather than a sick man. He wouldn't let anyone know except Grandfather and he made Grandfather promise to keep the secret."

She stopped then. I thought of a question to prime the pump, but Owens motioned me to silence. We waited. Martha stared ahead at the picture she made for herself. She winced, but she kept looking.

"My father was very busy then. Most jazz men were finding it difficult to make a living, but The Prince," her voice stumbled but she brought it back under control. "The Prince," she repeated proudly, "was top of the heap. I imagine he was just as pleased that I wasn't around too much though.

"Later on, I think I must have hurt him terribly. I refused to stay here more than a week or two at a time. I know I said horrible things to him about his drinking. It's true that he did drink, too much sometimes when the pain was worst. Grandfather admits he didn't approve of it. He never drinks himself, you see, and I used to plan hurtful things to say to my father about it. He never said anything. He would get up and leave me, but he never defended himself.

111

"So I went on, being smugly superior and sneering at my father, at The Prince, when he was in pain."

It was a long hard session for Martha and she was showing the strain. Maybe it was good for her. She was shoving the needle pretty deep, but maybe it had to go deep to relieve the pressure. Owens' face was fixed, drawn and sad, but there was a solemn pride in his eyes.

Martha looked squarely at me then. "Mr. Wilde, Larry says you have a fine reputation as a private investigator. I want you to show Magee's charge against my father for the false, dishonest thing it is. I'm not sure how much money father left, but I know it is quite a lot. I am perfectly willing to spend every cent of it to insure that The Prince's memory is clean and shining. I behaved as badly as a daughter can behave while he was alive. My pride in my father is very great now. I want this slander disproved. You can have anything you need, any help you need to do the job."

Owens dropped his bruised right hand on the arm of Martha's chair and she stroked it gently, smiling at him.

"That's a big compliment to a man in my business, Miss Prince," I said after a long moment. "But I haven't earned the money I've had from Doctor Owens.

"Now, about your father. I have a couple of questions to ask. You may not like answering them. But I have to know. First, I want the Doc to tell me if the story about the brain tumor is sound, medically speaking?"

"You mean," Owens asked bluntly, "could Mr. Prince have had a tumor, or was his father lying just to make Martha feel better? Would that about sum it up?"

I nodded. "You're ahead of me, Doc. And rougher."

"Medically, such a condition is possible, of course. I

112

don't want to guess what the specific symptoms might be, or the possible danger of the tumor, but we will certainly have to compel his doctor to tell us now, before we talk about it further. I do not believe his father would lie—even for Martha. The pattern is true and it rings true. Also, and probably more important as an element of proof, the last letter from The Prince to his father bears it out. Martha saw it, a brief little note mentioning severe pains coming on and warning his father to get things ready for him, because the pain was worse than he had ever felt before."

"Okay, Doc," I said. "Now tell me this: Why in hell didn't he get rid of it? Whatever he had? Can't you sawbones do anything about brain tumors?"

"Not so fast, not so fast," Owens objected. "Let's find out from his doctor before we try any wild guesses."

I bowed. "Doc, you're in the wrong racket. Or maybe I'm in the wrong racket. But if that crack about wild guesses was a pun, I quit."

Martha laughed, high soprano laughter. "Oh, no, Mr. Wilde. If that was a pun, we'll both quit."

Owens grinned. His face was wide and innocent to the point of burlesque. "I'll confess," he said, grinning, "that I'm convinced a pun is a fine thing. But that was unintentional. So you can stick around. Next question?"

"The next one is really wild, Doc. What does The Prince's illness mean as far as his death is concerned?"

Owens' face went sober again. "I read Magee's affidavit rather hurriedly, but I do remember that he stated that he was making his claim at this time because Mr. Prince might die any moment. Possibly that is true. And possibly Mr. Prince told him about it. However, it occurred to me as a vague chance that Magee's knowledge of the illness might have some bearing on all this. If it was kept secret from everyone else, it should not have been known to Magee."

I thought about it while I lit a cigarette. I shook my head slowly. "It's a thought, Doc, but it sounds thin. Maybe it does have a bearing, but I can't see how it could be important."

Owens flashed a bright smile. "Well, I'll not become a detective just yet then, Mr. Wilde. I'll stay with medicine."

"But what about your grandfather?" I asked Martha. "What's his opinion of Magee? He must have seen him often enough."

"But Larry said . . ." she began.

"Yes," he interrupted. "I've given orders that no one is to mention his son's death to old Mr. Prince. Possibly he didn't see the gun beside the body. He did see his son lying there dead and he collapsed from the shock. I don't want him disturbed any more until he recovers."

"Why not?"

Owens frowned slightly. "Look here, Mr. Wilde. I'm his doctor. He has a cardiac condition that isn't unusual in a man his age, but it could become critical with shock. I plan to let him up next week and then I'll tell him about it. Then if anyone wants to question him, I'll permit it, but not before next week."

I nodded. "You're the doctor."

Owens grinned suddenly. "Now we're even, Mr. Wilde."

"Okay, Doc, I'll stick to my problem." I leaned back in the deep leather chair.

114

"And I'll stick to Martha," Owens said softly.

And that really broke up the party. Glowing gazes met and melted and poor old Wilde sat out in the chilly emptiness. I stood it as long as I could and then I climbed clumsily to my feet and offered a hand to Owens.

"Congratulations, Doc," I said. "You're moving in on quite a family. When is the wedding?"

"Tomorrow, if I have my way," Owens said firmly.

"Larry, you fool," Martha giggled. She clutched my arm tightly. "Next month, Mr. Wilde . . . no, I won't call you Mr. Wilde any longer. What is your first name?" she demanded.

"Carney, ma'am," I mumbled.

"Carney," she repeated slowly. "Carney. Fine. Then, Carney, you shall come to the wedding. I'll throw my bouquet right into your hands."

"I'll be there," I grinned. I backed away and headed toward the door. Martha raised a hand quickly and stopped me.

"Not through there, please. I had the maids put Randolph on a couch. You wouldn't want to meet him now." I didn't argue about it.

"I'll go quietly," I said. "Which way?"

Martha walked to the opposite door. She went through and lifted my coat from the rack in the hall closet.

"Oh, Carney. I had a call from Manny Brenner last night. He is planning an All-Prince Night tomorrow. He wanted me to come and maybe to play. I wasn't going to, but now . . ."

"Sure," I grinned. "I think you should. I'll come, too,

if you'll play *Smite-um, Daniel* for me."

"Oh, I will," she said eagerly. "You just come and listen. Us Princes."

"You Princes," I agreed.

Her pale amber skin was alight with pink tones. Her long strong face was spread in the broad grin that had made The Prince a familiar and favorite citizen for a long time. The resemblance was close enough to be shivery when she grinned like that.

"I'll play the *Nathan Hale Rhapsody,* too," she said solemnly. "That's a really *big* piece."

I pulled the door open.

"Okay, Prince."

CHAPTER TWELVE

It was nearly six o'clock when I pulled down the drive away from The Prince's sprawling fieldstone homestead.

Possibly the session at The Prince's house had put me ahead in my chore, but I couldn't quite see how. I knew more about The Prince, and that was worth the bother. I began to like his daughter and I hadn't expected that would happen. Either she had changed radically or she was a fine enough actress to fool me. The new manner might be something she could put on as easily as her lipstick.

So far as useful information was concerned, I had hardly anything that helped. Maybe I had a better idea of Magee's motive for murder, but that wasn't precisely my job. It didn't show me how to prove that Magee was a phony with a slick conman's claim to The Prince's music. And that was the only job I was working on.

I couldn't get my mind off Owens somehow. I kept seeing that loose, relaxed expression that came just before he swung on Greene. That was a really satisfactory clout he threw. I thought back through the incident and saw the gaps where my knowledge didn't quite catch up with the party. Owens blew his top for a crack that didn't make any sense to me. Maybe Greene's phrase meant something particularly nasty, but you couldn't prove it by me. It was a language I didn't know and it grew from a bitterness that wasn't natural to me.

I brought myself back to my driving just in time to make the turn from South Gilmore Drive into Chester Boulevard. I could keep straight and wind up in The Bend, down along the docks and close to the place where Gene Marigny's band was playing. But a few blocks detour west would bring me to my apartment and that idea won out. I swung left at Sycamore and wound my way through the involved pattern to my house.

In the sitting room I glugged together the makings for a brace of dry Manhattans and carried the jug with me into the kitchen for some ice. I let the mixture sit idly while I shucked my coat and hat. Then I took the pitcher of grog into the sitting room with me. I still have two unbroken cocktail glasses left from the original dozen, but I seldom bother with them. I slammed the icy mixture, ice and all, into a tall highball glass and stretched on the couch.

I let the telephone ring three times before I shoved off the couch. Every time it rings when I'm in the sitting room, I make a solemn promise to get an extension. I'll probably never do anything about it.

I sat on the edge of the bed, took a deep swig at my glass and lifted the phone.

"Wilde?" a voice whispered. It was the old handkerchief gag, I suspected. Stuff a handkerchief into the mouthpiece of a telephone and whisper through it and you have a well disguised, thready voice. That way any voice sounds like any other. But it's hard to make the voice carry a threatening tone, and that's what this voice was trying.

I grunted nastily. "I'll tell him when he comes in." I banged the phone down and waited for it to ring again. It was a two-second wait.

"That's two nickels wasted," I said the second time.

The voice was stronger this time, but still well muffled. "Lay off, wise guy," it said thinly. "Just lay off that business with The Prince. Get me? Lay off or get hurt."

I manufactured a yawn and let it stretch out.

The voice snarled at me. "That's all for you, wise guy. Don't forget."

This time he beat me to it. His receiver snapped down with a bang. I put mine back and fished a cigarette from the box beside the phone. I sat there, staring at the floor, reaching back through my memory for anything that justified the threat. I've had too many anonymous threatening phone calls in this racket to let any of them disturb me, but the motivation for them can often be important—to someone. I couldn't see anything in my job to frighten anyone, unless it might be the Joslin

118

woman. I picked up my drink and sprawled back on the bed, reminding myself that a private detective's life is a life of constant peril, much as the sailor's. I drank a toast to my romantic existence, making a wide strained grin at the ceiling. But the skin on the back of my neck stayed tense and watchful.

Shortly before seven I heaved myself upright and got my clothes on. I didn't know whether I was playing it smart or not in going down to Hollie Gray's night club that early. It seemed like a good idea at the time. Hollie Gray's isn't a place where you go to dinner. Business wouldn't move there until ten. But musicians have a way of hanging around the place where they work. Maybe they don't get paid enough to drink any other place.

I shrugged into my coat, picked up my hat. I stopped at my dresser and reached under a pile of fresh handkerchiefs for the small square persuader I kept there. I bounced it up and down in my palm, remembering where I had got the idea.

During prohibition, when I was a lot younger than I would admit, there was a bouncer at the old Bohemian Club who used a persuader in both hands. In that grimy little place he wore glistening white kid gloves all the time. The rest of his clothes never came up to his gloves. He was called Buster. Maybe he had another name but I never heard it. Buster's white kid gloves held a tight pocket of chamois sewn snugly around an ounce of bird shot. In his gloves, the persuaders were lethal. Once I saw him pat a hefty bruiser's cheek with a motion that looked hardly more vigorous than an admiring tap and the lad who caught it went sliding on his keister right out the door.

I slipped the heavy wad of bird shot into my glove and worked it in toward my palm where it fitted without a bulge. It felt like ten pounds of bother, but I didn't mind that. I don't want to wander around The Bend even in daylight with no more protection than my fists. It's that kind of neighborhood. Every city has them. The Bend had a series of night clubs all within a few blocks and they pulled suckers from miles around. If you didn't know better, The Bend might seem glamorous. If you didn't know better, Hitler might have seemed glamorous. When I had to snoop around in The Bend, I wore my .38 most of the time. The persuader seemed to cover the problem for now.

I aimed my car away from the curb near my apartment and stayed in the right-hand lane, letting the commuters take over the highway. By the time I reached the center of the city, cars were bumper to bumper for dozens of blocks. I turned left at Ransom and headed toward The Bend, leaving most of the personal traffic behind and getting myself tied up with a confusion of heavy produce trucks and semi-trailers hauling shipments outward bound from the docks that circle The Bend.

Hollie Gray's night club is a clip joint with little to recommend it. Hollie is a character far too common in every city. He started in business with a wheezing farm truck that he stole from his father. With it he met the speed-boat pilots who ran the shuttle from the liquor ships hull down beyond the legal limit. He took small portions for the rest of the distance. Hollie was arrested as often as seemed proper. He paid his meager fines with a confident smirk for the newspapers. Hollie wasn't big enough to make the papers often. He was never in any shooting scrapes. If the wad of large denomination bills on his hip wouldn't buy him a free trip, he was willing to come along and pay a legal fine. During that long and enterprising career, Hollie learned whatever one needs to know to become a restaurateur. A restaurateur has no resemblance to a man who owns a restaurant, or even to a headwaiter. He is the man whose name is on the canopy, who counts the profits each week and whose major assignment is to mingle with the local yokels who think that conversation with a small-scale hard guy is a night's entertainment. Hollie fitted into the scheme nicely. I had been to his place several times, usually because his manager often booked some fine orchestras, and once to pull out a young punk who had worked over one of my clients. Hollie didn't like me very much.

I pulled into a parking lot a block from his club and parked as close to the attendant's cubicle as I could get. My car isn't worth much and its chrome work is hardly noticeable, but what there is of it, I would just as soon keep for a while longer. I picked a slow stumbling route along the snow-clogged streets. A block later I turned in at Hollie Gray's club.

The check room girl wasn't on duty yet. I went through the foyer and down past the bar. Two tired-looking men in dark suits were huddled at one end and the bartender was as far away as he could get without leaving the room. His ear was bent close to a radio that was tuned too low to carry to me. I kept going in to the restaurant section.

The color scheme was something exotic and bilious. The chairs and banquettes were padded in a striped fabric with the white portion nearly blanked out by constant rubbing. The band shell was the usual gimcrackery thing. A plyboard base, flimsy cardboard shields painted with silver gilt for holding music and extra instruments. A piano that had once been respectably black was now coated with flat white paint that had begun to chip at the edges. At the piano was a long bent man. He held a fat stack of sheet music on his lap and thumbed through it with no apparent interest. Near him at a table beside the stand was another man, sleepily peering at a paper spread flat on the table. A short fat black instrument case weighted one side of the paper. I worked my way through the crowded tables and came up behind them.

"We ain't got it, Harry," said the man at the piano.

The man at the table shrugged without looking up.

Sheet music slapped the scarred top of the piano and the bent figure straightened with a long sighing yawn. His hands fell lightly on the keyboard and his fingers flashed through a bright arpeggio of dancing notes.

"That's the theme structure," he said in a nasal voice. He turned toward the man at the table and saw me.

"Sounds good," I said.

The piano player nodded. "Lost the music. Have to work out a head arrangement, I guess." He slapped the keyboard with a peevish hand. "Damned thing is out of tune," he muttered.

His face was long and pale with that chronic indoor pallor that is the musician's badge. His back seemed to have no backbone in it. Instead of stiffening occasionally, it just collapsed again like a well-pulled bow. His eyebrows were black and stiff, with a sharp angle near the far ends. He had fine eyebrows for asking questions. He asked me a few with them.

"I'm looking for Gene Marigny," I said.

He shook his head. "Out. He never gets here before show time."

"Maybe you'll do."

"Maybe." He rose in a flowing motion and stepped to the floor. "Want to leave a message?"

"Nothing that fancy," I said. "I'm trying to find a singer who used to work with you."

The piano player lifted his rounded shoulders once and let them drop. "Just came with Marigny last month. You better ask Gene yourself." He sat at the table near the man with the newspaper.

I pulled out a chair opposite them and sat. The man with the paper looked up briefly, yawned widely, said "Parm me," and went back to his reading, moving his lips as he read.

I fumbled awkwardly in my pocket with my bare left hand. The first bill I could get separated was a five and I suspected that might be enough.

I twisted the bill into a butterfly and sat it on the table where it rocked gently in the warm moving air. The piano player looked at it and at me with casual suspicion.

"For what?" he asked softly.

"Just suppose I buy a bottle," I said. "Then maybe we could talk about a singer for a minute."

He touched the bill with a pale finger and moved it a short inch away from him. "That buys two bottles of what I drink, but it wouldn't buy you a thing." He pushed at the bill again and nudged his literary friend. "Harry, you got five bucks' worth of information?"

The reader shrugged with his eyes hard on the paper. "What I know ain't worth a dime. Unless you want a tip at Hialeah." He marked the end of a paragraph with his thumb and raised his eyes. They stopped at the bill, regarded it dimly and then came up to my face. "Private cop?" he asked hoarsely.

I nodded. "Nothing important, boys. I'm looking for a singer named Bella Joe. Blues singer."

"A dog," Harry said easily.

"I wouldn't know," I said. "I never heard her."

"A dog."

"Okay."

"A real dog." Harry wobbled his head sadly. "She can't beat. She ain't got a tone and she can't sell. A real dog. What in hell you want her for?"

"Not for singing," I said. "Not after that. She's just a witness to an accident. I need a statement from her. You know where she is now?"

Harry stared at the five-dollar bill. "Cheap job?"

I nodded. "Not worth much to anybody. There could be another one to go with that, if you can give me her address."

Harry turned to the piano player. He leaned far over the table toward me and asked softly, "No rumble?"

"Not so far as I know," I said.

"I don't know that answer anyway, peeper," he said with a tight smile. "Least I ain't sure. What do you pay for a guess?"

I pushed the five toward him with a forefinger.

"Okay. I'm sitting in a session with Manny Brenner and some of the boys from Herman's mob about a month back. I'm coming out maybe four, five o'clock and I see

Bella Joe going up a stairs to a crummy house right around there." Harry looked at me with speculation. "That a good guess?"

I leaned my finger heavily on the bill. "Guess a little more about where the house was," I suggested.

He grinned. "Onna corner, maybe three blocks down the alley."

"Maybe?"

"Aincha goin' to ask me how I know, peeper?"

"Sure," I said. "How do you know?"

"Because I'm looking at this broad-beamed babe pushing up the stairs and I wonder where I seen her before. And I cross the street and I see that music store onna corner there. Bell Music. Bell Music. Get it? Bell Music. Bella Joe. Got it, huh?"

I lifted my finger. "Got it," I said. "Thanks." I got my left hand around to my wallet and took it out. I swapped a ten for the five on the table. "That's a help."

Harry fingered the ten with close interest. "Any time, peeper. Any time."

I buttoned my coat. I picked up my hat and waved it toward the bandstand. "Much of a play, these days?"

Harry grunted heavily, "Stinks. Le jazz hot is no living. People got records. They got the radio. And they won't pay the freight for hot crews no more."

"The Prince was doing all right," I said absently.

Harry snorted. "Sure. And why? He's a curiosity. Just like Armstrong. Now I don't say there's a better horn than Pops today, but that ain't what drags in the crowds. He's old man History. He's just about the last horn that come up from Storyville, played the river boats, blew Chi all to hell. For my dough, The Prince ain't a jazz man like old Satchmo. He's more the classical type. Like Bix got to be in his later days. You know *In a Mist?* The Prince was like that, too. Awful big, but it wasn't always jazz." Harry heated up and his eyes came alive. He nudged his friend. "Whatcha say there, Box?"

The piano man roused himself. He made a rude noise with his lips. "I say *Still Water Blues* beats even *Royal Garden.* And if that ain't jazz, I'll start playing a horn like the other eggheads." He scowled deeply at Harry.

Harry leaned back perilously in his chair and hee-hawed in a high voice. "See, peeper? All these rhythm ticklers is nuts."

The piano man prodded the table with a rigid finger. "I got a record back there," he said grimly, nodding his head toward the rear of the club. "Bunk Johnson doing *Still Water Blues.* Johnny Dodds, Minor Hall and Dutrey with him. That," he said insistently, jabbing his finger at the table, "that, you slot-brained bastard, is jazz. You hear me?"

"You're right," Harry said soberly. "I hear you, Box. I remember that one. I play me a little trombone, too. I'll go some to get close to Dutrey on that one. The Prince really hit it there."

They regarded each other with loving forgiveness, forgetting I was still there. Harry banged his friend on the shoulder, flipped the ten in front of his nose. "Let's pick up some corn before we go to work," he offered. He winked at me as they rose. "Come back real soon, peeper."

I said I'd be back to hear them some day, but Harry didn't look as though he believed me.

The bar had a dozen new patrons as I came through

again. The bartender's radio was turned off and he was working hard. I stopped at the far corner, leaned across the mahogany and ordered a straight rye.

"Put your money away, Wilde," a hard voice said. "We don't serve finks in here."

I turned slowly. A wide, hammered-down man scowled up at me. A good thick scowl for the paying customers. "Hello, Hollie," I said. "You're putting on weight."

He moved closer. "Too much weight for you, Wilde." Both hard wide hands clutched the edge of the bar tightly and ropy muscles bunched against the wood. Hollie had to lean his head back to keep his gimlet stare boring at me, but he was used to that by now. He stood about five-and-a-half feet. Now and then some jerk would make the mistake of trying to take him. The outcome was always the same. The jerk was slammed from behind while he was still winding up. Hollie hadn't done his own fighting in years. I didn't bother to look behind. Someone was there, I knew. I probably wouldn't know him, anyway.

"I don't like cops bothering the help," Hollie said tightly. "What the hell do you want here, anyway?"

I shrugged. "Ask the help, Buster. It's no secret."

One meaty finger stabbed at my chest. "I'm asking you, bright boy," he said nastily. "What's the pitch?"

I leaned my left elbow on the bar and shoved back my hat. "Cost you a drink, Hollie."

He didn't want to play games. His wide flat face went white and stiff. He hadn't been needled often enough lately to know how to take it. He was being insulted. His eyes glared at me tensely and then they lifted, moved to a focus behind my back. I didn't wait any longer.

I moved just a whisper ahead of the sap. I rolled on my elbow, spinning down the bar toward Hollie while the blackjack artist behind me swung where my hat had been. His sap swept down the loose folds of my overcoat and he followed through, stumbling after me. I used the momentum of my movement to get both arms around Hollie Gray.

Hollie hadn't expected that. He was standing flat-footed with both hands still on the bar. I braced one foot on the brass rail for leverage and laid my persuader solidly along the base of his jaw. The bird shot in my glove landed with a satisfying clunk. Hollie slumped, staggering toward his blackjack operator. They held each other lovingly for that flash of a frozen moment. Then I swung my loaded glove at the back of Hollie's skull. He sighed softly when it landed, wrapped his wide arms around his boy and fell with him to the floor. I didn't wait to see what they looked like.

I got away from the bar as fast as I could. When my back hit the wall, I stayed there, half-crouched, facing the bar, with my loaded right hand tucked in the V of my overcoat. That stopped all movement.

The bartender had one hand on the bar and a foot lifted ready to leap. He held it right there like a broken movie film. Only one of the barflies appeared to be one of Hollie's crew. He was just inches away from me, hands reaching forward. He tried to stop, but he couldn't make it. The force of his charge carried him into me, but there wasn't anything behind it. He was trying to get away and I helped him with a left hand bouncing off his nose. He stumbled to the bar and stayed there.

My right hand was getting all the attention. They seemed to think that no one would be stupid enough to mix it with Hollie unless he were loaded for big game. I agreed that no one should try it. I slid carefully along the wall, keeping my hand under my coat. My face felt hard and cold and my nerves were tight, eager for movement. I held my motion to a crawl toward the door. I turned with my hand on the knob. No one had moved. "Just hold it there for a while," I said tightly.

I banged the door behind me and jumped into the first doorway up the street. My breath popped in a faint explosion and I realized I had been holding it still, breathing with the top of my lungs. I dragged down a few snorts of the icy breeze and tried to get my pulse down to normal.

I could see the entrance to Hollie Gray's night club without moving. I would still have a slight edge if anyone came after me. I wouldn't have a chance in the long empty block between me and my car. I stayed there until the cold air came reaching through my heavy coat. No one left the club.

I stared blindly at the misty neon light over the door, trying to bring back a memory of the anonymous voice that had called me on the phone. Just then I wanted to see a resemblance to Hollie's voice. I tried to convince myself, but a thin edge of doubt stayed with me. The handkerchief gag is effective. All the wishful thinking I could manage wouldn't point a definite finger at Hollie Gray.

I stepped quickly out of the doorway, moving swiftly and as quietly as I could manage, up the cold quiet street toward the distant corner.

CHAPTER THIRTEEN

I BATTLED my way through the early evening traffic to my usual space in a lot near my office building. That left me about eight blocks to walk to reach Bella Joe's address. I decided to go on foot rather than fight any more traffic.

I had given my trouser cuffs an extra turn up when I got out of the car, but they were rimmed with soggy street slush by the time I reached the Bell Music Shop. I could see why Harry would know it well. The dusty glass displayed a collection of pictures of the great hot men. They were mostly trumpet players, which is logical enough. The hard powerful drive of a jazz trumpet makes you notice the men who can play it right. Some time later you hear the counterpoint harmony that holds it all together and then you begin to look for the other instruments.

I pivoted with my back to the music shop and looked across the street. The house on the opposite corner had a door set flush with the sidewalk. The one next to it had a short curling run of steps that jumped the half-basement and went toward the second floor. That seemed to be the one I wanted.

Tenants were listed on a row of mail-boxes. Half the boxes had illegible smears of block printing in faded ink or pencil. Number Seven slot held a neatly printed name, "A. B. Joe." The boxes were brass and all except the one marked "Joe" were dingy and green with age. The "Joe" box glistened coldly from frequent polishings. I didn't like any part of that. The woman I wanted should be living under the hat. The clearly printed name, the polished box, were things that looked like a law-abiding taxpayer. I pushed the bell above Number Seven with a reluctant finger. I had a bad hunch that Arabella Joslin was going to be hard to find.

No one answered. I leaned on the bell for a long moment. I could hear no ringing, which wasn't surprising in an old well-built house. I thumbed the bell push again just for luck and twisted the door knob. It moved back easily.

A narrow dim hall stretched back from the door. There were just five doors on the first floor. I climbed a dark staircase to the next floor. Number Seven was one of two front apartments that faced the intersection. I knocked heavily on the panel.

There was no answer. The house was still. The freezing air made old boards groan slightly and the window glass murmured. No one moved. I knocked again, a police knock this time, two brisk peremptory raps that speak of arrogant impatience. That brought an answer, but not from Number Seven.

The next door, Number Six, snapped back against the wall. A sleep-frowzeled head leaned around the opening. The man was heavy, dark and tired-looking, with red-rimmed eyes, a sleep-swollen face. He regarded me with weary disgust.

"She ain't home, mister. How's for letting me get some shut-eye?" He was big enough to put it in stronger language, but he made it a mild request.

"Sorry," I said. "It's pretty important. Do you know where I can find her?"

"Naw." He reached a dark calloused hand for the door and pulled it back toward him. "I ain't seen her in a week."

I watched the door close. Heavy steps crossed the room and old springs complained when his heavy body sank on them again. The name on the door was "H. M. Godfrey." Why that seemed important, I couldn't say.

I gave Number Seven mail-box a quick rub for luck on my way out. It still didn't make much sense to find that the woman I was looking for was living quite that openly. Not unless she was sure she had kept herself clear of the whole thing. If she wasn't in with Magee on the fraud, her behavior was reasonable. I was hoping that wouldn't be the answer. Usually, on a job, I'm just digging for the facts that make the story. I don't give much of a damn how they come. I give my clients a break, but none of them get breaks when the facts go against them. But this one was different. I wanted to sink Magee. I wanted to see The Prince's reputation stay something shiny and fine. If Bella Joe were also Arabella Joslin and she wasn't trying to duck, it began to look as if Magee might be on the level. That would make me as wrong as I could get. I didn't want to think about it.

I stumbled along the sidewalks, heading for Sam's Grill and something hot and alcoholic before dinner.

Long winter shadows already darkened the narrow streets and the uneasy footing of the daytime had become perilous hazards now. I slid and staggered to Sam's, picked up an evening paper and sat far back in a rear booth, grateful for warmth and silence.

It still lacked a few minutes of eight o'clock when I got out of the booth and paid my tab. I had things to talk over with Manny Brenner and it seemed to be a good idea to catch him before he got steamed up with his music. Yesterday I was keeping Magee's claim a secret from anybody. Today I wanted help. I was willing to swap for it.

I stopped at the parking lot for my car and drove back, leaving the car around the corner from Bella Joe's house. I went through the door-banging routine once again with no result. I turned left coming out and went on down the alley to the HOT BOX.

The bar was getting a little play tonight but everyone there was quiet. They were all men and they all seemed tired and discouraged. Manny was behind the bar, counting the money in the till. He had a short, wide-mouthed glass beside him. He counted a few bills, sipped at the drink and counted some more.

"I'll have a little of both, Manny." I climbed on a stool near him and leaned over the bar.

He looked up with a wide grin. "You better have the rye, kid, it's still as good as it ever was." He locked a sheaf of bills between two fingers and poured a generous gollop of Canadian Club into a short tumbler. He ignored a chaser and I knew better than to ask for one. He licked his forefinger and finished his counting. He laid the bills carefully in the cash drawer and slammed

133

the register shut. He looked at me, shaking his head. "Takes three of them these days, steada one." He lifted his drink in half-salute. "One of these still does the work."

I agreed with no reservations. We drank to his noble thought. I put my empty glass down and spoke to him quietly, "Can you get away for a minute, Manny?"

"You wanna see me?" he asked with light sarcasm. "I thought you was just killing time till Nancy got here."

"That, too," I admitted.

Manny's face grew sober and pinched. "I got things to talk to you about, too, Hawkshaw. Let's go upstairs." He tipped a thumb to indicate that the bartender had it all for himself. Then he lifted a hinged section of the bar and came out.

Manny's office was a room on the second floor. It was the only room left there when the ceiling had been lifted to make a larger room downstairs. We climbed stairs and I waited while Manny fumbled for his keys.

That room could tell you everything about Manny. It was all there somewhere. Manny was a souvenir saver and the square cluttered room was a shambles of personal junk. Pictures covered every wall and a short ton of gadgets had been pinned on top of them. There was an old-fashioned glass-doored bookcase full of sheet music, probably each piece autographed. An ancient iron safe that would take a good peterman five minutes to open had a place of honor beside Manny's rosewood desk. The desk was almost clear. Just a few oddments, three clarinets in locked cases, a desk-pen set with marble ends, a vivid orange blotter in a padded leather holder. Manny pointed to a rump-sprung leather chair near the desk. He let me admire the room and watched me with proud eyes.

"Pretty fine, huh?"

I put my hat and coat on the desk and sat. "It's fine, Manny," I said. "It hasn't changed much."

"Won't neither," he said firmly. "The old lady always tries to throw the stuff away. I have me a hell of a time before I get this place. Nice to have a place to keep things." His round pink face waited for a smart crack from me about his room. I didn't want to make any cracks.

"Wish I had one," I said.

Manny smiled rosily. He slid into his chair with a quick motion. His hands locked automatically behind his head and both feet came up to a restful posture on the desk.

"This babe you was asking about, Carney. Bella Joe. Maybe you better tell me about her, huh?"

"Sure, Manny. And thanks for giving me the tip. I haven't found her yet, but I think I will pretty soon."

Manny grinned widely. "I found her for you, kid." He leaned far back and spoke toward the ceiling. "Little Nancy comes in and tells me you really want that old babe, so I give you a hand. Okay?"

"I should say it's okay. Any time. I know where she lives now, thanks to you. But I haven't seen her yet."

Manny let me dangle a little longer. He had a triumph and he meant to savor it. He watched me slyly from innocent eyes. "I hadda talk with her this afternoon."

I gave him his triumph. We listened to the silence while Wilde registered surprise in wholesale lots. I let Manny milk it for a moment longer and then asked the question.

"Why?"

Manny shrugged. "You get me all curious last night, I guess. I told Nancy about this babe I remember. And then she sees you and I find out it's got something to do with that job you got for young Doc Owens. And then when I talk to Martha today to ask her to come on down here tomorrow night, I say something about this Joe babe and she acts kinda funny about it. Then the Doc takes over and says it's under the blanket for now. He says it's maybe big stuff about The Prince. So I got a little hot about it. Nobody asks me nothing. Nobody comes to me and says I should get busy and help. Just some half-smart gumshoe that don't know Hines from Heifetz comes around asking if The Prince wrote his own stuff. You think I didn't notice that?"

"Okay, Manny," I said softly. "You noticed it. Then what?"

"So then I phone around a while and find this Joe babe. She lives in a flea-bag just downa street, so I go talk to her."

"And then?"

Manny brought his chin down and looked obliquely at me. "What's it all about, kid?" he asked gently. "I'm the best friend The Prince ever had. And the oldest. What's the score here?"

"You get it all, Manny. And right now," I said quickly. "That's really why I came here today. But what did you talk to Bella Joe about?"

He shrugged easily. "Hell, I'm scared to talk to her much. I figure maybe you're cooking up a king-sized plot and I'm scared I'll step all over it. I shoot the breeze

136

with her about how I hear she is hot with the warbling and maybe I can use her. We kick it around for a while and then I leave."

"That's all?"

"Hell, gimme time, kid," Manny grinned. "I case the joint pretty close while we're chewing it over. There's a coupla pictures on a little table but I don't get close enough to see them good. That big babe is pretending to be listening to me, but all the time she's kinda keeping me penned in near the door and I don't want to tip my mitt. But still I get a look at something that makes it a good bet she's the one you want."

He was waiting for the question. I asked it.

"You remember that high school book I showed you?" he asked. "I got it around here somewheres." He pawed aimlessly around his desk and looked quickly about the room. "Oh, well, maybe I left it down in the bar. Anyway you remember it. That babe, Joe, she's got one, too."

I nodded. "Yeah," I said slowly. "I guess she has Magee's copy."

Manny shook his head firmly. "Nope. Couldn't be. This Magee was three-four years older then me and The Prince. He had a job swamping out a saloon when me and The Prince was in school. I don't even think he graduated anyway. But that Joe babe sure had one. 1915, too. I notice it and I point at it and say, 'My, was you a Western girl, too?' And she don't fall for it. She mumbles something about her brother or maybe a friend of her brother's. She ain't sure. And, like I said, I'm scared to push because I don't know where you want to go."

"You did fine, Manny. What else?"

"That's about it. I say something about that being my yearbook. Same year. We talk a little about how you never get tired of looking at the old pictures and then I tell her she should come down here sometime and let me hear her go over some songs. She says she will and then I blow."

"When is she coming here?"

"No time special. She's going to call me first. Now, what's it all about, kid? What's this old babe up to?"

I searched my pockets for the picture Al Gilman had given me. "This the woman?" I tossed it to Manny.

He looked at it briefly, flipped it back. "That's the one. So what?"

"So I still don't know whether she really is Arabella Joslin, but that Chicago yearbook makes it look probable. I'll give you the story now, Manny, but let's get this straight first. It's all under the hat. Every bit of it. I want your help and I especially want your guesses, but it can't go any further. Okay?"

Manny bobbed his head silently.

"When the cops grabbed Magee, he was running out the back of his house with documents that seem to prove that Magee and not The Prince wrote most of the music that has been credited to The Prince. The police agreed to keep the documents secret because they don't mean anything particular to their case. They have Magee for murder. The rest they were willing to let alone for a while.

"The Joslin woman comes in because there were two affidavits in the stack that were signed by an Arabella Joslin. She swears that Magee wrote a couple of songs

138

for her some years before The Prince published them. And that's our problem. Magee's case won't stand up in court, but we don't even want to let it get that far."

Manny's round face was tight and angry. His mouth was twisted down at the corners and he looked at me as though he were peering under a damp log. I lifted both hands in a peaceful motion and waited for him to come out of it. After a moment he smiled sheepishly and nodded. I let my hands drop.

"Magee is still in the hospital," I went on. "I probably won't be able to question him for another day or so. That leaves the Joslin woman as my only lead. And if Bella Joe is the same woman, I want her bad."

Manny's voice was grim. "Me, too," he said flatly.

"Nope," I said. "It's my show. I'll have to handle it."

There was thick silence in the cluttered room. Manny stared blankly at the far wall with lost, angry eyes. "It makes me sick," he said softly. "You don't even have to know The Prince for it to make you sick."

I didn't say anything. Manny wasn't talking to me.

"He used to sit down at the piano some days, just sorta resting his fingers, you'd think. And he'd fumble around a minute. And then he'd look up and say, 'Manny, boy, you play like this.' And he'd shape up a light little pattern for me. Then he'd turn to whoever was on trumpet and he'd outline that man's part. And so on, real old New Orleans head arrangements, nothing on paper. You don't see that any more. He'd just take a little bitty eight-bar idea he got. Something that didn't sound like anything at all. Then he'd build it up. We'd boot it around for a while and before we were finished, we'd have ourselves a terrific sock. And by the time we had it set, The Prince had most of the words ready for the singer. That's a composer, kid. He mighta been other things, too. Maybe he wasn't the best man in the world. Maybe he was a nasty drunk sometimes. Okay. I won't argue it right now. I'm just saying that was a composer, see?"

"I see," I said in a low voice. Manny didn't hear me.

"We start playing in school and my old man don't like it. He's got a trucking business, doing pretty good, too, and he wants me to work into it. And he don't like colored people worth a damn anyway. Just after I get out of school, he puts it up to me cold. I work on the trucks or I blow. I never even thought about it. Me and The Prince, we were hot men. I blow out of the house and I ain't been back since. And me and The Prince, we made a hunk of music. But The Prince made most of it. Right out of his head."

"Tell me about Magee, Manny," I interrupted in a loud voice. I didn't like to watch that concentrated stare, that low insistent murmur of Manny's voice that sounded too much like a man whipping himself up to something. Manny turned slowly and looked at me. His eyes focused slowly on me and he blinked several times before he answered.

"Yeah," he said hoarsely. "Magee. I never knew him very well. He lived next door to The Prince and him and The Prince were all the time together. I never gave a damn for him, though, even then."

"Was he really a good arranger?"

"Sure," Manny said firmly. "He even did a tour with old Pops Whiteman. Damned good, I guess. Nothing like as good as The Prince, though."

140

"But why did The Prince keep him around, if he didn't need him?"

"Hell, I didn't say that," Manny objected. "The Prince could make arrangements, all right. It's a job of work. The Prince didn't like to bother. He just worked out the piece and then he threw it over to Magee to work out a big orchestral arrangement. Took a lot of time. Lot of talent, too. When Magee finished it, The Prince would clean it up and then it would go to the publisher."

"Did Magee ever write anything under his own name?"

"I never heard of it," Manny said. His eyes watched me. They were hard and bright.

"Lay off the hard-guy stare, Manny," I said wearily. "I'm on The Prince's side."

Manny looked away. "Sorry, kid. I'm all keyed up, I guess."

"Sure. Me, too." I offered him a cigarette and lit it for him. We smoked for a while, staring at the souvenirs on the walls, thinking of nothing in particular. "Got a good show for tomorrow night?" I asked casually.

Manny looked at me brightly. "Sure thing, kid. You really don't want to miss that. Martha's going to play some of The Prince's stuff and I've got some of the old hot men coming down to play with me. We're going to cut a piece of cake."

"I wouldn't miss it," I said.

"Invitation only, kid. I'm locking the door. This is just for the guys that know. Most times, I'll put up with the squares, but not tomorrow night."

"I'll bring my pitch-pipe." I climbed to my feet and stuck out my hand. "Thanks, Manny. Just sit on it for a while, until I know more about it. I'll keep you posted."

Manny stood briskly. His round hand pressed mine hard. "Do that, kid. Don't forget. And if you need any money, or . . ."

I waved away the suggestion. "Thanks anyway."

"You keep me up on it and I'll tell Nancy something good about you," he said with a wicked grin. "If I can think of something good, that is."

"It's a deal, Manny," I said. "Just tell her how I love animals and read the best books. Stuff like that."

"How you love blondes and only the best bookies," Manny repeated solemnly. "I've got that. What else?"

"Go to hell." I got my hat and squirmed into my coat. "Just tell her I'll be back later tonight, huh?"

"Will do, kid." Manny reached up and thumped my back. "Don't forget to give a shout if you need me."

We kicked it around again and then I managed to get out the door and down the steps. It wasn't necessary to go through the bar again. A door led straight to the street. I walked back down the clumsy alley paving, aiming toward Bella Joe's apartment.

After one more attempt at the door, I climbed into my car and started the motor. I eased the clutch in slowly, moving it forward to a point where I could see her windows across the street. I cut the motor and turned off my lights. I hoped Bella Joe would come home before the heater ran my battery down. I slumped low in the seat and leaned sideways against the door. I could just see the darkened area where lights should come on when Bella Joe arrived.

CHAPTER
FOURTEEN

THE car grew warm quickly. I opened a fresh package of cigarettes, stretched to a comfortable position and leaned back to watch Bella Joe's window. It was a long wait.

Three times during the night I went over to the all-night coffee pot at the corner for a hot drink and more cigarettes. By two o'clock my battery was reading a discharge point that warned me I would have to turn off the heater fairly soon if I ever wanted to start my car again. I snapped the control button and gave it another hour in the cold.

Shortly after three o'clock I pushed down the door handle and slid out. I walked down the alley on numb feet toward Manny's HOT BOX. According to the law, it was closed. According to Manny it was closed unless you were willing to walk up to the second floor and down the fire escape to the back entrance. I wasn't particularly willing, but I managed. I stopped in the hall and snuggled against the steam radiator for half an hour before I could make myself go any farther.

Inside, the world was warm and rosy. There are always a few die-hards who won't go home and Manny loves them all. He was weaving a lacy fretwork with his clarinet, laying it gently on top of a solid four-four beat the sleepy pianist was pounding out. There were five people at a table near him, a few more leaned at the bar.

Manny blew the farewell, "That's all" on his clarinet. He twisted it apart, flipped out the moisture and laid the two pieces on the piano. He picked up his glass, waved languidly at the crowd at the table and walked down the room toward me.

"You're late, kid," he grinned. He sat beside me. "You see that Joe yet?" he asked quickly.

I shook my head. "She won't come home."

He laughed at me. "You been waiting outside all this time?"

"I've been chasing rainbows," I said sourly. "Where's Nancy?"

Manny tossed off his drink and winked at me. "I tell her you'll be around so right away she disappears." He regarded me solemnly. "What is it you got that frightens women so bad?"

"I do all right," I said with no interest.

"Who do you do all right with, mister?" asked a light voice behind me.

I didn't need to turn. "Me and my big mouth," I said. "It's a cold nasty night and Manny is needling me. Sit down and defend me."

Nancy snickered. "To quote your favorite quoter, 'You're doing all right.' Why don't you stay home these nasty cold nights?" She snaked a chair over with her foot and sat across from me.

"Mine is a bleak and chilly hearth without the warmth of a light-haired woman," I chanted. "Am I too late for a song?"

144

Nancy turned to Manny. "We knocked off, didn't we, Pops?"

Manny nodded. "These snake dancers don't give me no audience tonight. We'll save it for tomorrow." He snorted scornfully at his late customers.

Nancy patted his hand gently. "Don't fret, Pops. You were real gone with *Cherokee* tonight."

"That wasn't bad, was it?" Manny brightened for a moment. "We had it there for a while but we couldn't get the bounce heavy enough." He yawned widely. "Well, go on home, kids. Let's have a big night tomorrow." He stood slowly, looking pudgy and cheerful in the frowsy atmosphere. "You kids go on home," he said lightly.

I fiddled with a drink while Nancy brought her gray fur coat out of her locker and wrapped her head in a light woolen Indian sari. Manny waved from the table near the bandstand.

"Tain't a fitten night out for man nor beast," Nancy said with a shiver. She took my arm and shook me awake. The heavy air, the overheated room, were beginning to fog my brain. I wobbled my head around to start the circulation and got to my feet before I lost my ambition.

The cold air brought the roses back to my cheeks, the shivers back to my shoulders. I pinned Nancy's hand tight in my elbow and aimed the expedition toward my parked car.

"I'll bet it won't start," I muttered.

"Don't be cryptic, Hawkshaw," Nancy said softly. "What won't start?"

"My car," I said. "I've been running the battery down

145

on a long wait out here."

"So you'll have to push it," she said briskly. "Now get to the point. Why were you so late? I turned down three rides home before you came."

"That's just what I was trying to tell you," I grinned. "My clever reasoning indicated that I should sit out in a freezing street and run my battery down while a long lovely blonde waits for me just three blocks away. You couldn't be expected to understand it. I am a very great detective and I just figured it out myself."

For that I got a kick in the shins. Nancy smiled angelically. She didn't break her stride. But I'll carry the dent for another year.

"Next time you'll come early," she said serenely.

"Next time I'll . . ." I reached for the door of my car and stopped quickly. Bella Joe's light was on.

I pointed toward the light. "That's what I've been waiting for. Do I take you home first, or will you wait for me?"

Nancy smiled. "You tell me, Hawkshaw. Which?"

That slowed me down enough to think about it. If Bella Joe became just the least bit argumentative, Nancy would freeze before I came back. And the coffee pot across the street was no place for a solitary girl to spend any time. She went home. Bella Joe would probably stay home now that she had come in. After all the time I had put in, I wouldn't mind waking her when I got back. I opened the car door.

Nancy entered with a graceful motion. I closed the door and walked around, crossing my fingers for enough power to start. It didn't help. The motor churned like a fat woman easing into a girdle. Nothing happened.

Two more tries and each time the battery delivered a lesser charge. I was ready to quit when the motor caught for a brief flash. I turned off the ignition, let it rest for a moment and tried again. I barely made it. The last push from the battery kicked it over. We sat gratefully, letting the motor warm up. I didn't dare use the heater right away. After a short wait, I snapped on the lights. They burned with a villainous yellow cast, but they burned.

Nancy hid both hands in her wide fur sleeves and pulled her neck down into the coat. "My mother warned me against you stage-door johnnies," she said. "Fancy cars and jewels and probably etchings."

"That makes me an honorable cuss."

Nancy laughed lightly. "I liked you better the other way."

"That's Manny's idea of a build-up," I said bitterly. I eased in the clutch and dragged the car away from the curb. "Which way?"

Nancy leaned closer. "The Berkeley," she said softly. "If you're in a hurry."

"Within limits," I said, "it's a hurry." I dropped my arm around her shoulders and pulled her close.

I brushed the curb outside the Berkeley and pulled off the lights. Just to save the battery. The heater had warmed the interior fairly well. I turned it off. Just to save the battery.

"Carney," Nancy said gently, years later. "Don't you have to get back?" Her voice was deep and husky. I could guess what power she would have in her lower singing register.

"I'm on my way," I said without moving.

She pushed up from my chest and brushed back her bright hair. She kissed me lightly on my right eye and sat back where she could see herself in the rear-view mirror. There was a little female business with a handkerchief which I watched carefully. I got another kiss for my attention and then I got the handkerchief swabbed over my face where it was needed.

"You're coming tomorrow night?" she asked softly.

"I'm coming to take you to dinner," I said in a firm tone. "Eight o'clock?"

She nodded. Her hand rested gently on my cheek for a brief moment and then it was gone. The door closed quietly and I was left in the car, staring out at a slim erect figure that moved like a dancer.

I let the world come back to me slowly. The growing cold helped speed the process. I had a moment's uneasiness but the warm motor started without complaint. I drove back to Bella Joe's house with my mind busy with other matters.

I parked in the space I had found earlier. The cold streets were deserted. A few wind-busy papers flipped around the corners. Nothing else moved. I pulled the throttle out to the lowest point and left the motor running. I wanted no part of a stalled car at that time of night.

As I approached the lighted entrance to the house, I looked at my watch. In a few minutes it would be six o'clock. A million alarm clocks would shortly declare a new day for a million hard-working citizens and here was Wilde still puttering about with the old day. I gave the door a casual push. One objection and I was ready to kick it in. So naturally it opened immediately and let

148

me and my bad temper in without any trouble.

I climbed the stairs quietly and found Bella Joe's door. I rapped softly with the back of a gloved hand. There was no light under the door, no movement inside. I banged again. I waited.

The hall was cold and still. Just then a normal man would begin to feel a trifle guilty about bothering people. A normal man would go home. I didn't feel quite that guilty and this time I used my feet. I kicked on the bottom panel and made a hell of a rumpus. I was working away with a good rhythm when the neighbor's door opened.

Mr. Godfrey's dark swollen face peered around the corner. It frowned heavily when he recognized me.

"You get me up. You put me to bed." His voice had no expression. "Now what?"

I aimed a thumb at Bella Joe's door. "She was home a little while ago," I said flatly. "It's important, so I'll wait. Any objections?"

Mr. Godfrey was a peaceable man. "Sure not," he said hastily. "How's for being a little quiet about it? Fellow's got to sleep, you know."

"I said it was important. Did she leave again?"

"Hell, I don't know. I just got home myself." He leaned against the door jamb. "Even her old man don't know when he can find her. Or where." He put a cigarette in his mouth. "Got a match?"

I fanned a lighted match under his cigarette. "How come?" I moved over to his door and blocked the opening with my foot, trying to make it look accidental. It didn't work.

He stared down at my neat number ten and blew a

stream of smoke at it. "Look, mister, I work nights. I gotta get some sleep now."

"Only a minute," I said quickly. I shucked my glove and fished around in my pocket. I pulled out a thin folded wad of bills, three or four dollars in ones. I held out the wad to him. "Just for your time," I said. "Can you tell me anything about her?"

He shook his shaggy head. "I don't know her at all, mister. I seen her once, twice, maybe. I wouldn't recognize her on the street, even." He didn't reach for the money.

I stretched my hand around the door and tucked the wadded bills in the pocket of his faded blue work shirt. "What about her old man?"

He rubbed a thick calloused knuckle slowly in his eye. He looked at me with a blank stare that I hoped was a thoughtful expression. "I think he said she was his wife. I only seen him that one time."

"Tell me about him," I said quickly.

"Sure." One thick black finger prodded the pocket where I had rammed the money. "He's a little guy, maybe five-ten. Skinny. He bangs the door just like you. Madder'n hell. I stand all I can, then I get up and yell at him and he gives me a song and dance about how he is trying to find this woman. He won't let me go for a while. He's a sour-looking bastard and I almost hang one on him. Anyway, he takes off and then I can't get back to sleep. I go back and listen to the football game for a while. It's five o'clock first thing I know." He looked at me with some despair. "I never get no sleep around here."

"Tough," I said. "But I paid my way. And I said it was

150

important. Now, when was this guy here?"

He shrugged helplessly. "Friday."

"What time?"

"Hell, man, I don't know for sure. Afternoon sometime. Three-thirty. Four, maybe. I don't know."

I thought about it for a moment. I couldn't see that it mattered much. Then I got a minor idea.

"What game were you listening to? What quarter?"

He shrugged. "Some little colleges. You don't get the big games on Friday. Never heard of them before. Something Teachers and somebody else. They cut it off just a coupla minutes after I tuned it in. No score. This Teachers outfit is on the four-yard line, second down coming up. So that's when they cut it off for some damned cowboy story."

"Okay, thanks," I said wearily. I reached for the picture I had been given in Gilman's office. "This what she looks like?"

He had the picture in his thick workman's hand, studying it carefully. The door behind us opened swiftly and a large dark-skinned woman stood ominously in the entrance. "This is what she looks like," she said nastily.

The heavy man shoved the picture toward me and slammed his door quickly. I turned to face the woman.

"You're Bella Joe?" I asked. There wasn't any doubt.

She looked at me tensely with hot suspicious eyes. "Who wants to know?"

"My name is Wilde," I said slowly. I flipped my pocket folder and waved it at her. She caught a flash of the sheriff's badge, but it didn't sell her. What convinced her was my tiredness. Only official cops are weary and bored. The private boys have fire and zeal.

She stepped back. "I should have known. Come on in, copper." She backed into the room and waited for me.

She was tall, for a woman. She stood at least five-eight and she had the weight to go with it. Her face was nearly round and slathered with lavender powder that gave her a faintly decayed look in artificial light. Her clothes were just clothes. A thick wool dress that would keep her warm and not do another damned thing for her.

She walked regally across the room and sank into a deep chair. It was the only comfortable chair in the room. I shoved my hat back, just to keep up the police illusion. I lifted a straight-back chair and carried it close to her before I sat.

The room was just something you rent furnished for twelve bucks a week. The bed was rumpled and the bedclothes were twisted where she had pitched them when she rolled out. The mattress would be thin and lumpy. The blankets would be slightly warmer than Grant's Tomb, but not as clean. A few fly-specked pictures were nailed to the walls and the room had three chairs, a rickety reed table and one lonely lamp with a carefully measured cord to discourage reading in bed. I guessed that the wide soft chair the woman was sitting in belonged to her. Except for that, you could have bought the furnishings for a brand-new five-dollar bill.

A blond maple phonograph was just barely visible on the table under a stack of records and sheet music. I looked around quickly to see if I could spot the high school annual Manny had seen. It wasn't in sight. I did see something that looked promising. On the bedside table, a spindly affair that seemed to be made of maple splinters, was a picture framed in red leather with a lot of gold inlay around it. I reached over for it.

The picture had been made out-of-doors with a box Brownie and later enlarged. It could have been any two people. I felt fairly sure that that large dark woman was the same one who was sitting across from me with a heavy boredom. The man was short, slim and very dark. He had a large mouthful of teeth. The man had a stiff sailor straw in his hand and he wore a tight jacket over peg-top trousers and knobbly shoes. The woman had a high pompadour of shellacked hair and a long skirt with a tight busty shirtwaist. That was all I could be sure about. But I felt like gambling.

"Magee looked better in those days," I said casually. I put the picture back and brought out my cigarettes, keeping my eye on the woman. If there was a reaction, I missed it.

"Next question," the woman said in a dull tone.

I blew a streamer of smoke and made a wise face. "You're Bella Joe?"

She shrugged.

"You're Bella Joe," I said flatly. "You are also Arabella Joslin. What other names do you use?"

She watched me with flat dead eyes. "Abraham Lincoln, George Washington, Theodore Roosevelt," she said. "I forget the others."

I pointed a thumb at the picture beside the bed. "That's 'Stuff' Magee in that picture."

"No."

"Don't kick it around too hard, Arabella," I said easily. "I saw a picture of Magee in Manny Brenner's high school annual. Same guy."

Her large face suddenly tensed. "Stuff wasn't . . ." Then she stopped short and looked at me warily.

"That's right," I agreed. "Magee wasn't in it. But you wouldn't know that unless you knew Magee pretty well, would you? Now let's get to the point. You're Arabella Joslin and you and Magee were planning a stupid swindle of the Prince family. I want to know all about those phony affidavits."

She leaned forward and rested her meaty forearms on her knees. "Let me see that badge again, huh?" she asked tightly.

I tried a smoke ring and a smile. Both of them were too thin. "Private, Arabella. It isn't city, but I can get the locals if you insist."

She moved quickly. I don't think I ever saw a large woman move faster. I couldn't have done anything about it, anyway, but I didn't even get a chance. I saw the movement, looked down and stared straight into the barrels of a ugly, outsize pistol. It was a vicious little over-and-under derringer like the ones that river-boat gamblers used to wear up their sleeves. It had two barrels and the caliber would be at least .41 and possibly larger. It took the trick.

I was careful not to move suddenly. "It's gone beyond that now, Arabella. You'd better talk."

"Out," she said thickly.

I rose slowly, keeping my hands in front of me. "Unless you actually knocked off The Prince yourself, this won't buy you a thing, Arabella. You'll be picked up two seconds after I put in a call."

She leaned back and grinned broadly. She let the pistol drop in her lap. "Go away, white boy," she said.

"I'm not running. Go play your games with somebody else."

"Then . . ." That was as far as I got.

"I'm going to shoot a burglar in just about a second," she said pleasantly. Her strong fingers lapped around the stubby gun and it aimed just under the knot in my tie. "Just about a second."

I pulled down my hat and waved good-by. I like to think that I can hold my own in any argument, but I can be convinced. I was on my way.

CHAPTER FIFTEEN

THERE was a dead, disgusted flavor in my mouth as I left Bella Joe's house, and much the same feeling in my head. It had been a long dreary day without much to show for my time. I was positive that Bella Joe was the woman I wanted, but there were a lot of questions that still needed answers. She wasn't afraid of me or anyone else who wanted to ask questions. She wasn't running or hiding and I would have expected to find Arabella Joslin deep in the darkest hole she could discover.

I stopped with my hand on the door of my car and held a brief debate. I decided in favor of going down to Grodnik's office. The local precinct might give me a hand and it might not. Somehow, I didn't think that the woman was going to make us work to find her again.

I was willing to bet on it for an hour or so, just long enough to make a stop at my apartment and check in with Grodnik when he came downtown.

Only occasionally do I envy Lieutenant Grodnik and the other city employes. Right now was one of the times. I wanted a long cozy chat with Arabella and Grodnik was the man I knew who could fix it. In fact, he would probably be happy to take it out of my hands entirely. His opinion of private detectives was no higher than the law requires.

I climbed into my car and headed toward my apartment. My collar was wilted to a soggy mass. I was carrying the usual morning beard and the noises my stomach made were warning signals for a time-out.

I put the coffee pot on to perk while I stripped off my clothes and aimed for the bathtub. I drank three glasses of cold water while the tub was running and then I stretched out in the steaming water and tried to forget about everything for ten minutes. I struggled awake with some effort and got wearily out of the tub to shave.

Fresh clothes and dry shoes made the day look possible, but only a little brighter. I adjusted my tie while the coffee made its last few burbles. I drank a scalding black cup. Then I had the remains of a quart bottle of tomato juice that had the icebox all to itself. More coffee and a piece of stale bread finished the breakfast. Either I shopped for groceries today or I went dieting.

According to my watch it was nearly eight o'clock. With just the reasonable time allowed for the drive, I would reach City Hall by eight-thirty when Grodnik should be in. I wasn't sure whether a Detective-Lieutenant bothered to punch a time clock, but I was sure that

Grodnik hadn't forgotten any of the patrolman virtues, or any of the vices.

Grodnik was in. He looked sleepy, but he was available for business, feet on the desk, a thick file of papers in his hand, eyes fixed thoughtfully on the ceiling.

"You're late, Lieutenant," I said.

"You're nuts," he said amiably. "Whatcha want?"

"I found Arabella Joslin for you."

Grodnik widened the opening between his large feet and looked at me through the aperture. "Not for me you didn't find her," he said mildly. "I don't need her."

"I found her just for kicks." I matched his gentle tone. "Do you want to hear about it?"

"Sure," he said readily. "Always interested."

I sat in the chair beside his desk. I lit a cigarette and put it out after the first raw taste. I rubbed my eyes and brought them to focus on Grodnik's beaming face. "It's awful early, Lieutenant," I complained. "Let's leave out the punch lines for now, huh?"

Grodnik didn't answer. He brought his feet down and stared at me calmly. He offered a small, early-morning smile. "Have a bad night, Wilde?"

"Bad enough," I admitted. "It was a long day."

"We get them in this racket," he said agreeably.

"It was a long day, Lieutenant," I said wearily. "Mostly I was doing your work. So let's talk about it some."

Grodnik grunted deeply. "Tell me how you were doing my work, Mr. Wilde," he purred.

"Yeah. Be happy to. First, as I said, I found Arabella Joslin. You may not exactly need her for your case against Magee, but you should have found her, just to clean up the loose ends."

"Case is closed," Grodnik interrupted. "Glad to help, but it isn't anything to me."

"That's fine," I said nastily. The long tiredness began to work on my eyes. I kept them closed just for relief. "I'm glad to hear it's all over, Lieutenant. But you left out a few minor details when you told me the story. Do you think you could tell me about what time The Prince was killed?"

Grodnik slammed the top of his desk with a heavy hand. I opened my eyes. "Don't get fancy with me, Wilde," he said grimly.

"Nothing fancy, Lieutenant," I said. "But what's the answer?"

Grodnik reached to the right and opened a drawer of his desk. He brought up a manila file folder and spread it on his desk. I could see the carbon copy report. He flipped a few pages to reach the medical section and ran a thick finger down the statement. He looked up. "It's a good point, Wilde, but it won't work. Time is a little vague, maybe, as I told you Monday. The cook, Lily, says she heard the fight about two o'clock. She heard the old man, The Prince's father, when he turned over his night table or something just before he found the body. Then when she didn't hear anything more, she went in to look. She called the police at three-eighteen, P.M., Friday. Is that all right, Mr. Wilde?"

I shrugged. "So far," I said. "This maid saw Magee leave the house. Is it all right if I ask what time that happened?"

Grodnik turned back one page and read from the record. "She says it was just about two-thirty. She was baking some cakes and that's why she knew the time.

158

What else?" He was not disinterested any more. He was a good cop and the discrepancy hadn't passed by him without notice. He was a good cop with a closed case and a man sitting in front of him who might punch a hole in his answer. He didn't like me. His eyes said so.

I let the tension grow a little longer. I don't get many chances to sink the hook in Grodnik. I wanted to enjoy this one. What I knew might be a very simple matter to explain away, but I knew Grodnik would have to investigate it. I wanted to trade my information for an interview with Arabella Joslin. And I wanted Grodnik to bring her in for me.

"I'll swap, Lieutenant," I grinned.

Grodnik dropped a heavy hand on his telephone. "For what?" he asked tightly. "With what?"

"I want to talk to the Joslin woman. Here, where she will loosen up."

Grodnik eyed me tensely. "You'll swap what?"

"I'll swap the name of the man who says he talked to The Prince after Magee left the house."

It wasn't the bombshell I thought it was, but for Grodnik, it was an earthquake. His eyelids barely trembled. They drooped sleepily and he smiled a thin unhappy smile. "And what would that name be?" he asked placidly.

I shook my head. "Get the woman first, huh, Lieutenant?"

I could almost see the wheels whirring behind his peaceful tan eyes. The narrow lines of restraint were barely visible around his mouth. After a long moment, he nodded briskly. He lifted the telephone. "Where is she?" he asked. He called the police radio bureau and

159

authorized a pick-up for Bella Joe, or Arabella Joslin. He relayed the address and read her description from the reverse side of the picture I handed to him. He flipped the picture back to me.

"Al Gilman," I said quickly, not waiting to be coaxed. "I saw him while I was trying to get a line on the Joslin woman. He was The Prince's booking agent. He was talking to The Prince on Friday. At two-thirty or thereabouts, he said. It's close, but . . ."

Grodnik snorted. "Close?" he said in deep disgust. "That's what you swap? Why, I should . . ."

"Why not check it first, Lieutenant? Gilman may have it cross-referenced with something else that sets the time definitely." I spoke quickly, hoping that Grodnik wouldn't rescind the pick-up order. I wasn't paid to worry about the murder of The Prince. All I wanted to know was that Magee's claims were phony. Arabella could tell me, if she wanted to. And I felt she would probably want to, in a police station.

It was the fast talking that did it. I was sitting humped over Grodnik's desk, trying to think of sound reasons for him to help me and trying to act as though I had something concrete for him to work with. From Grodnik's suspicious face, I could guess that I wasn't doing too well. Just then the first edge of the idea hit me. Largely wishful thinking, probably. If Magee were strongly alibied for the time of The Prince's death, the case was wide open again and Grodnik would need the Joslin woman as badly as I did. Just because I would have liked it to be that way, I toyed with the notion. And then I remembered something that made it look possible. It looked good and it fitted my plans perfectly.

I leaned back and thumped my fist on the arm of my chair.

"By Gawd," I said softly. "That's it! I'll bet Magee is out of the whole thing."

Grodnik pushed up from his chair. "Wilde, I warned you before . . ." he said tightly.

"It's no gag, Grodnik," I said quickly. "I just put it together. Now get this: When I walked into the Joslin woman's house, she was out and I walloped the door loud enough to get the man next door out to see what I was up to. I won't give you the blow-by-blow, but the upshot is that when I came back later, that same man told me he saw another guy pounding Joslin's door on Friday afternoon. About three-thirty or four o'clock. Somewhere around that time anyway. His description of the man could fit Magee. According to him, this guy said he was Joslin's husband. And we know that Magee and Joslin have been close enough on this phony deal with the papers. They could be married."

"And I could be Harry Truman," he snorted. "Nuts!"

"Yeah, maybe it is screwy." I lit a cigarette and grinned across the table. "But you have to check it, don't you, Lieutenant?"

Grodnik glared at me. His bushy eyebrows were a straight line over his watchful eyes. "Tell me why, smart guy."

"Sure. You have to check because it's entirely possible that the guy might have been Magee. No matter what the time was, you have to know what Magee was doing every minute on Friday afternoon until you picked him up. The D.A. would have some bitter comments if the defense had some information you had missed." I grinned widely at him. "Right?"

Grodnik bobbed his head sedately. The long fringe of hair between his ears flapped lazily. He wasn't angry any more. He had a job to do and personal feelings weren't going to have any meaning for a while.

"What time did you say this was?"

"The man next door said it was about three-thirty or four, as I recall. He tuned in a radio broadcast of a football game when he went back in his room. He says it lasted just a few minutes and then it was cut off for a network program. Just some minor league game. One team was a Teacher's College. You could find out what time the broadcast went off the air."

Grodnik's pencil made swift motions across a desk pad. "Did this man next door have a name?"

"Card on the door said, 'Godfrey.' Number Six."

Grodnik put through a call to the Homicide Bureau office next door. He asked for a detail of men, giving no explanations. He wouldn't want to put his neck out until he had checked everything backwards and inside out.

He aimed a pencil at a chair in the corner. "You take your gear and sit over there. I'll need you later, maybe."

Three men in plain clothes answered Grodnik's call. He didn't give them time to take off their hats before he had them assigned to jobs. One was ordered to check with the precinct and go along with the local men if they hadn't yet made the pinch. If they had, he was to search the room and bring in anything that looked interesting. Another man was given a brief outline of my conversation with Al Gilman. He was sent off to take a deposition. The third man, a slim sergeant who looked like a tie salesman, drew The Prince's cook. Grodnik

162

gave him the cook's statement. The sergeant was to double check all the times mentioned just in case something might be slightly wrong.

Grodnik had his men assigned and out of his office in less than five minutes and all of it without the least sign of hurry. I waited until the door closed behind the last man and looked around from my paper.

"Lieutenant," I offered quietly, "just in case Magee is out of this, you'll need a new angle, won't you?"

Grodnik didn't look at me. He rustled papers on his desk. "Well, let's have it," he said grumpily.

"The Prince's doctor is dummied up about whatever it was his patient had. I can't see why. His daughter tells me The Prince had a brain tumor, but his medic won't even tell Doctor Owens about it. It might just mean something."

"How?"

"There you got me, Lieutenant. I can't do all your work for you. I'll make a guess if you like."

"I won't like it, but go ahead and guess," Grodnik said.

"Owens had a notion that Magee should not have known The Prince was ailing. From everything I've heard, no one else knew about it, except The Prince's father. I didn't think much of it yesterday, but now it might have some meaning. I don't see just how it could fit in, but maybe we better find out."

Grodnik brought a thoughtful gaze down from the ceiling and stared at me blankly. He lifted his telephone without speaking to me. "Who's on the bench right now?" he asked sharply. "Yeah. Yeah. Okay, send me Connolly." He hung up. He wrapped his stubby fingers around his pencil and eyed me placidly. "Do some more guessing, Mr. Wilde."

"That's all for now," I grinned. "The picture has changed a little, Lieutenant. I'm happy with it as it is."

"Tell me about the changed picture, Mr. Wilde," he suggested mildly.

"Well, Lieutenant, when I first talked to you about Magee, you were just moderately interested in Magee's documents. They didn't mean anything to your case, because you had Magee cold for murder. Now it's a little different. Now you need Arabella Joslin more than I do, so you'll bring her in for me. You need to know about The Prince's illness and how Magee found out about it. So you'll get the answers." I spread my hands wide. "So, I'll ride for a while. You carry the load."

Grodnik nodded with no enthusiasm. "Like I said, we were in a hurry with this one. Maybe we skipped a few points. I happen to think they are still little points, but we have to make sure." His heavy fingers snapped the pencil with a dry crack in the quiet room. "You may get some leg work done for you, Wilde, but you won't last long if any of it looks queer. You know that, don't you?"

"I know that, Lieutenant," I said.

Grodnik's door opened quietly. A tall wide young man with a coffee-colored face came in and closed it behind him. He took up a rigid stance the prescribed distance from Grodnik's desk and threw a crisp salute. "Acting Detective Connolly reporting to the Lieutenant for assignment, sir," he snapped.

Grodnik looked up in surprise, fumbled his hand at his forehead in response. "We don't bother much with salutes here, Connolly," he said gently. "Sit down."

Connolly relaxed slightly and sat beside the desk, half-

164

facing me. His back was poker-straight and his hands were tensed in his lap.

Grodnik leaned back comfortably in his chair. "First assignment, son?" he asked kindly.

The tall man bobbed his head. His sharp Adam's apple jumped twice but he made no sound.

Grodnik smiled. "Just sitting there on the ready bench, huh? That's no life for a young man."

"That's for sure, Lieutenant," Connolly answered. Grodnik's quiet manner had erased most of his tension.

"Gentleman in the corner," Grodnik waggled his thumb toward me, "is Mr. Carney Wilde, an eminent private detective of our city. You will under no circumstances offer him violence within the shadow of City Hall."

Connolly grinned suddenly. He nodded once toward me and turned back to Grodnik. I guessed he was just about as tall as I am, which made him six-two. He would weigh a little less. He was obviously wearing his best suit for the job. A rich dark blue suit that was nearly black, a glistening white silk shirt and something very special in gray-barred neckties.

Grodnik said, "Connolly's the guy that bounced the baton off Magee's noggin. Damned fine pitch."

Connolly fumbled with his fingers. "Lucky," he mumbled.

"Sure," Grodnik said readily. "Sure, you were lucky. And if you stay in plain clothes, you'll have to stay lucky. Now let's get on with it." He brought out a fresh pencil and made notes on his pad. "I want you to hike down to the Medical Arts Building and talk to Doctor A. K. Warner. He was The Prince's doctor. You may have to chase around to find him, but get him as soon as you can. I want a complete report on his treatment of The Prince. And I want to know how Magee found out about the illness, whatever it was. You ask the doc. If he starts flubbing around about ethics and no-talk and that kind of stuff, bring him in. You get it?"

"Yes, sir," Connolly said briskly. His tan fingers slid a new leather notebook and a silver pencil from his pocket. He asked for the spelling of the name, checked the address. Then he stowed his pencil and notebook, snapped another fine salute and got out of the office.

Grodnik grinned at the closed door. "Good boy," he said happily. "He should do fine. He's hit just the right time, too. He wouldn't have had a chance of getting above Patrolman ten years ago."

"That's fine," I said. "I'm happy for both of you. Now I want to get over to my office for a while. How about it?"

"Sure," Grodnik said placidly. "Check back with me later on. I'll want a detailed statement from you sometime today. Maybe about two-thirty, thereabouts."

I pushed up from the chair, shook my head to clear the sleepiness and moved toward the door. I waved my hat to Grodnik and went out into the corridor. I went out the back way to get my car, propping my eyelids wide to stay awake. I turned left at the rotunda and stumbled down the worn marble stairs that led to the police quadrangle.

CHAPTER SIXTEEN

I PICKED up a cardboard container of coffee from the stand downstairs, fought my way through the cluster of twittering stenographers at their midmorning recess and took the elevator to my office.

The coffee was watery and the soft cardboard of the container melted in my mouth like wet blotting paper. After choking down three gulps, I threw the rest of it into the corner sink. Then I dropped my hat and coat on one of the customer's chairs. I wanted to settle down in my swivel seat, but I suspected I would fall asleep if I did. Parking one thigh on the edge of the desk, I pulled the phone toward me.

The receptionist at Owens' clinic recognized my voice, but she was still brisk and businesslike. I waited for Owens, holding the phone with one hand and trying to strike a light from a paper match with the other. I burned a ring of cinder on one thumb and cussed softly while I lit my cigarette.

"Those kind words for me, Mr. Wilde?" Owens asked softly.

"Nope. Sorry, Doc. Trials of a private dick. I've got something I want to ask you."

"Go ahead," he said easily.

"The day The Prince was killed—that was Friday—you went out to the house when the cook called you.

How long did you take to get there?"

"Why . . ." he paused. I could almost see his forehead knotted in concentration. "Why, not more than ten minutes, I should say. I was on a call in the neighborhood then. The clinic relayed the message and I came straight over. But why is it important now, Mr. Wilde?"

"Dunno yet, Doc. Just ride with me a while. Now then. You beat the cops there, didn't you?"

"Why, yes. Lily hadn't even phoned them. She hadn't done anything at all except call for me. She just waited."

"Okay," I said quickly. "Now this is the big question: Did the old man say anything at all to you before you socked him with the needle?"

"He was in shock, Mr. Wilde," Owens said coldly. "People seldom speak coherently when they are in shock. I examined him on the floor, gave him the injection there and then Lily and I put him to bed. He did mutter a little when we were undressing him, but he didn't actually say anything; he merely made sounds." Owens' tone was wary now. I didn't like hearing that note of caution.

"Relax, Doc. I'm just digging. Thanks a lot. I'll see you tonight." I hung up before he could answer. I put the phone back in its cradle and stayed in that position, leaning over the desk, staring at the phone.

I didn't care for my thoughts just then. Doctor Owens was a fast man with a hypodermic needle, maybe too fast. It hadn't mattered when Magee was the choice for the murder rap, but now it seemed significant. I didn't need much brilliance to see that Owens was on the possible list now. And Grodnik would spot it fast enough.

A stiff finger prodded my back. I hadn't heard a

sound. I'd been leaning my weary head over the desk, full of thoughts, full of sleepiness. I hadn't heard a thing. I turned and straightened.

The man was short and squat, twice as wide in the beam as I was. His deep jaw was massaged to a high blue gloss with a grainy surface like rough marble. His skin was a pale tone with greenish shadows at the temples. He was something that lived in the dark. This was far too early for him to be up and about. He didn't even have the clothes for daytime. That purple-blue serge coat was a nighttime thing. His voice was a nighttime voice, too.

"You Wilde?" he whispered.

I started to move away from the desk. I had one foot on the floor and then I stopped there. The short man's right hand was in his coat pocket and when he moved it, something else moved, something that wasn't hand or coat. I stayed where I was. The short man nodded amiably.

"Like I said," he mouthed. "You Wilde?"

I said I was Wilde. The drowsiness left my head. I was awake now. It was a little late, but I was awake.

The short man moved away from me. He pulled a chair to the far side of the desk and sat there lightly. He waved his free hand toward my swivel seat. "Sid-down, friend. Let's kibitz awhile."

From his chair, he could see the drawers in the desk. I kept my hands on the arms of the chair and waited for him to give me the next cue.

"How's business?" he asked softly.

"It was good up till now," I said.

He smiled thinly, very thinly. "Don't kid," he whispered. "Just play it straight, like a smart boy, huh?"

"Sure."

"That's fine," he said easily. "Who you working for these days?"

Then it seemed to make some kind of sense. The night club clothes didn't necessarily mean anything. The short man was a rented gun. He would hire out to anyone, but, from the question, I guessed he belonged to Hollie Gray.

"I'm on a confidential job," I said. "But tell Hollie there's nothing for him to be worried about."

Nothing moved in the short man's face. "Don't be fancy, friend. Who you working for?"

I leaned back in the squeaky chair and hoisted my legs up on the desk. I locked my hands behind my head and grinned widely. "Everybody in the case knows who I'm working for, Buster. It hasn't been any secret. The people outside the case don't know. One of them is Hollie Gray."

The short man moved slightly in his chair. He shrugged. "I'm just a working man myself, friend," he whispered. "Just a job to do, you know? I do it anyway I have to. Now, who you working for?" His voice was still a light rasping whisper. He wasn't tense or indignant. I was showing just the normal sales resistance. He would be willing to talk about it—for about one more minute.

I reached down between my legs for my cigarette. It lay on the rim of a clogged ashtray and I sent two fingers toward it. The short man watched negligently. I missed the cigarette, bunting it into the tray. My fingers closed around the glass base and I flipped it into the short man's face.

A thick screen of cigarette ash swept through the air. The short man got his arm up in time to stop the ashtray, but he didn't see my foot coming. I rolled sideways in my chair and aimed my toe at his chin. I missed with the toe, but my heel caught the side of his head and bounced it back against the leather cushion.

The force of the kicking threw me out of my seat and I scrambled toward the short man on my hands and knees, just getting to him before he recovered. I pounded my fist twice under his ear, as hard as I could swing. That was enough.

When I came to my feet, breathing hard, my heart pounding like a leaky boiler, I had his gun in my hand. It was a useful model, a Banker's Special .38, with a one-inch barrel. I thumbed the latch and dropped the loads on the floor.

The short man grunted once, deeply. His eyes opened slowly.

"It's a stand-off," I growled. "Friend."

He looked up at me tightly with no expression and he nodded. "You ain't hard to find," he said hoarsely.

"Next time make an appointment." I hauled him to his feet and kept him off balance toward the door. He went out without resisting, without looking back. I heard the elevator bell ring before I reached my desk. I pulled the door open again and heaved the empty .38 down the hall. The short man picked it up slowly and put it away. I closed the door.

I leaned against the wall until the tense reaction left my muscles. My face was still stiff but the wobble had left my legs when I picked up my overcoat and doused the lights. I saw no sense in a local red-hot coming to call on me. I wasn't working on that kind of a job, as far as I could tell. But if he belonged to Hollie Gray, that would make sense. No more sensitive flower ever bloomed than a semireformed bootlegger. I pulled on my coat and left the office.

I got my car from the parking lot and drove through the slushy streets to my apartment. One stop at a neighborhood beanery for sandwiches was the only delay. Just then I wanted no more of the world. I'd been trying to get by with no sleep for too long. I wasn't thinking very clearly and I was beginning to make mistakes.

I left my car around the corner, hiked up to my two-room home and stripped. I pulled both window shades to the bottom, snapped off the lights, dropped into bed and hauled a sheet up over my head. The alarm clock next to my ear was set for six o'clock, which would give me five hours' sleep if I corked off with no delay.

I was thinking about that five hours' maximum sack time I was going to get when the alarm went off. Someone was playing a time machine trick with me. The clock read six, the alarm was blaring, but my raw throat and aching back insisted it was still noon. I rolled to my feet and stumbled into the bathroom.

I gave the dressing problem more than the usual thought that night. I was due for dinner with Miss Lucas and I had vague suspicions that no small elegance would go unnoticed. My new brown suit, polished British oxfords that glowed like redwood, a red-and-silver necktie that had cost more than my watch. Maybe Miss Lucas wouldn't be impressed, but I certainly was.

It was still a few minutes short of six-thirty when I

172

turned in at the police quadrangle at City Hall again. I knew Grodnik could catch me up on developments if I came around. I was particularly hoping for a long chat with Arabella Joslin. I walked up the stairs and through the connecting ramp to the Annex.

Grodnik was in and he had most of his team with him. The slim sergeant was caught in the middle of a phrase when I opened the door. I walked into the sudden silence with a cheerful wave.

"Have a seat, Wilde," Grodnik said briskly. "I want to talk to you. Go ahead, Sergeant."

The sergeant eyed me from half-closed lids. "Well, Lieutenant, I was just saying that she shouldn't be hard to find. She didn't take anything with her. Not even a toothbrush. So maybe she just went out for the day. Hell, I'll bet we pick her up easy tonight, what with the X-call on the radio and a precinct man sitting in the room."

"All right, Sergeant," Grodnik said heavily. "I won't say you're wrong. Put all the reports in writing before you leave. That goes for all of you," he added to the others. "You can take off for the night. All except Connolly."

The tall Negro detective fidgeted beside the door while the rest of the men left. Grodnik waved him to a chair.

"You hear that, Wilde?" Grodnik asked.

"Was it about Joslin?" I asked.

"Skipped," he said bitterly. "Why didn't you get the precinct on her last night? And what in hell did you scare her with anyway?"

"Go soak your head, Lieutenant," I said elegantly.

"You know damned well the local precinct would have snickered at me last night. Even you didn't want the woman until today. And another thing: That woman wasn't scared of anything last night. She wasn't running and she wasn't hiding."

Grodnik looked at me with deep disgust. "It's really a beaut, the way you make everything look messy every time you stick your fingers in police business."

"Ain't it the truth?" I marveled. "You alibi Magee?"

"Not tight," Grodnik said. "Al Gilman talked to The Prince, all right, but he can't pin the time on the button. But it could be after the time we think Magee left the house. I'll give you that. Magee could have left, but nothing kept him from coming back."

Grodnik had an idea, but it wasn't a good one. Just the same, I nodded with great interest. "And what about the man next door to Arabella?"

"Three-forty-four. That's when that football game stopped. But we don't have a positive identification yet. Just a picture identification. We'll set up a group and see if that guy Godfrey can pick out Magee tomorrow. Still, Magee could have gone back to the house, killed The Prince and gone downtown afterward."

"Sure," I said. "Now you find out where he rented the airplane."

Grodnik frowned heavily. "So?"

"Look, Lieutenant," I said soberly. "I've made that drive out to Seneca Park and then downtown. Magee might have done it in about an hour, if he poured on the gas. But if he went much over forty, those roads would have thrown him in the ditch. Remember they were covered with glare ice and heavy snow. That

174

makes for slow driving."

"It could be done, couldn't it?" he insisted.

"I suppose so," I said wearily. "It's giving Magee every break to assume he might have done it. The timing is too close for my taste."

Grodnik rubbed a thick hand over his face. He sighed deeply. "Well, don't push it too far, Wilde. I'm inclined to agree with you." He opened his pale tan eyes and stared at me. "On behalf of the police department," he said tiredly, "I suppose I should thank you. For myself, go to hell."

"I see your point, Lieutenant," I said slowly. "Still, it's better for me to spot it than someone else, isn't it? You'd look a little sick if Magee's lawyers turned up that alibi."

"You think so?" Grodnik snorted. "Now what do we hold Magee on? We were going to book him as soon as the doctors would let us. Now, we'll have to move to-morrow and we can't charge him. We stall and his law-yer hits us with a writ of habeas corpus and Magee walks out. See?"

"If he has an alibi, why not?"

Grodnik waved his hand angrily. "I forgot," he said. "You didn't hear all of Sergeant Thompson's report. The Prince's cook recognized a picture of the Joslin woman. Says she has seen her around the house. Twice. A month ago when Joslin came in with Magee and again about a week ago when the cook saw her with Magee and The Prince's father in the studio. Cook says she didn't see her come in or go out either time."

"I don't get it," I said. "What does that mean?"

"Hell, how do I know?" Grodnik snorted. "The woman

175

is tied with the blackmail pitch, with Magee, and now with The Prince. And we can't find her. I don't like that a bit. Maybe Magee is clear, maybe not, but I don't want him running around until I get somebody to take his place."

"Material witness?" I suggested.

Grodnik shook his head. "Not unless I have to. He'd get bail in an hour, if he's got any money."

"What does The Prince's family say about Joslin's visits?" I asked. "As I understood it, none of them had seen her."

"That's right," Grodnik said glumly. "The girl and Owens had never heard the name. Don't recognize her picture. Owens asked the old man and he says she was just a visitor Magee brought. Doesn't even remember what name she used, he says. That's that."

"I guess so," I agreed. "If Magee should be out of it, who can you move into his slot?"

Grodnik lifted one widespread hand and counted them on his fingers. "Martha Prince. The old man. Doctor Owens. Randolph Greene. Maybe Joslin." That used up all five fingers and Grodnik stared at his clenched fist morosely. He relaxed his grip and dropped his hands on his desk. "No alibis that mean anything. The girl was out driving. No one with her. The old man was having a nap. The doctor was between calls and within a possible range of the house. Greene—and what a punk he is—says he was home and working. He lives in Seneca Park, too, not far away. Joslin I don't know about yet. We do know she wasn't home when Magee, or whoever it was, went to her room a little while later." Grodnik looked up blandly. "Then there's the cook. She

176

was the only servant in the house just then. So, take your pick. That's on alibi. Everybody had a fair opportunity. If Magee is out, we don't know the motive, unless somebody else was in on that blackmail deal with Magee and Joslin." His voice dwindled off gradually.

Grodnik shaped the pile of notes together with both hands and slid them into a file folder. He put the folder on the corner of his desk and seemed then to notice Connolly for the first time. He stared blankly at him for a moment. Then he nodded toward me.

"Tell him about that fancy business," he said sourly.

"Yes, sir," said Connolly smartly. He half-turned in his chair. "Well, I persuaded Doctor Warner that he should tell me about what he was treating Mr. Prince for. He gave me a written report finally and I gave it to the Lieutenant." He looked hopefully toward Grodnik, but the Lieutenant didn't move. "Well," Connolly coughed twice. "Well, in simple language, Mr. Wilde, The Prince had this brain tumor that was growing larger just recently. It gave him a lot of pain sometimes and it made him go a little screwy when it hit him hard. The pain was pretty bad, I guess." Connolly sounded a trifle apologetic about it, as if it were his fault in some way.

"The Prince wouldn't have an operation until he had to, because there was just a chance that it would leave him blind, and maybe even deaf. Doctor Warner says The Prince just wouldn't take any chances about it. He was a musician, you know," he added softly.

It seemed to make a lot of difference to Connolly whether or not I understood that The Prince had a very difficult choice to make. I tried to indicate that I saw the point.

177

"Sometimes The Prince could tell when he was going to have a bad spell and then he would come and live at home where Doctor Warner could watch out for him. He wouldn't tell anybody about it, except his father. Nobody else knew about it. Doctor Warner says he can't even guess how Magee found out about it. He knows he didn't tell him and he's sure neither The Prince or his father would have told him.

"Well, anyway, when this pain came to him, he used to hit that old bottle awful hard. That's why most people thought he was such a lush. Doctor Warner says he was hurting himself bad with all that drinking and he says he gave The Prince his choice, either he was to have the operation pretty soon, or he could find another doctor. Doctor Warner says the tumor was getting too big to live with much longer." Connolly had his hands laced tightly together and his voice was growing gradually thinner. He looked at me nervously.

"Thanks, Connolly," I said. "That's rough to hear about The Prince. I can see it was a bad time for him."

Connolly nodded eagerly. "Yes," he said quickly. "Years of it, Doctor Warner said. Like to drove him crazy sometimes."

"I'd think it would," I said. I turned to Grodnik. "What do you think, Grodnik? About Magee, I mean. He sure as hell knew something about the tumor, according to that statement in his affidavit."

"The hell with it," Grodnik said mildly. "He was The Prince's secretary, remember. Maybe he just overheard somebody on the phone. Or maybe he was around when the doctor came one day. Something like that would explain it normally enough." He yawned widely and stretched his arms toward the ceiling. "I'm going home for dinner. I need to do some thinking on all this. You certainly opened up a barrel of cats for me. How about dropping in later this evening?" He rose slowly, still yawning.

"Not tonight, Lieutenant," I said. "Large evening at Manny's. All-Prince Night. Big doings. You can get me there if you want me."

Grodnik nodded silently. He worked his wide shoulders into his overcoat, stuffed the file folder into a large pocket and clamped a battered gray felt hat on his head.

He dropped a thick hand on Connolly's shoulder. "You can take off, kid," he said. "Check with me in the morning."

Connolly jumped to his feet briskly. "I can come in tonight, Lieutenant," he said eagerly. "If you want me?" His eyes were hopeful.

Grodnik smiled briefly. "Sure. You come in about eight," he said. "Matter of fact, I got a coupla things you could check for me."

Grodnik waved at me from the door. "Keep in touch, Wilde," he grunted sourly. He didn't wait for an answer.

Connolly looked at me warily. I buttoned my coat and picked up my hat. "Like working for Homicide?" I asked casually.

"Better than walking a beat," he answered carefully. "Takes a lot out of a man though. Lots of head work."

"You've got a good boss, though," I said. "Jack Grodnik is just about the best in these parts. May not look like much. Doesn't act like much, come to think of it. But he's good."

Connolly pulled open the door. He snapped the locking catch and doused the lights while he waited for me to leave. "I know about him," he said easily. "He's got a big reputation. He got that Black Hand gang down in The Bend. You hear about that?"

"I heard about that," I said. "That was a long time ago."

"He's been good for a long time," Connolly said firmly.

I nodded. "A lot of people don't remember that," I said softly.

"No cop would forget it," Connolly insisted.

"That's where you're wrong, kid," I said. "A good man on the cops makes a lot of enemies in this town. You've probably seen that already. You'll see it more on Homicide. Grodnik will never make Chief of Detectives. Not in this town."

The big young Negro grinned happily. "Give me the same kind of enemies as Lieutenant Grodnik and the same kind of friends. I'll make out like that."

I looked back at him standing large on the step above me. From that angle his jaw looked like the working end of a sledge hammer. "I'll bet you will, at that," I said.

CHAPTER SEVENTEEN

THE All-Prince Night at the HOT BOX was bound to be Manny Brenner's top effort. He wanted Nancy ready to go at ten o'clock and that gave us very little time for anything more than a brace of cocktails before a fast

180

dinner. Somehow, I had the notion that a singer could charge in at the last moment, try a few mi-mi-mi's on the way and be ready to take off. Apparently there was more to it. At any rate, Nancy scheduled herself for a nine-thirty arrival and that cut into my plans considerably.

Nancy and I reached the alley entrance of Manny's club just about the right time and I let her out of the car. She waved back at me and scampered in. I drove down the alley and turned to the first parking space I could find. I walked down a few steps and looked up toward Bella Joe's windows. Somewhere in the room was a large discontented cop waiting patiently, hardly breathing, not daring to smoke or cough. I sloshed back up the alley to Manny's HOT BOX.

The bar was packed solid by the time I came in. Manny had promised music by ten, but he had invited a mob for dinner and several others had come early. A rough customer at the door held a thick arm just under my nose and looked toward Manny. Manny nodded to me from his perch behind the bar. The thick arm dropped.

"Kinda thought you'd be early tonight," Manny chuckled. He poured a jolt of rye for me and pushed it forward. Bottles of water were spaced along the bar and all the customers were drinking whatever Manny grabbed at the first try. "Onna house," he grinned. "It's a party, kid."

"Good one, looks like," I said amiably.

"Gonna be, any minute now. Haveta have rubber walls, if everybody I invited actually gets here."

The HOT BOX had a new treatment. The virulent

181

murals were gone for the evening. Tonight belonged to The Prince and everything in the club reminded you of him. The walls were covered with Manny's collections of pictures and souvenirs of The Prince. Everywhere you looked, his wide cheerful grin jumped toward you. The juke box was loaded with The Prince's music recorded by Manny and his various teams.

The feature of the room was a huge blow-up of The Prince which served as a background for the bandstand. I was studying it when I noticed Owens sitting at a table toward the front of the room. I stood up on my toes and saw Martha Prince with her back to me, and Randolph Greene, looking rather subdued, sitting across from Owens. Owens spotted me when he looked up.

I held a finger to my lips and motioned for him to join me. He leaned toward Martha, murmured something, smiled at Greene and stood. He worked his way smoothly through the crowd at the bar and joined me at the far end, near the pin-ball table.

"Mr. Wilde," he said pleasantly, "it's good to see you here. I hope you have some good news for us?"

"News, maybe," I said. "I wouldn't call it good." I looked toward the table where Martha sat with Greene. "What gives there?" I asked. "Last time I saw him he was flat on his back."

Owens rubbed his chin and shrugged. "He's all right, really, Mr. Wilde. He . . . well, he feels things very keenly."

"Your business, Doc," I said flatly. "He's a punk in my book."

Owens leaned soberly toward me. He tapped one long forefinger on the bar. "Mr. Wilde, Randolph Greene is a brilliant young man. With any other skin, he might not be so . . . recalcitrant. He . . ." Owens studied me carefully. "There aren't enough brilliant Negroes, Mr. Wilde. We can't afford to lose even one through bitterness."

It made sense. I nodded. "You playing papa?" I asked. "Like old Mr. Prince?"

"There's nothing paternal about my interest, Mr. Wilde," Owens said tightly. "Greene's a rather objectionable fellow, I find. But I know him better than you do. Remember, he graduated Phi Beta Kappa. That should mean something. And since then the best job he could find was running an elevator." Owens spoke tensely, well under control, but with an edge of identity.

"Okay, Doc," I said as easily as I could. "I still think you have more patience than I have."

"I've had to learn patience, Mr. Wilde." Owens smiled thinly. "I don't consider it so much a virtue as a necessity —for a Negro." He grinned at me suddenly. "Randolph's a good boy who hasn't had a chance to do the things he knows he can do and do well. Old Mr. Prince has great hopes for him. He put Randolph through college, you know. I'll help Randolph, if I can. If he'll let me. But to get back to the subject, Mr. Wilde. What news?"

I smiled back. "Good for you, Doc. I guess the boy will be a little easier to handle now that he knows you can clout."

Owens nodded, a wide grin on his thin face. "I did bust him good, didn't I?" he said in total amazement.

"It was a pip, Doc," I said firmly. "Well, about the job. I've spent most of my day with Grodnik. The Joslin woman has been found and lost again. We should get

183

her tonight and then . . ."

A trumpet blare broke in. The horn blew a frantic fanfare and all the noise in the bar stopped as quickly as though it had been turned off at the source. Manny stood with widespread legs on the podium, holding his clarinet high above his head and waving for attention. He got it.

"Folks, the meeting will come to order," he shouted. He waited for complete silence. "Tonight is for The Prince," Manny said quietly. "And it's going to be just the way he would want it. Plenty of grog at the bar, plenty of fine music from fine musicians and everybody happy. Now let me introduce you to the boys who are going to play for us tonight . . ."

One by one, Manny called off the list of musicians, each of whom broke away from his party and came to the stand. The list read like *Who's Who in Hot Music.* Manny introduced each, not by the man's basic reputation, but by his relationship with The Prince. Apparently every hot man in the business had played with The Prince at one time.

An angry voice sounded close to my ear. With no warning, Greene's dark ugly face was scowling down at me, snarling with a young, half-drunken intensity. "Can't we go anywhere without being hounded by you?" he demanded with great indignation.

Owens touched his sleeve gently. "None of that, Randolph."

Greene pulled his arm away with an impatient movement. "I'm warning you, Wilde . . ."

I'd had my fill of young Mr. Greene. I didn't wait for the rest of it. I hooked his right arm toward me suddenly, spun him around and used a hand against his back to send him stumbling along the bar.

"Keep him away from me, Doc," I snarled at Owens. "I'm in no mood for him tonight."

Owens flicked a brief look at me and went after Greene. He caught the younger man at the end of the bar, steadied him with a solid arm and held him there for a moment, speaking earnestly to him. It took some little persuading apparently, but Greene eventually saw the point. He followed Owens back to their table.

Manny was nearly finished with his introductions. He presented Sweets Claxman and even I stood to shout. Sweets was oldtime almost as far back as Bechet. The grizzle-haired old man stood with a wide black-leather face stretched in a wondrous smile and waved his soprano sax case at the mob.

A sprightly old boy with close-cropped white hair and faded blue eyes slid along the bar and nudged me. "That Claxman," he said from the corner of his mouth, "that's really a horn. I remember him from the old days. He used to play with Buddy Bolden and Jellyroll Morton. Way back at Frisky Maud's in Storyville." He looked at me closely. "You wouldn't know about that," he added sadly.

"Those were the days," I said agreeably. I sipped at the drink Manny had poured for me. I put down the empty glass and the sleepy bartender filled it almost the moment it hit the bar.

"You don't know," the old boy said. "The beginning of American music. Red-letter days, my boy. Too bad the Army cleaned out Storyville in '17. A generation or two there and American hot music would have had a proper start."

We shook our heads at the sorrowful tale. We had a drink together to old Sweets Claxman. The old boy wanted to lament about Storyville. He wanted to tell me the ancient and fancy yarns about the New Orleans red-light district that had been the breeding ground of jazz music. They were fine stories and I had a hard time turning him off.

Manny had all his players identified by that time. "And now," he shouted eagerly, "now, the girl who sings like The Prince used to play, Nancy Lucas!" He round-housed his arm toward the side of the platform and Nancy stepped up for her bow. She was the only woman on the platform, but even so the applause wasn't merely the usual extra noise for a girl. It had some noticeable feeling in it.

Manny waved at the restive crowd. "Just one more," he promised. "Folks, we're going to start off the program with my favorite of all The Prince's songs, *Red Devil Blues,* and to start us off right—and brothers, I mean right—we've got The Prince's little girl to bang that box and take the second chorus. Ladies and gentlemen, a little girl who makes most of us look like Three-Fingered Fred, Martha Prince!"

Martha stood hesitantly and the noise was something solid. Tonight, Martha was The Prince. She had a tough audience. Everyone in it—except me—was a sound musician or an accomplished amateur. They knew their stuff and Martha would have to work hard at any normal time to come up to their requirements. But just a good try would be enough tonight. She was The Prince.

She walked slowly to the stand, stepped up and took

186

Manny's hand. With Manny beside her, she bowed to the crowd, waited for quiet.

"Tonight we pay our respects to the great man who was my father," she began. For some reason, I looked toward Randolph Greene, who was scowling a fierce young scowl at the tablecloth. Martha's voice was high and happy. "I must confess that most of you here tonight knew him better than I. Understood him earlier and better, and possibly even loved him more. But that was long ago . . ."

The old sport beside me murmured, "'. . . and in another country and besides, the wench is dead.'" He seemed happy to remember the phrase.

I didn't look at him. I joined the rest of the mob in watching Martha Prince. She stood high and serene in a silver-gilt dress that dropped low on her pale tan shoulders. She stood stiffly in the posture of the newly converted Christian. The sort you see in the old chromos that were made in the Dark and Evil Ages when the differences between men were determined and magnified by concentrated stupidity. Martha smiled and almost anyone could guess what that smile cost her.

"No one here," she said calmly, "can now compete with my admiration for The Prince. Tonight is a coming-home for me, a recognition of much that is finest in our world and a fierce rebellion against much that is filthiest. That I have learned from my father's music and learned well." She bowed quickly to the audience. "The remainder of the evening belongs to The Prince. Mr. Brenner has offered to let me play *Red Devil Blues*, the first," I could see the pause here, "the first and, I think, the finest of his great jazz songs."

There was no applause. I don't know why. Sometimes things strike an audience that way. Martha had said what there was to say and the crowd wanted no noise to disturb the feeling she had built. Everyone watched Martha seat herself at the piano and look toward Manny.

"Gawd, what a team," the old boy beside me whispered. "Just look. Manny Brenner, Sweets Claxman, Joel Cuffee, Bob Taylor, Harry Bierwagen and Martha Prince. Boy, what dough they could drag down in any spot in the country!" He smiled rosily at me. The high flush of the steady drinker lay thickly on his cheeks.

"Should be fine," I offered.

He looked at me as though I had sprouted two heads. "Fine? This is the best mob you could get," he insisted. "Oh, maybe you could argue it, but there couldn't be many changes." He banged down his newly charged glass and stared challengingly. "Maybe Armstrong and Bechet, okay. No argument there. Who else? Hines, maybe, because we don't know much about the kid. Who else? Go on, smart guy. Who else?"

I held up both hands peaceably. "Not me," I said. "Not me. I'm a chopsticks boy myself."

"Huh," he snorted. He glared with cross-eyed intensity. "Huh." He subsided against the bar and looked down the room where the six people on the stand were huddled around the piano, getting the order of precedence established.

Joel Cuffee hammered a flaring introduction for Manny's clarinet. Cuffee's press roll on the drums ended in six hard fast rim shots that set the tempo. Manny's clarinet caught it in the upper register and the combination behind him built up a solid beat and a stable har-

188

monic pattern that gave him freedom to roam over his instrument.

All the force and drive of fine jazz was in that song and the band playing it was adjusted to show it off well. Manny's tone was clear and true, with a hard, pulsing surge that made *Red Devil Blues* seem fresh and newly minted, which is just what it was. The Prince wrote it. You can see it on paper and you can buy a full eighty-man orchestration of it, but what Manny and his crew were playing was jazz, an inventive departure from a fine song. Manny's hard attack, his clever, wheedling phrasing, built the first chorus to a flare-up that brought all the instruments into the picture almost equally and then they faded to leave the insistent clarinet on top for a brief flash. The trumpet behind him hit a heavy dominant seventh. Manny wove a minor third through it, developing a keen wailing moan that worked, note for note, accent for accent, into the fast rocking piano and then faded under to let the piano carry the load.

You'll hear a lot of hot music people, and people who should know what they are talking about insist that the piano doesn't really belong in a jazz combination. They argue that jazz derives from fast march-time basically and the piano's place is only in the rhythm section, to help build a rich harmonic background for the horns. It could be. Maybe musically it can be proven one way or the other. But tonight, the piano belonged as a dominant, forceful instrument. Martha Prince had the touch of a concert pianist, a determined crispness that cut clearly through the harmonic thread and made its own way with the same incisive clarity that Manny

189

brought to his clarinet.

It was spirited teamwork we were listening to. Joel Cuffee took over the rhythm assignment. For a long while he rumbled a heavy press roll with both hands working furiously and at the same time he was accenting the second beat with his foot pedal on the bass drum. It was a wonderfully lively pulse and old Sweets Claxman rolled his eyes happily, half-grinning around his golden sax. Taylor's trumpet and Bierwagen's trombone were in the background. The trumpet was powerful and the trombone insistent, but the piano was carrying the thread. The straight simple pattern of the horns gave Martha a strong base for weaving contrapuntal harmonics and she swept into a dazzling series of rich chord progressions that had the room throbbing.

From the third chorus on to the end, the fabulous team on the stand left me behind. I could feel what they were doing. I could hear it perfectly, but musically there was too much for me to understand. Especially Sweets on his sax. He worked himself into a rising development of chords that seemed to be a complete blind alley to me. There wasn't anything I could see that could bring him logically back to home base. The piano and trumpet flared high with him, picked up his harmonic balances and together the three instruments worked out a vibrant solution. Over it all, Sweets' light pure tone pointed the way. I didn't understand how he did it, but it isn't necessary to understand that sort of work. The old boy beside me gasped quietly and poked my ribs. We shook our heads together.

The explosive finale came almost without warning and I looked up to see Sweets standing on the platform, grinning hugely at the crowded room, gasping slightly with an old man's struggle for air, holding Martha's hand high in the air. The Prince was back. The rolling applause left no doubt of that.

Even Randolph Greene was caught in the excitement. He pounded Owens heavily on the back, waving toward the stand and shouting. Owens obviously couldn't hear him. He looked back toward me for a brief moment, holding both hands high in the boxer's handshake.

There should be no more confusion for Martha. Not in her career, at least. I could see that tonight's reception could solve a lot of problems for her. From her radiant smile, her wide happy grin that reminded everyone of The Prince, I knew she was home. It's a rare thing to see and it comes only to a few people, but there was no doubt that Martha Prince was home.

The evening continued almost as well as it had started. The band membership changed constantly, with one man slipping away and another moving in with no break. Manny stayed through most of the evening's work, even when there were three other clarinetists on the platform. But only Martha stayed the limit. Some hours later Owens and Greene were leaning over the back of the piano, working happily on a joint bottle of champagne and singing softly with the band.

The music was almost evenly divided between the old Dixieland boys and the latter-day Chicago stylists. The old men carried the younger ones to a high pitch of effort. Too many people have done far too much talking about the difference between the two styles. There's a lot to say, but mostly the difference lies in the fact that the Chicago boys simply weren't good enough.

191

They tried and tried damned hard to play as well as the Dixie Negro units, but they weren't the instrumentalists in the first place. There isn't a single Chicago style trombone that has any of the wild freedom of the New Orleans tailgate. The Chicago boys couldn't play that well, so they replaced it with a honking tenor sax, but it isn't the same thing. And the hard drive of the Chicago men doesn't mask their occasional flat and sour harmonics that came just because they couldn't always hit the subtler blues notes of the Dixieland bands. All the gutty wobble, the low, aching, "dirty" tones of the best Chicago bands developed just because they couldn't reach the simple conviction of the New Orleans units. Quite a few drummers, a couple of trumpets and a few clarinets—that's about what Chicago managed to produce in competition with the Dixie bands. Most of the good ones were on hand.

It was a night for instrumentalists. The men Manny had rounded up were the best in their business, with very few exceptions. They were playing the best basic jazz they knew, with no exception. Everyone of them had an idea, a new arrangement, an inventive notion for a chorus, for almost every one of The Prince's pieces. On *Beginner-Brown Blues*, Sweets took eight choruses without once repeating himself or coming up for air. The evening went like that.

Nancy Lucas was good. Almost as good as Manny had said she was and much too good for anything less than the league she was with tonight. She had the quiet deep sincerity that the jazz idiom demands and seldom gets. Her control was what impressed me. Her glides and skidding elisions were far more the work of an instrumentalist than a singer. While she sang, the band had another instrument and her tonal range was wide and sure enough to let her sing duets with Sweets and his soprano sax or Bierwagen's deep tailgate trombone. She stood tall and sure on the stand with her arms down. She had no phony mannerisms, no wiggles and no contortions, no cheap attempt to use beauty and appeal where talent and work were needed. It was fine to listen to and her low register was as low, as definite and as mournful as Kid Ory's wonderful horn.

Later in the evening, as it worked its way toward daylight and fatigue, Nancy was finished. Instrument or no, a human voice will not stand the pressure. Where Manny's clarinet was warm and true, where Martha's piano was still gay and sprightly, Nancy's voice was beginning to strain. Manny kissed her good night and shoved her gently off the stand. I had my biggest battle of the night, beating my way through the mob to rescue her from all the people who offered drinks, who wanted to talk or just wanted to look at her. Half an hour later we wormed our way out into the hall for a breather.

"Oof," Nancy grunted deeply. "That's an audience that swallows you." She leaned wearily against the doorjamb and shivered in the sharp air.

"I'm part of it," I said slyly.

She giggled. "Not just now, me lad," she said, waving me away. "Let's get out of here for a while, huh?"

"Let's get out for keeps," I suggested. "It's been a long night."

Nancy looked up lazily and nodded. "But my coat. It's way back in there . . ." she pointed in through the bar.

"We'll leave it," I said quickly. "Get it tomorrow." I reached back through the door for my overcoat and hat hanging on the rack there. I draped the coat over Nancy's shoulders, pulled on the hat and hauled open the outer door.

The snow had stopped and a thin glistening sheet lay on top of the world tonight. We walked quickly with crackling steps down to my car, choked it into life hurriedly and headed for the Coronet Restaurant to pick up where we had left off the evening earlier.

It was late when we left Manny's HOT BOX. It was much later when we left the Coronet and it was far too late when I let Nancy out in front of her apartment building. There had been intervals filled with this-and-that, which as everyone knows, is time-consuming. The night kept a lot of magic from the splendid music at Manny's and the atmosphere almost pulsed in rhythm with the strong jazz beat. Nancy and I moved slowly through it until the city began to wake up and make the busy noises that open a busy day.

It was almost six when I reached my apartment. I called the switchboard, left instructions about being awakened at nine. The girl didn't seem impressed, but she was willing to make an effort. I authorized an expedition by a bellboy, if I didn't answer. I was asleep by the time I got the phone back in its cradle.

CHAPTER EIGHTEEN

THE phone was ringing with a nagging persistence that convinced me it had been going for some time and wouldn't stop until I answered. I shoved an arm out for it, dragged it over and mumbled, "Okay, thanks," and hung up.

I was thinking about getting up when the phone rang again. This time I felt no gratitude. I snatched the receiver and grunted at it.

"Mr. Wilde," the switchboard girl wailed, "there is a Mr. Connolly here to see you. He says he is a policeman." Her tone held a deep suspicion.

"Yeah," I grunted again. "He's a cop, all right. Send him up, sugar."

I dropped the phone and rolled out of the sack. I couldn't find my slippers. My new robe seemed to be missing, too. I settled for a faded red robe that still had Army Medical Corps insignia on the left pocket, the souvenir of a malarial holiday. I got into it and tied the frayed cord. I was near the front door when Connolly knocked.

He was the new look in city dicks. He wore a dark brown tweed that made his pale tan skin look like a Florida special. A figured gold-and-red bow tie fell loosely over a white shirt. He carried his hat and coat, which is not regulation precedure for a cop. He smiled diffidently and waited to be invited in.

"Morning," I mumbled. "Late night."

Connolly's smile grew stronger. "Sorry to bother you, Mr. Wilde," he said. "Lieutenant Grodnik sent me. He wants to see you."

I closed the door and went back to the bedroom. Connolly dropped his things and followed me.

I fumbled through my dresser for a fresh shirt and laid out my clothes on the rumpled bed.

"He got something?" I asked sleepily.

"I don't know, Mr. Wilde," Connolly answered. "He called me at home and asked me to stop here on my way down. He said the people here refused to let him get through your switchboard."

"Good," I said readily. "I'll have to slip the gal a buck for that."

"Not so good," Connolly objected. "It's a homicide, the Lieutenant said. He really wants you downtown fast, Mr. Wilde."

I nodded slowly. "Who's dead now?"

"He didn't say. He just said to hurry." Connolly eyed me. He wanted to see some speed but he was willing to be polite for a while longer.

"Sure," I said. "Suppose you go in and brew us some coffee while I get dressed, huh?" I pointed toward the kitchenette.

My percolator takes seven minutes to make coffee after it reaches the boil. It needs possibly four minutes to heat up. The glugging solution had a dark rich tone by the time I joined Connolly at the table. I had a brief scratch from my razor and my throat was lined with sandpaper, but I was ready. My black eye was just about finished. There was just one little purplish dot like a beauty mark at the outer edge. I decided it was becoming.

Connolly had one cup with me just to be sociable. He sat tensely in his chair, trying not to squirm while I had a second cup. I choked it down as quickly as I could. I sneaked a look at the morning paper. There was no murder featured there.

"You driving?" I asked Connolly.

He shook his head. "Lieutenant said for me to take a cab here. I paid him off outside."

"Sure," I said. "You can ride in with me. I'll bill the city. One trip—here to City Hall. Fifty bucks. Plus expenses."

Connolly grinned widely. "Not City Hall," he said. "But I'd like to see what happens to that bill."

"You're too young to know things like that," I said. "Where do we go?"

Connolly slid his new notebook from his pocket and thumbed through. He read the address. I knew that address. Connolly repeated it.

"Down in the old section," he said. "I can find it."

I cleared my throat. "I know it, Connolly," I said thickly. "That's Manny Brenner's HOT BOX. Let's get moving."

I don't know why I stopped for my gun. I just wanted to have it handy, I suppose. I stripped off my jacket and gave it to Connolly to hold. Then I unlocked the bottom drawer of my desk and got the pistol. I twisted the straps around my shoulders and adjusted the wash-leather holster under my left arm. I swung the cylinder out and checked the shells. I put it together and shoved it under my arm. I liked knowing I had it with me. Whatever was waiting down at Manny's was something I wasn't going to like. The .38 might be useful for a change. I seldom carry it. A permit goes with my job but the gun isn't really necessary. But today I wanted to have it with me.

I took my jacket from Connolly, got into it and grabbed my overcoat and hat from the couch. Connolly had the door open when I reached it and we wasted no more time.

I may have made the trip downtown in better time, but I don't think anyone could have gone much faster on those streets. I turned in at the alley and parked three doors down from the HOT BOX. The rest of the space from there was taken up by three black police cars. Connolly and I climbed out and walked up the narrow path to the door.

Only one driver was left with the cars. He looked up with no interest. I pushed open Manny's outer door and we went in. A bulky uniformed patrolman waited just inside the door. He grabbed my arm tightly before I could get inside.

I didn't feel in the mood that early. "Take him out, Connolly," I said over my shoulder.

"Please do not finger the taxpayers," Connolly said tightly. He flashed his buzzer at the cop and tapped his arm gently. It went away. Connolly let the cop see he was displeased. "Where is Lieutenant Grodnik?" he asked.

"Now look," the cop said quickly. "How was I to know . . ."

"Where is Lieutenant Grodnik?" Connolly asked

again, ignoring the excuses.

"Upstairs," the cop said glumly.

Connolly waved one slim hand and the cop moved aside. Connolly let me go first.

I shoved on the door to Manny's office and went in. Grodnik stood beside the desk, leaning slightly against it. He looked up. He ran a thick hand over his wide bald head and ruffled the fringe of hair at the back. Two other men were busy in the room. One was puffing an insufflator at the glass doors of the bookcase. The other was cataloging a small stack of belongings, just the mixture you always find in any man's pockets.

Grodnik's hand moved forward to rub at his eyes. He spoke without emphasis. "Manny Brenner got shot this morning," he said heavily. "Right between the eyes."

He waited for me to speak. I didn't have a thing to say.

"You in on that shindig last night?"

I nodded. "Part of it. Left about three, I think."

"He always leave it beat up like this?" he asked absently.

"Not quite this bad," I said. "He kept a lot of things here. Souvenirs, music. But it was fairly tidy when I saw it."

The room had obviously been searched and searched clumsily by someone in a great hurry. Music and books had been hauled from the cases and dumped, pictures had been torn from the walls, desk drawers pulled out and spilled on the floor. Whoever had been through the room had made a lot of noise and left a hell of a mess.

Grodnik sat wearily, letting his chin drop forward on

199

his chest. He looked like a modern-day Buddha, brooding over the sins of the world.

"I got a statement from one of the people here last night. You can read it over and see if you can add anything."

"Any time," I agreed. "When did it happen?"

"Dunno. This morning some time. Couple of hours ago anyway."

"How did you find him so soon?"

Grodnik shut his eyes and stretched his legs out. He yawned, showing three gold inlays in his back teeth. "'Scuse me," he said vaguely. "No sleep last night. I was reading over that statement of yours where you told about Manny talking to the Joslin woman. So I figured if he could find her once through the people he knows, maybe he can find her again. Besides, I figured maybe he might have left something out when you talked to him. I sent a man down to see him. Manny wasn't home this morning so my man came here. He found him." Grodnik shifted his weight and yawned again. He struggled to his feet. "If I sit down any longer, I'll never get up."

"You any closer to Joslin?" I asked.

He shook his head and said quietly. "She didn't come in last night. Precinct man waited all night."

Grodnik shoved his hands in his pockets. "Let's blow and let the working men finish up," he said mildly. "We can go downstairs."

Connolly opened the door and followed us downstairs into the bar. Grodnik levered himself up on a stool and Connolly sat on the one beside him. I walked down to the far end, lifted the partition and came back up inside the bar. Most of the liquor compartments were locked, but on one ornate little glass shelf was a row of elegant liqueurs and two bottles of vintage brandy. I chose the twenty-year-old Courvoisier.

"This one's on Manny," I said. "He had a good party last night. He didn't know what a smash finish he was going to have."

I poured several ounces in each glass and held mine up. It wasn't exactly a toast. No one said anything, but Manny would have liked it that way. He was a round little man with a genius for a vibrating reed. He didn't adjust very well to his culture. He wasn't much of a citizen, as we reckon citizens these days. But he was a hell of a fine guy. And he could play wonderful music. He had a sensitive and gentle nature that was apparent mostly in his music, only slightly with people. I liked Manny and what little I knew and appreciated of American music came from his high enthusiasm, his scorn for the shoddy and his real love for honest work in his field. I poured down the velvety old brandy.

Grodnik stared at his glass for a moment and then lifted it and threw the brandy against the back of his throat with a quick twist of his wrist. He put the glass down quietly and watched me refill it. "Let's not drink it all," he said quietly. "It's damned fine brandy, though. Makes me feel more alive." He looked around the empty room, staring ahead toward the deserted bandstand. "He was a nice little guy, you know it? We used to have a joke whenever I came in. He'd play something and if I could tell him the title, the bill was on the house. Kinda silly. The missus always liked to come here Friday nights. He was a nice guy. I never guessed right once. What do you think about that?"

"He was probably inventing new ones for you," I said. I downed my second drink.

"Yeah, that could be," Grodnik said softly. He sipped at the brandy.

I gave Connolly another charge in his glass, poured just a drop into mine and corked the bottle. I put it back on the shelf. Stuck in between the cash register and the wall was a dull blue leather book with a cracked finish. I pulled it out. It had "Western High School, 1915," on the cover. It was Manny's annual. I brought it back to the bar with me and opened it. The book fell open naturally to the page where Manny and The Prince were featured. That was probably the only page that continued to have meaning for Manny. I turned it around and pointed to the picture of The Prince and Manny.

"That was the first show they did together, Manny told me," I said.

Grodnik leaned over to look and Connolly twisted in his seat so he could see. Connolly sighed heavily. The sound was deep and solemn in the still room. "They really had it, didn't they?"

Grodnik nodded silently. He pushed up from the bar. "Better phone in," he said.

I folded the book together. "Think I'll take this out to Martha Prince, if you haven't any objections, Lieutenant. She would probably like to have it."

"Guess it's okay," Grodnik said. He forced a smile. "It's stealing, of course. I wouldn't want to hear about it."

"You won't," I promised.

Grodnik wedged himself into the phone booth near

the door and dropped in a nickel. I sat leafing through the book, sitting beside Connolly, while Grodnik spent ten active minutes with his office.

I was reading The Prince's athletic record in the sports section of the annual when Grodnik came back from the booth. The Prince was just average at sports. That made sense. Not many high school boys have more than one developed talent. Most of them don't have even one. I marked my place with a fingernail and looked up.

Grodnik's face was lined and tense when he left the booth. He leaned solidly against the bar. "Magee's lawyer cut our water off," he said. "No statement. No nothing. He's on his way to get a writ now. We'll have to book Magee or let him go."

"So you'll try the material witness charge," I suggested.

"Sure, if we have to," Grodnik said slowly. "I'd like something stronger though. He'd be free in an hour on that. Sergeant Wentworth phoned The Prince's daughter, trying to get her to charge Magee with attempted blackmail. Wentworth says that guy Greene was in the room with the girl and he heard them kicking it around. Greene must have persuaded her not to go for it. Wentworth is just guessing, of course, but that's what it sounded like to him and he's a pretty smart kid." Grodnik's eyes blinked twice. He rubbed them with heavy fingers. "Hell, I got to get some sleep. Can't take it any longer like you young guys." He stared glumly at the floor for a moment. "Look, Wilde, why don't you take that book out to her? Tell her what we're up against and see if she won't give us a hand? Make sure she keeps it under the hat. Don't tell her any more than you have to, but be sure she knows where the Department stands on this. How about it?"

"The blackmail charge, you mean?"

"Yeah. She has the estate to consider, after all. She has what you might call an insurable interest. I'll make sure no one will question her basis for the charge."

"What does that give you?"

"Dammit, Wilde, you know as well as I do," Grodnik snorted. "We want to keep Magee on ice but we can't do it for long without a good strong charge."

"And my client makes a good strong charge of blackmail and what happens if she can't make it stick? Can you keep her clear of a countersuit?"

Grodnik looked at me and shook his head. "No, I guess not. Just put it up to her anyway, huh?"

"Sure, Lieutenant," I said. "Always glad to oblige. As a matter of fact, I think she might be willing to chance it. I'll let you know."

He dropped a tired hand on my shoulder for a brief moment. He walked to the door and spoke to me as he moved. "I'm going home till noon or maybe a little later. You can get me there."

I searched my pockets for a nickel and climbed into the telephone booth. I found Doctor Owens in his office. I don't know how he managed it, but he sounded brisk and vital. I was sure he hadn't had an inch more sleep than I had and I was just as sure that he hadn't been able to knock off a snort for assistance.

He didn't ask questions. He was willing to meet me at The Prince's house at eleven. He had a friend who could take over his clinical work for him.

Connolly was still perched on the bar stool when I

came out of the booth.

"You coming with me?"

"Guess not, Mr. Wilde," he said slowly. "Lieutenant didn't say. He looks awful tired. I think I better stick with him."

We agreed that was the best notion. Connolly stayed on his stool where he could watch for Grodnik to leave. I pulled my overcoat collar high enough to break the sharp wind that whistled down Manny's alley.

CHAPTER NINETEEN

MARTHA PRINCE and Doctor Owens were in The Prince's studio. One of the maids took my hat and coat and led me through the corridor.

Martha sat at one of her father's pianos, the mahogany one with bright nacre inlay. She was half-turned to Owens who sprawled lazily in a deep chair near the liquor cabinet. Martha was still riding the wave of her performance at Manny's. The piano was spread thickly with old yellowed sheet music and the area around her had the look of a long session. She still wore the silver slippers that matched her evening gown. The gown was replaced by a pale gray wool robe that swept to the gray-tiled floor. It had a daring square bodice cut low from the shoulders. I kept my eyes studiously away as I crossed the rug and held out the annual to her.

"Small gift from a nameless admirer," I said.

Martha reached greedily. "How nice, Carney," she smiled. "Everybody has been so very nice."

"Not so damned nice," I muttered. "Not everyone."

Martha didn't hear me. She tumbled the book about in her hands. I tipped my mitt to Owens and dropped into a chair near him. I leaned over. "Manny Brenner was murdered this morning," I said softly.

Owens froze. His long face grew longer and harder. He said nothing. His eyes involuntarily reached toward Martha.

She sat happily on the piano bench with the book. "It's The Prince's, isn't it?" she asked. He wasn't just her father now. Even to her, he had become The Prince.

"High school annual," I said. "Manny Brenner had it. I thought you might want to keep it. Sort of a souvenir."

Owens touched my arm to stop me. "Martha," he said tensely, "Mr. Wilde has some very bad news, my dear."

Martha looked up with no more than polite interest. "Yes?"

"It's Mr. Brenner," Owens said. "He's been killed."

Martha looked with horror toward me.

"It's just that bad," I said. "Somebody killed him after last night's show. Down at the HOT BOX. But that's not all." I turned to Owens. "I haven't done you much good, Doc. I've spent a lot of time and some of your money, but so far the only concrete thing I've come up with is an alibi for Magee."

Martha sat in stricken silence. Owens dug tightly at the arms of his chair. "He's free, you mean? He's out?"

"No, not yet, Doc." I spoke with all the confidence I had left. "Grodnik wants to keep him and he will if he can. There is little doubt he figures in both the death and the blackmail. Both Grodnik and I are sure of that. But just on the basis of time, it looks as though he can't be touched for the killing."

I lit a cigarette and then broke into the tense silence with an explanation of the time factor that seemed to eliminate Magee as a suspect for murder. "With that information," I concluded, "Grodnik can't charge him with murder. He could hold him as a material witness, but even I know three local judges who would give him bail in ten minutes on a witness charge. So that's why Grodnik wants Martha to reconsider signing a complaint for an attempted blackmail charge against Magee. It's a rough chance and I couldn't advise you. I'd hate to see Magee go free though, and he will, if he's charged as a witness. With blackmail, the bond will be too high for him to meet and we can keep him around."

Owens moved over to the piano bench and took Martha's hand. "I think it would be best, my dear," he said gently.

"But isn't it dangerous, Larry?" she asked. "Randolph said . . ."

Owens made an impatient gesture. "Damn Randolph," he snapped. "You didn't know that Magee had an alibi when the police phoned this morning. I suppose it might be dangerous if Magee can substantiate his claims. It's dangerous even if you aren't able to prove he did actually attempt to blackmail the estate, but it isn't a question of finding the safe course. I think it would be far wiser to keep Magee under control until this whole business is cleared up."

"I'd back that judgment, Martha," I said. "I think

207

the doc has it on the button."

Martha stared at the floor. She pivoted on her seat to face the keyboard. She made a sudden grab to catch the annual that was sliding from her lap. She put it on the music rack and began to leaf through it. After a long moment, her hand reached for Owens. She touched his sleeve and patted softly. "All right, Larry," she said firmly. "That's what we will do."

Owens smiled and his whole body seemed to relax. "That's fine," he breathed.

Martha riffled through the album with one hand. Her thumb found the double-page spread where Manny had broken the spine. The book lay flat there under her hand and she peered closely at the picture.

"It's The Prince, Larry. At school. See?" She looked toward me. "Isn't that Mr. Brenner there?" she asked. "Beside him?"

I said it was. I wanted to get her started for Grodnik's office and take care of the formal complaint against Magee but I didn't think that was just the moment to push. I smoked my cigarette and let her get used to the idea first.

Owens and Martha bent their heads low over the spread page and I could hear Martha humming in a low throaty voice. She was picking the misty faded notes from the piece of sheet music that the publisher had used as a background for the spread. She hit one hesitant chord on the piano softly, then a run of four bars. There must have been a picture at that point, because she merely beat time on the music rack for a few bars and then picked it up again. It sounded like nothing at all to me at first. Then she struck a chord progression that nudged at me with thin remembrance. She hit it lightly and the same progression was repeated. Then I knew it.

"Hold it there," I snapped.

Martha's hands fell to the keyboard and she looked up with mild surprise.

"That last phrase. Try it again. Faster this time."

Martha searched for the phrase. Her long thin fingers hit it with precision and power. She repeated it in a faster tempo.

"It *is!*" she said with complete conviction. "Oh, Carney! It *is!*"

"*Red Devil Blues,*" Owens whispered hoarsely. "Even I know that part. Then that means . . ."

"That means Magee is a phony," I said. I kept my voice under control, but I felt like jumping through hoops. "That's a 1915 annual. Magee claims he wrote it in 1916. So if that song in the high school annual was written by The Prince, we got him. Got him cold."

"But wasn't it?" Martha asked. She turned swiftly and held the book toward the light. "*Red Devil Blues,*" she read slowly. Her eyes ranged down the page. "But there isn't any name," she wailed. "Oh, Larry, there isn't any name."

Owens took the book from her limp hands. He brought it over to the strong lamp near my chair and bent over it. His lips moved faintly as he read. Then he straightened confidently. "It's all right, Martha," he said firmly. "It's there. Enough anyway."

We followed his finger as he traced the outline of three faint initials that were barely visible beneath the title line. "H.M.P." meant Harold Morton Prince to me and to the rest of the world. Magee was halfway down the drain right now.

"That's it," I said with heavy relief. "Now we get this to Grodnik right away." I didn't ask for permission to use the phone. It stood in a niche in the main hall and I was nearly there before I had stopped talking. I dialed Central Police and asked for Homicide. I knew Grodnik wouldn't be back yet, but I hoped they would give me his home number. Like most sensible cops, he keeps it out of the phone book.

The duty sergeant at Homicide would not give me the number. He was willing to admit that Grodnik was expected at two o'clock and from his flat, slurring tone, I knew that was all I would get. I figured it could wait that long. I hung up and went back to the studio.

"Grodnik will be in at two," I said, ignoring the close huddle on the piano bench. "Can you come downtown then?"

Martha smiled happily. "Yes, of course we can, Carney, but . . ." she hesitated. "I mean, are you sure it's really enough?"

"Hell, yes," I said flatly. "All Magee had was a stack of claims that had a certain vague possibility because of Arabella Joslin's affidavit. I don't think he had anything he would have dared to take into court. He wasn't working on the strong edge of probability, remember. The Prince, or rather Martha, had that. Magee had a claim that was so preposterous it took your breath and you couldn't tell how to fight it right away. Now you have one definite piece of proof that he was lying about one claim. I'm no lawyer, but I'll give you a thousand to one that he wouldn't get anything more than that first day in court. Then he goes out on his ear. And that's just where you want him."

Owens nodded briskly. "That's exactly it. I won't pretend I'm not relieved, Mr. Wilde."

"And me, Doc. And me." We grinned at each other and we both bowed toward Martha. "This," I pointed to the annual, "this also gives us the good solid excuse we want to charge Magee with blackmail. It isn't proof enough, of course, but it's the prima facie evidence that shows good faith. We've got him, Martha."

She grinned widely. "We make quite a team," she said happily. "Do you want to wait while I dress? Then we can all go downtown together."

I shook my head. "I'll meet you there, if you don't mind," I said. "I'd like to stop at my office first. I haven't seen it for a couple of days."

We agreed on that. I reminded them to bring the book along and got out.

Traffic was light on the way downtown. I brought my car to a halt in my usual parking lot and traded it for a ticket. After a quick sandwich at Sam's Grill, I turned down the street toward my office building.

Nothing seemed changed since the last time. The elevator cage looked a little cleaner and my door looked a little dirtier. It all evened up. I coaxed the stiff lock back and went in, feeling along the wall for the light switch.

There was faint movement in the room. I thought something had moved on the floor behind me. I turned with my finger still reaching for the lights. I never found them.

Sudden heavy darkness fell over my eyes. Something

exploded with colorful sparkles in my head. That was all.
I knew when I began to drop, but I didn't feel a thing
when I hit the floor.

CHAPTER
TWENTY

A THICK pulsing rhythm beat in my head like the ringing
of bells. I opened my eyes a crack and stared dimly at
the dusty floor. My hat lay just in front of my nose with
a deep crease along the back.

The ringing was not merely in my head. The telephone bell jangled insistently again. I pushed up a short
distance from the floor, squeezed one dusty hand across
my eyes and stood slowly, while waves of dizziness
came and went around me.

I half fell toward the desk, braced one hand hard on
the top and fumbled the receiver toward me. I kept my
eyes closed. I mumbled something.

"Wilde? Wilde?" It was a snappy, fast voice, vaguely
like an excited Pomeranian. I couldn't identify it, but
I didn't have to try. He told me. "Al Gilman," he barked.
"Where the hell you been?"

I cleared my throat roughly. He didn't wait for an
answer.

"I see in the papers about Manny Brenner. That the
right stuff? Cops think Bella Joe had something to do
with it, huh?"

"I haven't seen the papers," I said thickly.

"Uh-huh," he snorted. "This is mixed up with The Prince, too, I'll bet. Well, listen here, I got a line on that babe if you want her."

"I want her, all right," I said clearly. The heavy fog lifted slightly.

"Lenny Boxer seen her," Gilman said. "He's got a spot at the Fortunatus. In the café. Lenny says she was having dinner there. She signed the check so she must be living there." Al's voice picked up speed and pressure but he spoke distinctly. "Don't look like she's trying to duck, but if you want her, there she is."

"Thanks, Al. Does Boxer know her well enough to recognize her?"

"Yeah. Yeah. Usedta work inna same combo once." Al's tone was crisp and short.

"Okay, Al. Thanks," I said. "I'll let you know what happens."

We said our good-bys and I depressed the space bar for a moment and let it up again. I stood there fighting off sudden waves of nausea. I choked them back and dialed Central Police. I asked for Grodnik's office. The phone rang twice and then Acting Detective Connolly identified himself at the other end.

"Connolly," I said hoarsely. "Carney Wilde. You know where Grodnik is?"

"On his way, Mr. Wilde. Be here in half an hour, I should think."

I didn't want to wait. "Well, tell him I've got a tip on Arabella Joslin. Maybe I'll be able to bring her in." Then I thought of Connolly. "Wait a minute. You want to bring your badge along, Connolly? Might make it faster that way."

213

"Sure thing, Mr. Wilde," Connolly said readily. "That is, if it isn't too far. Lieutenant Grodnik will expect me to be here when he comes in."

"It'll work," I said. "She's supposed to be at the Fortunatus. Leave a note for Grodnik just in case and tell him that Miss Prince and Doctor Owens will be there at two. Then meet me at my parking lot right away." I gave him the address and hung up.

I stood straight and went back to the door for my hat. My fingers found a thick welt on the top of my head. No professional thug had put it there. Anyone who knew his job would have laid his sap behind my ear and used half the force. It was an amateurish clout with half the effort wasted on my hat, but it hurt enough anyway. I wiped my hat against my coat and eased it onto my head gently with both hands.

I checked my pockets. Whoever had sapped me hadn't touched a thing. My gun was still in the holster and still loaded. No money was missing and my wallet showed no signs of a search. I had obviously received another subtle warning. I thought of my telephone warning. The heavy dim voice meant nothing even now. Both warnings were clumsy and almost meaningless. Anyone could have phoned me. Anyone could have forced my office lock that had been warped away from the jamb for years. And anyone would have had enough muscle to bang my skull. I thought quickly then of Arabella Joslin's wide heavy arms. Plenty of muscle there, too. I suddenly wanted to talk to her again.

Connolly was waiting at the entrance when I came sliding along the icy pavement of the parking lot. I handed him my keys and motioned him toward the driver's seat. I told him how to reach the Fortunatus and he turned the car down the ramp into the street and turned south toward The Bend.

The Fortunatus had once been a fine hotel, just as The Bend had once been my town's best residential district. In the days when John Paul Jones docked just down the street, The Bend was the only place to live. The Fortunatus had been built when the first Roosevelt was in the White House and The Bend was for the last time a neighborhood for the city's respectable folk. Now the Fortunatus was eight floors of weathered rose brick that badly needed pointing. It took what it could get by way of tenants and in The Bend that wasn't much. The Bend had become an area of dingy rowhouse tenements; all-night garages with smirking ,wise-eyed young men lounging in the doorways; dirty, fly-infested restaurants, fish markets and small groceries that sold limp produce, uninspected meat and even nastier things. Most of the city's night clubs were in The Bend.

I pointed to a clear space a block from the Fortunatus and Connolly parked there.

"Manager first," I said. "Since we can afford to be legal."

Connolly looked worriedly at me. "You okay, Mr. Wilde?" he asked. "You look kinda beat out."

"I'm all right," I said slowly. "Let's go haul her out."

We climbed the streaked granite steps to the lobby and pushed through the doors.

An elderly man was sorting mail behind the desk. He had the thin shoulders, the sour face and the spurious concentration of the lifetime clerk. A sign above his head listed the manager's name as "H. K. Stevens." A

215

smaller one under it said, "On Duty: Mr. Johns." I rapped on the desk top but Mr. Johns was too busy to notice. He squinted at an envelope and deposited it carefully in a numbered slot.

Connolly lifted the registry pen and flipped it neatly smack in Mr. Johns' lap. The old man started back wildly from the table. He turned suddenly and found Connolly's blue-and-gold buzzer just under his nose. He needed just one look. A police badge would be a common sight in the Fortunatus. He bobbed his head up and down and tried painfully to smile.

"Very sorry, Captain," he whined. "Awful busy these days. Very sorry . . ."

"Get the manager," Connolly said coldly. "Just get the manager."

"Yes, sir, Captain," Mr. Johns said quickly. "Yes, sir." He walked quickly along the desk to a closed door, opened it without knocking and slipped through.

Mr. Johns stayed inside. The manager appeared a moment later. He was the blue-jowled, well-massaged character who always can be found in a place like the Fortunatus. Connolly let him see the buzzer and then he put it back in his pocket.

"You have a woman here," Connolly said. "Negro woman. Five-foot-eight. Weighs about one-eighty. Big woman. What room?"

Mr. Stevens frowned just to prove he was thinking. "I'll ask around," he said smoothly. "I don't remember myself."

"Name might be Bella Joe," I said. "Or Arabella Joslin."

Stevens opened a loose-leaf notebook and turned to

216

the J's. "No," he said, "I'm afraid not . . ." He turned the page. "There's a Bertha Johnson," he offered. "Registered last night."

"Check the description," Connolly said. He leaned against the desk and made a bored face.

The manager turned quickly and went back to his office. He was gone about two minutes and then he returned with a wide glowing smile. He smirked at Connolly.

"She seems to be the one you want, gentlemen," he said. "Shall I come with you? Do you want me to ring first?"

"No—to both of them," Connolly said easily. "Just send someone with a passkey."

"Certainly. Certainly, sir," the manager said quickly. He hammered petulantly on the desk bell. "Front!" he called in a commanding voice. "Front!"

A small man with a bland secretive face eased up to the desk. "Yes, sir," he said to the manager. His tight eyes measured me, then Connolly, and moved back to the manager.

"Take these gentlemen to Room 427 and stay with them as long as they need you," the manager said briskly.

The bellhop said "Yes, sir," again in the same blank tone. He led us to the openwork elevator cage in the corner and rang the bell. "Cops?" he asked me from the corner of his mouth.

I pointed at Connolly. The bellhop squinted at the tall Negro and shook his head sadly.

Room 427 was the last door down a long dim corridor toward the rear of the Fortunatus. I stopped the procession when I spotted the door. I held out my hand for the key. The bellhop was glad to get rid of it.

"Knock first?" Connolly asked in a whisper.

I shook my head. "She had a gun," I said softly.

I pulled my .38 out of the holster and held it low against my leg with my left hand. Connolly got up close to the door so he could come in with me. I took a deep breath, rammed the key in quickly, turned it and shoved the door back.

Connolly and I came through like a pair of blocking backs. If you are ever going into a room where you expect trouble, that's the best way to enter. Just as fast as you can. Stay up on your toes and be ready to get the hell out if it's too much to handle. There wasn't any need for precaution in this room.

It was long and narrow, overlooking a busy alley. A soiled paper blind with a torn corner was the only covering at the window. Besides the bed, the room held a chest of drawers in peeling veneer, a shadowy mirror, one spindly chair and a thin-shanked bedside table. The bed was the thing that held me.

It was the usual white-painted iron affair with sagging springs and badly ironed coverings. Arabella Joslin—Bella Joe—Bertha Johnson—lay peacefully on it, fully dressed, smiling pleasantly with open eyes at the cobwebbed ceiling. Her right hand was pressed closely against her left breast and was partially hidden by a fold of her dress. I touched her other hand. It was stiff, cold and waxy, with the dead-body texture that is like nothing else in the world.

Connolly moved around beside me. He motioned for the bellhop to come in and close the door. He lifted the

218

loose fold of her dress from her right hand and then we could see the gun. It was the same stubby derringer she had shown me. She had held it tightly when she fired. Hardly any blood was showing. The Fortunatus was out one mattress and attendant fixings, but everything looked quite tidy. Connolly looked slowly around the room, as though he were searching for something in particular.

The woman's blue-cloth suitcase was against the wall. She hadn't bothered to unpack. Her handbag was balanced near the old-fashioned telephone set on the bedside table. The key to the room was beside it. I saw the paper just as Connolly lifted the bag. Weighted by the bag, but protruding a few inches toward the body, was a strip of pale green paper. That was what Connolly had been looking for. Everything said suicide and nothing was suspicious, but all bets were off if there wasn't any farewell note. A suicide has the last word. Few pass up their chance.

Connolly put the cloth handbag on the chair. He bent over the paper without touching it. It was a piece about four by six inches that had printing on the reverse side that showed faintly through the flimsy paper. It looked like a department store sales slip. It was probably the only paper handy when the note writing urge came on her. I stowed my .38 in the holster and bent with Connolly to read it.

"Just tell the old man I never meant to hurt The Prince," she had written in heavy pencil. "I never meant to hurt Manny, neither. He came in when I was trying to find that book. I knew he still had his and it would have ruined Stuff's plans. I'm sorry I shot. I didn't mean to and it's a sin that weighs me down. But I didn't want him to prove it against Stuff. Tell Stuff I'm sorry, too. But I guess sorry won't help now though. Manny knew what I wanted the minute he saw me. He said so. I guess Stuff hasn't got a chance now. He was so sure. Tell him I'm sorry for it all. Tell old Mr. Prince, too." It was signed, "Arabella Joslin Magee."

"Magee," Connolly breathed softly. "She was his wife. That's how come . . ."

"Yeah," I interrupted. "We better get Grodnik here, kid."

Connolly looked toward the dark still woman on the bed with sad lines in his young face. He batted his eyes twice and looked away. He slid two pencils from his outer pocket. He braced one pencil on each side of the fluted receiver and brought it to his ear without smudging any prints it might have. He told the operator to send the manager to the room. He gave her the number for Central Police. After the usual delays, he was put through to Grodnik's office.

"This is Connolly, sir," he said. "Mr. Wilde and I found Arabella Joslin. She's dead. Suicide, looks like . . . Yes, sir, at the Fortunatus. Room 427 . . . Yes, sir." He listened for a moment and then turned to me. "Really hopped up," he whispered. "Bringing the whole team with him." He listened again, said "Yes, sir," and hung the receiver carefully back on its forked rest.

The bellhop stood flat-footed, leaning slightly against the door and he was thrown nearly across the floor when the manager slammed into the room. He scrambled up quickly and found a safe spot against the blank wall. The manager didn't even notice him.

"What's this?" he barked. "What's going on here anyway?" His entering charge carried him well into the room. He spotted the body and his voice dwindled away. "Oh," he said dully.

"Just sit down, Mr. Stevens," Connolly said slowly. "The Lieutenant will want you pretty soon."

Stevens stared wide-eyed at the still body. He cleared his throat with a hard rasp and got back most of his spurious confidence. "Now, see here," he said, "I'm . . ."

"Sit down," Connolly said bluntly.

Mr. Stevens sat down. Connolly was no man to argue with just then. He was a new dick on his first case and all alone as far as official help was concerned. He would be as tactful as a hungry leopard if anyone bucked him. Mr. Stevens pulled the spindly chair over near the window beside the bellhop and sat there cautiously.

"Is it all right if I call my office?" he asked timidly.

"No," Connolly said. "We'll all wait a while." He moved to the chest of drawers with the handbag. He knocked the simple catch open against the top, holding the bag by the cloth part. He used one of his pencils to fish around in the collection. I didn't bother to look. It would be the usual stuff. I leaned against the foot of the bed and tried to ignore my headache. Connolly spread out the things from the handbag and left them where they fell. The only thing of interest that I spotted was a box of cartridges that would probably fit that stubby derringer the woman had. She had been prepared to do a little shooting. I was just as glad she had changed her target.

The Fortunatus was a twenty-minute drive from City Hall, but Grodnik made it in ten, using his siren all the way. It died with an angry snarl as the cars stopped at the hotel.

Grodnik had left in a hurry, his driver had kept the gas pedal hard down all the way, but when he came down the hall, you would have sworn he was an elderly gentleman out for a lazy constitutional in the morning sun. He led a slow procession along the hall to the room. Six men in all, which seemed a few more than were really needed. Grodnik was giving Arabella the full treatment.

Connolly saluted when Grodnik reached the doorway. In a few sentences he gave Grodnik the background and made a special point of telling him that nothing had been touched. He was a little proud of that. Grodnik nodded placidly.

"Let's see that note," he said when Connolly had finished.

Mr. Stevens and his bellhop stood when Grodnik entered the room. Connolly waved them back impatiently. He walked to the bedside table and pointed at the note. "We didn't touch it, Lieutenant," he insisted.

Grodnik smiled amiably. "That's fine," he said. He raised one finger in greeting to me and then leaned over the note. He read it through with minute attention and then again. Slowly he straightened and sighed deeply.

"That's it," he said gratefully. "That's it, thank Gawd." He swept back his hat and ran thick fingers over his head. His face lost its deep, strained lines and he smiled easily at me. "That was nice work on that song business, Wilde," he said. "I was just talking to the girl and Owens.

They make a real nice couple, I will say. They're dictating a statement for me now. The D.A. will be pleased to hear about it."

"That's fine," I said. I leaned against the wall and blinked my eyes to keep them clear.

"You really pulled a fancy Hawkshaw there," he sighed again with wide expansive contentment. He looked toward his men in the hall. "Well, let's clean it up," he said briskly. "We'll take the people out and give you a chance. Get the prints on that note and the stuff in the bag first thing. Then bring them to me." He turned to the manager. "You got a spare room we could use for a while?"

"Yes, indeed," Mr. Stevens said readily. "Indeed, yes. Next door should be empty, I think."

"No, it ain't, Mr. Stevens," the bellhop said quickly, "but 418 is."

Stevens smiled with forced cheerfulness. "Well, anyway, you're welcome, I'm sure."

Grodnik thanked him. "Let's just go along in there, huh?" He nudged Connolly to go with them.

Grodnik laid his hand on my sleeve and held me in the hall. He leaned against the wall and smiled serenely. "Not much need for a really sharp detective when your suspects confess and knock themselves off," he said softly.

"You're right, Lieutenant," I said. "I didn't get much done. But I managed to stay five yards ahead of you all the way."

Grodnik smiled thinly. He jerked a thumb over his shoulder. "That's a break for us all," he said. "Damned good thing, too. Magee is alibied tight and the D.A. is popping his cork."

"What more have you got for Magee?" I asked.

"Kid in the street. Saw Magee getting his car out of his garage. That was three o'clock. Kid was just leaving school. That puts Magee at his house about three. He couldn't have gone back to The Prince's house and still gone downtown. Not a chance. That's why we should be thankful about this."

"You be thankful, Lieutenant," I said harshly. "Do you like that confession she left? To both murders?"

Grodnik's thick finger rested against my necktie. He jabbed hard twice. "I like it, Wilde," he said grimly. "I like it and you like it. You've been a help. I'll admit that. But it's over now. The D.A. gets off my tail and you get paid off. It's finished." He dropped his hand and let his hard stare relax. "It's not so hard to figure," he said calmly. "This woman calls Magee after he gets back from his trip to see The Prince. She probably tells him she is downtown, but she isn't. She's right handy to The Prince's place in Seneca Park. Magee probably tells her he muffed the play and then she tells him to come on down and talk it over. That gets Magee out of the way and she slides over to talk to The Prince, puts it to him strong and gets shoved around, so she shoots him. Probably held him under her gun at first and then saw his and used it to kill him. She gets in and out by those studio windows, where hardly anyone ever sees anyone come in or out. Nobody does see her. Then when the old man finds the body, everybody thinks it was Magee because the cook remembered about the fight. And that does it."

I nodded cautiously. "It sounds good that way."

Grodnik shoved away from the wall. "We both like

224

it that way, Wilde," he said easily. "And with the confession, everybody else will like it."

"Okay, Lieutenant," I said wearily. "Would it mean anything if I told you somebody sapped me down in my office a little while ago?"

Grodnik looked at me blandly. His tan eyes smiled easily. "It would mean somebody didn't like you, I guess," he said. "I heard down at headquarters that Hollie Gray didn't like you any more. Maybe that's it."

"Maybe," I said. "Has Hollie got a price on my scalp?"

"Don't believe it's gone that far," Grodnik said placidly. "I'll send one of the boys down tomorrow to cool him off. But if anyone makes a pass at you, let me know." Grodnik wasn't paying much attention to what he was saying. His mind was on his job and I had no further part in that, as far as he was concerned.

"Just one more thing, Lieutenant," I said quickly.

Grodnik frowned slightly. "Well?"

"When you went out to The Prince's house last Friday, what did you find in the old man's room?"

"Not a thing," he growled.

"You found a busted brandy bottle and a glass, didn't you?" I insisted.

Grodnik shrugged. "That's right. Slipped my mind. So what?"

"Anything else? Like cigarette butts, for instance?"

"Not a thing. Dammit, Wilde, I told you that. The studio was an inch deep in cigarette butts. There weren't any in the old man's room. He can't take it. Makes him sick, or something."

I nodded. "Thanks, Lieutenant."

Grodnik reached for the door of the room where Connolly had taken the manager and the bellhop. "Stop in again any time, Wilde," he said indifferently. "Always glad to see you."

"Sure, Lieutenant," I said. "I'll do that."

Grodnik closed the door softly. He would take off his coat and hat methodically, find a comfortable seat and go about his business with the same slow method. When he was finished, the story would be a sensible account and the District Attorney would be pleased with it. Grodnik was a good cop. He had been good for a long time, but I had to remind myself how good he was, how good he had been. He was missing a lot of items I thought had some meaning, missing some of them purposely, because he was in a hurry, missing some of them bacause he wasn't digging deeply enough. Through the slow trip out to The Prince's house for my last visit, I kept wondering whether Grodnik was really as good as I had thought, as sound and careful as he seemed.

Martha and Owens had left Grodnik's office just a few minutes before I telephoned. They left a message for me to call at The Prince's house and catch them up on developments. I thought I would be able to give them their money's worth this time, though maybe they wouldn't like hearing all of it.

CHAPTER
TWENTY-ONE

OWENS came to meet me at the door as I came up the driveway. He peeled off my coat and threw it with my hat on a chair in the hall. "We're in here," he said, pointing toward the drawing-room. "Be a little quiet, though. Randolph is in the library doing some work for old Mr. Prince." He walked softly past the library door to the drawing-room. I followed him.

Martha stood near the fireplace, holding out both hands for me and smiling happily. "Is it really all over, Carney?" She squeezed my hands tightly. "They told us downtown that it was the Joslin woman. I'm so relieved."

I sat on one of the pebbly gray couches and leaned back. I wasn't as happy as the last time I had sat there. "The cops are relieved, too," I said. "We found Arabella Joslin in a crummy hotel down in The Bend. She wrote a confession and then she killed herself. That's really sharp investigation," I said sourly. "I haven't done much of anything about this case. The Prince is dead, the old man is in a shock state, Magee is in a coma. I can't talk to any of them. Then Manny gets killed and before we get to Joslin, she knocks herself off. There's some fine detective work. Just three jumps behind the whole trip."

Owens grinned. He sat beside me and thumped his fist on my knee. "You have done a splendid job, in my opinion," he said. "The Prince's music is clear, his murderer has been found. What more could you have done?"

"I don't know," I said glumly. "I wanted to talk to Joslin." I lit a cigarette and drew smoke deep into my lungs. "The only piece of real evidence I got in this whole affair, I found by accident. Almost by accident anyway."

"That high school annual, eh?" asked Owens.

Martha broke in. "Well, I think you did a fine job, Carney. I'm going to have you for all my work."

"No divorces though," I grinned. I moved forward slightly to get my bruised head away from the couch.

"Not even one," Martha said firmly. She looked toward Owens and blushed faintly. "Well, I still say you were fine. And we have your fee all ready for you." She leaned forward and dropped a folded check in my lap. I opened it. The figures read, "One thousand dollars." I folded it again and tapped it with my thumbnail. "It's ten times what I've been worth to you," I said.

Martha shook her head. "Oh, no, Carney. I wanted to make it more, but Larry said you wouldn't take it if I did. It's all been worth so much more than that to me."

Owens laughed deeply, a happy chortle low in his throat. "Old fee-splitter Owens," he said. "But, seriously, we both think that's only a portion of what we owe you. You'll have to collect the remainder in food and liquor over a period of years."

"It's a deal," I grinned. I tucked the check down in my breast pocket.

Martha sat on the coffee table, just inches away and leaned eagerly forward. "Now, tell us all about everything," she urged. "I forgot to ask before. How did she do it? And why?"

228

I drew on my cigarette again and held the smoke as long as I could. "I don't know how she did it. I don't know why she did it. I know the official guesses and I have a few guesses of my own. Right now, they seem to be fairly sound. Here's the way they go:

"Joslin and Magee rigged this frame-up with the music. Magee got those early originals out of the files probably and between them they rigged a fairly plausible story. Now, obviously, they knew that background sheet of music that was printed in the annual would ruin their case, but they were counting on two things. One, the matter would not go to court anyway, since it would either be settled or they would drop it. At least, that's my guess now. They wouldn't dare take that flimsy case to court. The second thing they were counting on was the scarcity of those books. Manny Brenner saw one in Joslin's room. My bet is that was The Prince's copy. Magee would have pinched that just to be safe. He didn't go to school with Manny and The Prince. He wouldn't have a copy of his own. Having The Prince's copy, which they were betting was the only copy in this area, they felt pretty safe. It must have been a shock for Joslin when Manny told her he had his copy handy. But I'm getting ahead of my story.

"We don't know just when they made their pitch to The Prince. As Grodnik outlines it, first Magee was here and he muffed it. The Prince threw him out. The official line is that Joslin was in the neighborhood and called Magee at his home after he left here. She told him to come down to her house and then she came here to put the screws to The Prince. Grodnik thinks she told Magee that she was home and wanted to talk to him. After she got Magee out of the way, Joslin came here, killed The Prince and got away without being seen coming or going. That isn't improbable. She could come and leave by those studio windows with no trouble.

"Then comes Manny Brenner's murder. I asked Manny to help me find her and he did. He saw her before I did and he mentioned that high school annual. That's when Joslin lost her head. After the big doings at the HOT BOX, she went to Manny's office to find the book. She found Manny instead, killed him and ran. That was a bad break all round. Any other night and Manny would have been home by that time.

"After she killed Manny she panicked. She didn't stay long enough to find the book, which was downstairs in the bar. She holed up in the Fortunatus down in The Bend, brooded about her troubles, got worried sick and scared as hell. She wrote a hysterical note and shot herself, probably using the same gun she had used to kill Manny. Incidentally, she was Magee's wife, which explains their tie-up. I guess they kept it a secret. At least, no one in the business knew about it.

"Her confession gets Grodnik off a very touchy case that had a shoulder-high pile of political implications and also got me a thousand-dollar bonus for being around in time to get the story. And that's just about it."

Martha turned away. She sat with her face toward the floor. "That awful woman," she said in a choked voice. Her shoulders shook heavily. She slid over to the opposite couch, holding her face in her hands and sobbing quietly. A light brittle sound like a door closing made a crisp noise in the still room. Owens twitched uncomfortably beside me. His thin face was long and sad as he watched Martha. After a long moment, he tapped my knee and pointed with his eyes toward the door. We rose and left the room. Owens closed the door with no sound.

"I'm sorry, Mr. Wilde," he said soberly, "but I'm sure you understand. This has been more of a strain for Martha than you might think." He lifted my coat and held it for me. "I'll stay with her today and then give her something to help her sleep." He pounded a wiry fist at my shoulder. "We do appreciate your help, Mr. Wilde, and we will both expect you to come to the wedding, if we don't see you again before then."

"Sure thing, Doc," I said. "I wouldn't miss it. About Martha—are you sure she'll be all right now?"

Owens nodded vigorously. "She'll be fine. She's going on with her studies. She had an offer from a New York night club to do a series of The Prince's songs, but she turned it down. Maybe in a few years . . ." He let it go at that, but there was just enough indication of his serious respect for Martha's work. She would make a hell of a screwy wife for a young doctor, but I was willing to bet he would love all of it, good or bad.

"Just one more hurdle now," Owens said slowly. "Another shock. I really hate to tell her, but I suppose I will have to fairly soon."

I wondered, briefly, if Owens had been thinking the same thoughts I had been thinking, doing the same wondering about a number of minor items that didn't fit into the glib pattern I had built for them. For his sake, I hoped not. I raised my eyebrows.

Owens indicated old Mr. Prince's room. "He won't last long now," he said. "Oh, he looks fine and he's spryer than ever, but it's all been too much. His heart will stop one day soon. One day—hell, any hour. Just like that." Owens snapped his fingers in the quiet hallway. "I'll have to warn her to be ready, but I'll put it off as long as I can."

I nodded noncommittally. "Best thing, I suppose." I looked at Owens' tense, tired face, his thin, restive hands. "Tell me something, Doc," I said in a tone I tried to make casual. "Did you touch anything in the studio last Friday when you saw The Prince's body?"

Owens stared at me. His eyes blinked once as he tried to focus his attention on the new subject. He shook his head slowly. "No. That is, nothing but the old man. I moved him into his bedroom."

"You didn't . . . ah, tidy up anything?"

Owens said he had touched nothing. His eyes measured me carefully. I brought a grin to my face and shrugged as if I had asked the question from vague curiosity.

Martha's voice reached us in a plaintive note, calling for Owens. He shook hands hurriedly and went back to the drawing-room, leaving me in the hall, opposite the old man's room.

I should have gone away. It wasn't any longer my business—checking pieces that didn't fit the pattern.

I walked slowly to the front door, opened it and stood there. I breathed deeply of the cold clean air and then closed the door again with an audible click. I walked back the way I had come, back to the old man's room, twisted the knob cautiously, leaning my weight away from the lock. The knob turned silently and I went in.

CHAPTER TWENTY-TWO

THE old man was huddled in a baroque tapestry chair beside his huge tester bed. He looked up when I closed the door, staring at me with a shallow concentration, smiling slowly as recognition came. He closed the book and nodded with great dignity.

"It's nice to see you again, Mr. Wilde," he said in a soft thin voice. "I don't have nearly enough visitors these days."

"I want to talk to you, Mr. Prince," I said. "I'll take just a few minutes. I think it's fairly important—for both of us."

His frail eyelids raised briefly and his wide-domed forehead wrinkled. He waited for me to explain.

"Just one thing first, Mr. Prince. This is the one really important thing. Did you know that Magee had been arrested for your son's murder?"

His pale gold face tensed and his chin came up fiercely. "I did not, sir. And if he has . . ."

"I know," I said, interrupting him. "That's what I thought. You would have confessed if anyone had bothered to tell you Magee had been arrested."

For a moment of tense silence the old man's eyes watched me carefully.

Then I leaned forward and spoke as gently as I could. "Now listen to me, Mr. Prince. Magee is out of it. He has an alibi. But this afternoon a woman committed suicide in a little hotel down in The Bend. She killed Manny Brenner. There isn't any doubt about it. She left a note confessing. From the wording of the note the police assume that she also confessed to killing The Prince."

I straightened. "I want to get this said first off, Mr. Prince. The case is closed. The confessed murderess—and she is a murderess—is dead by her own hand. The case is closed from here on out, amen."

"I see," he said, almost absently. "Yes, now I see. Thank you for coming to me in this fashion. Can you tell me about it?"

"Your son was a famous man, Mr. Prince. He couldn't die quietly and unnoticed. The public wanted to see his killer caught and punished. The police had to furnish a killer and furnish him quickly. They got Magee. For reasons I won't go into right now, Magee had a good motive for the killing . . ."

"He was preparing to blackmail my son," the old man said, staring with great detachment over my head.

I looked at him. "You do get around. I thought that was a secret."

"My son told me," he said quietly. "He told me everything."

"Yeah, I guess he did," I said. "You may know this, too, but in case you don't, I can tell you that we have definite proof that there isn't anything to his claim."

"Of course not," the old man said firmly.

"But Magee had a confederate in the deal with him. His wife, a woman who called herself Arabella Joslin, Bella Joe, Bertha Johnson and probably a lot of other

234

names. You may have met her."

The old man smiled, a weak, precarious, old man's smile. "I thought her . . . disagreeable."

I seconded that.

"We found her down in The Bend, dead. She shot herself. She wrote a note saying she was sorry she had killed Manny Brenner. She said something in the note about being sorry about The Prince and asking whoever found her to tell you she hadn't meant to hurt him. The police regard that as a confession to The Prince's killing."

The old man folded his thin bloodless hands in his lap. "But you don't regard that confession as a useful solution, Mr. Wilde?"

"You're wrong there, Mr. Prince," I said readily. "I think it's a fine solution. I wouldn't want you to think otherwise."

He focused inwardly, looking at something that wasn't for me. His eyes fixed on me blankly, staring down a long corridor of time.

"You are very wise for a man of your years, Mr. Wilde, and very kind. I am grateful to you. As you remarked, I did not know that anyone had been charged with the responsibility for my son's death. I am now an old man and my body will not endure much strain. I am always forgetting that and attempting things that are beyond my strength. So it was on the day my son . . . died. I felt rather sure, probably because my granddaughter and her young man worked hard to convince me, that the whole affair was over and that there was no need to speak of it again. That was wrong of me. But I do not think it was cowardice, Mr. Wilde. I should not like to think that. Pride, possibly," he said with sudden fierceness, "which can often be just as damaging as cowardice."

I didn't speak.

"I suppose you wonder why it happened," he said after a long pause.

"No." I shook my head. "I think I know, Mr. Prince."

He looked at me sharply, his high-beaked nose seeming to jut more keenly from his tense face. He nodded slowly. "Yes. Yes, I think you might," he said quietly. His eyes fixed upon his wrinkled pale hands. He made a tight double fist and pounded it slowly against his knee. "It was such a waste," he murmured. "Such a waste. Harold Morton was a great man. All his people earned a little peace, a little pride, from his greatness. It would not be fitting for him to leave his living days in an unseemly fashion."

"No," I agreed hoarsely. I stared at the old man, sitting still and alone in his great age, his great sureness. There was no arrogance, no pity and certainly no fear in him. He was a little frightening.

"You did not know that it was quite accidental, Mr. Wilde, that I should kill my son?"

I said slowly, "I wanted you to tell me."

He smiled faintly. "I keep giving you credit for omniscience." He looked at me, remotely amused. "It was just after that woman left the house that I shot Harold Morton. It was quite accidental."

"You mean the Joslin woman?" I asked quickly. "Then she really *was* here?"

"Yes," the old man said. "First Magee, then the woman. Harold Morton had a bitter disagreement with

Magee. He told me just the mere outline of Magee's scheme. I was trying to calm him, make him rest. I didn't listen very closely. Just shortly after that Mr. Gilman, his agent, telephoned and he and Harold Morton had a pleasant chat. I thought he would be all right then, but the woman came and Harold Morton became . . . excited. I'm afraid he had been drinking too much just then. And, of course, he was not well. He was in terrible pain. The growth in his head was exerting considerable pressure." The old man looked up dimly. "I'm sure in the course of your investigations you learned about my son's illness?"

I nodded and he went on.

"We had kept it a secret, but somehow Magee found out about it. In any event, the woman's entrance was enough to enrage Harold Morton. Just the sight of her and Harold Morton reached for her. He staggered when he got up and the woman ran out the window the way she had come. Harold Morton fell against the bookcase and he must have remembered his pistol which was kept there. He took it out. I don't know whether he intended to shoot the woman or not. He was in awful pain and completely irrational just then. I struggled with him for the pistol. I had it in my hand and then it went off. He was killed."

The old man's voice was flat, without tone or spirit. He was reciting facts. "I saw that he was dead, of course. I straightened up the room a little—things had been turned over and broken in the struggle. I was in a rather distracted condition myself, as you may imagine. It was a few minutes before I thought of calling anyone. I was going to the telephone to call the police, and then my old man's body betrayed me." He sighed heavily and looked down at his thin wrinkled fingers with distaste. "The rest you know," he said in a clearer tone, "though I can't imagine how you do know so much."

"It wasn't magic, Mr. Prince," I said. "I didn't start out by thinking of your son's death. I was looking for the Joslin woman and that was all I was interested in. But when I found an alibi for Magee, covering the time of The Prince's death, I did begin to worry.

"Joslin's confession was clear enough about Manny Brenner's death, but it didn't make sense to me as far as The Prince was concerned. That is, it didn't make a psychological pattern. I don't think the police are going to bother with it, but what disturbed me was the motive for her suicide. No matter what motive you think of first you are going to come back to fear—and possibly remorse. Both figure strongly in her note. She wasn't really a killer. She didn't run away when The Prince was killed. And she certainly wasn't frightened or remorseful when I saw her. But after Manny's death she did run. She hid, and then she became frightened enough, or sorry enough, to kill herself. That doesn't add up to a pattern, any way you look at it. So I began thinking about it on the way out here. I might add, it's just about the first thinking I've done on this case.

"First, I wondered if we hadn't got the wrong slant on the matter of Magee's claim against The Prince's music. Maybe Magee and Joslin never intended to make their pitch while The Prince was still alive. They put the evidence together, such as it was, to give the impression they were prepared to move right away, but Magee knew The Prince was ill, remember. And he would have known that no matter how good a case he could frame, The Prince would be able to produce plenty of evidence to support his ownership. Evidence that no one else could know about. That's what makes me fairly sure that Magee and Joslin planned to make their charges the minute The Prince was dead. That way their claim would look fairly hefty and it might scare the heirs and assigns into a pay-off.

"All that points up something critical. If Magee and Joslin rigged their deal to operate after he was dead, something went wrong with their plans. My guess is that The Prince got wind of it somehow, braced Magee last Friday and booted him out. Now, both of them still had a motive for killing him, but it wasn't so strong as we had thought. The Prince couldn't do anything to them for attempted blackmail unless he had their documents. All Magee had to do to stay clear was to destroy or hide them. I'll bet that's what he was going to do when the cops came for him Friday. He must have seen them coming and thought The Prince was having him picked up for blackmail. So he snatched the load of papers and went tearing off to get rid of them.

"Now, all that doesn't change much, but it does indicate that our original emphasis was wrong. We were looking at those documents Magee had and seeing in them the motive. Just for a change, I tried to think about the case, leaving Magee and his papers out of it.

"A few things stood out then. I remembered the spilled cigarette butts in the studio when your son was found there. And the broken brandy bottle and glass here in your room. The bottle in your room, the cigarette butts in the studio.

"I didn't think much about that at first, but after a while I came back to it. You don't drink. So why was the bottle in your room?"

The old man didn't answer. I went on. "It isn't much of a fact, as I said, but think about it. In your room we find a broken bottle and glass where it obviously doesn't belong. In the studio we find a dead man with a lot of alcohol in his system. By any kind of logic the two go together. Either the man or the bottle was moved."

He made no attempt to confirm or deny. I took it another step. "The Prince was a chain smoker as well as a drinker. No chain smoker lasts long without a cigarette and especially not when he's drinking. I knew The Prince didn't smoke in here. I'd been told you have a toxic reaction to cigarette smoke. That points to the conclusion that he didn't do his drinking here, either.

"My guess was that the bottle came from the studio, that it was broken when it hit the tile floor, during the scuffle. Somebody cleaned it up and moved the debris into your room."

The old man smiled faintly and barely nodded. I went on.

"Well, what would it indicate if we assume the bottle had been moved? That somebody was covering up something. The only really important element to be covered up was The Prince's death—or the manner of his death.

"Who was in the house to move the bottle? The only people I knew about were you, the cook and Owens. The cook was the first one in here after you collapsed, but she had no motive for killing The Prince or for

240

hiding evidence. And she stayed with you and Owens all the time until the police came. That puts Owens out of the running—he couldn't have moved anything without her seeing it. That leaves only you. You were unconscious when Owens got here, but no one could be sure what you had been doing before you fainted.

"That still left a lot of items to cover. You were the best prospect as far as that bottle was concerned, but what motive could you have for killing your son? And why would you move that damn bottle anyway? What difference did it make where the cops found it?

"Taking the second question first was the way I got both answers. The only reason for moving the bottle was to hide the fact that The Prince had been drinking heavily. Whoever moved it knew The Prince was dead and knew the house would be invaded by newspapermen the moment the body was found. You couldn't hope to hide The Prince's drinking from the police, a routine autopsy would show the liquor in him. But you might—and did—hide it from the public.

"That's all the bottle moving could mean. The open french window took care of the brandy fumes. With the bottle in your room, a little brandy from the glass spilled around and your bedside table kicked over, anyone would think you had broken it when you heard the shot that killed your son.

"That's the point that really pinned it on you. Because no one in this case gave a solitary damn about your son's reputation except you. Martha hated her father just then, she wouldn't have hidden anything damaging about him. The cook wouldn't think about it and Owens didn't have a chance to do anything. You were the only person in this house who would be worried about The Prince's reputation."

He was silent, waiting.

"I knew The Prince's medical history by then and I saw that his illness was probably the answer. The cumulative effect of that tumor might have thrown him off his trolley any time—any time at all. He was under great emotional strain the day he was killed. Physically, he was in bad shape. And he was ten miles from being sober." I hesitated before adding those facts to their total. But The Prince's father already knew it, of course. "If anyone was going to do any killing that day I would have picked The Prince himself. But he was dead—he hadn't killed anyone."

The old man drew a deep, almost sobbing breath. I hated saying what I had to say.

"But I think in the state he was in he might have tried—and you would have tried to stop him. I don't think you meant to stop him for good. I don't think you meant to create any mystery about his death. But you would—and I think you did—try to hide anything that made your son look like something less than The Prince. Because, being The Prince, he wasn't just your son. He was a symbol of pride to his people."

I tried to smile at him. My face was tight and the skin felt stretched.

"I suppose you came out of your faint here in your bed and everyone told you that it was all right and not to do any thinking about it. Was that why you didn't speak up then?"

He nodded wearily. His fragile eyelids fell. A tentative pulse throbbed erratically in his temple. "I wanted to be sure that no one would say my son had committed suicide. That wouldn't do either. Owens told me that wouldn't happen and he promised to keep me informed. Apparently he didn't keep his word. I asked Martha to send young Randolph Greene in to see me. I knew I could depend on him to tell me everything. But Doctor Owens wouldn't permit that. But just in case someone should ever be blamed, in case I should die too soon, I wrote it all out. An old man is compelled to consider such things." His voice trembled to a full stop and I could see that he was slowly going to sleep. I had to delay that for a moment.

I tapped his shoulder sharply and his eyes opened just a bare crack.

"Where is that statement, Mr. Prince? The one you just mentioned?" I spoke harshly, driving the words through his drowsiness.

"Table . . . bed," he said weakly. His eyes closed again and his hands slowly relaxed in his lap.

His quiet wheezy breathing followed me to the bed. The table was low and wide. It was the same table the old man had knocked over after The Prince's death. It had a locked compartment. I didn't want to wake the old man again to get his key. It was an ordinary lock, like a good many others. The thinnest key on my key ring took care of it. There was just one thing in the compartment, a folded piece of sheet music, the piano part for *Red Devil Blues*. The back of the sheet had no printing and it was there that the old man had written his statement, in a frail copper-plate hand-writing that looked like spiderwebs.

I read only enough to be sure it was the statement I

wanted. I folded it again and looked toward the old man. He was slumped peacefully in his chair, his thin lips partially open, breathing heavily. I thought of several things I wanted to ask him about, things he might be able to tell me. But he probably wouldn't tell me anyway, once he saw where the answers might lead.

There was the problem of the gun. Originally, the police had assumed that Magee had worn gloves when he shot The Prince. Now they would assume that Arabella Joslin had worn gloves. That settled it for the police, but not for me. I knew that the old man had held that gun and pulled the trigger. The gun should have been covered with prints.

Then there was the anonymous phone call someone had made to me, and the anonymous visitor. And the heavy sap that slammed down on my head. All were supposed to make me withdraw from the case and crawl under the bed. The old man wasn't responsible for those things.

I found myself staring toward the hall door. The door that led toward the drawing-room where Martha Prince and Doctor Owens were sitting. I could think of a good answer to fill in all the gaps, but I didn't really want to find out. The police file was closed and they must have known there were some gaps they would never fill in. I was ready to close my file with the story just as it stood right then.

I scooped my hat from the floor and shoved it on my head. I doubled the old man's statement in my hand. It was still there when I pushed open the door leading to the studio. The studio with the private entrance, the secret way in and out for people with secrets. I walked through, turning to ease the door shut carefully.

I was half-turned when I saw him. I completed my movement and stood very still. His gun had a wide bore that seemed large enough for me to stick my head in. My .38 felt heavy and useless in my shoulder holster and the old man's statement in my hand seemed as broad as a blanket and just as noticeable. The painful ache in the back of my head began to throb again.

Randolph Greene was leaning tensely against one of The Prince's pianos, close to the door where he could have heard everything we had said in the old man's room. He held his revolver loosely, hardly pointing it at me. His eyes were fixed, his mouth hard and determined. The dark young sneer was gone just now, but I wasn't sure that meant anything. I was careful not to move.

Even in the warm room, with my heavy coat on, I could feel a thin edge of iciness along my spine. Here was the heroic situation. Here was the moment to bring one agile foot up crisply and boot the pistol out the window. I didn't think my knees were firm enough to try it. Just then all I could see was a large revolver with pale lead slugs in all the chambers.

"You're lucky, Wilde," Greene said softly. His voice barely carried to me. "I thought you were going to talk a little rougher in there." He looked behind me to the old man's room. "I was waiting for you to accuse him of murder. You wouldn't have left the house alive if you had."

I believed him.

"I've been listening to you for the past hour. First in the drawing-room and now here. You're a smart man,

245

Wilde. You're lucky."

I let my pent-up breath dribble out slowly. I took several deep gulps at fresh air. The air had a brisk cleanliness I hadn't noticed before.

"There's just one thing left now," Greene whispered. His gun indicated the statement I held. "You don't leave with that."

I nodded once. I walked slowly down the long studio to a smoking stand. Greene trailed warily behind me, keeping just far enough away from me. I picked up a silver table lighter, struck it and held the paper above the flame. We watched the paper catch fire.

There was a momentary flicker in Greene's eyes, an obvious relaxing. Just the faint possibility of an idea came to me at first. Only the first fine edge, but it worked like a knife on stretched fabric, splitting a sudden long seam that let the light pour through. I knew then why Greene had been waiting for me. I knew what he was afraid of.

"You thought he murdered his son," I said thickly.

Greene's eyes were held by the slowly moving flame that crawled along the paper in my hand. His head moved up and down.

"You were the one who wiped off the gun. You phoned me, trying to scare me off the case. And when that didn't work, you tried a club. And you sent a hired bully-boy down to see what I was doing." Greene didn't look up. "I suppose you were here earlier today and heard me say I was going downtown. It wouldn't have taken much to beat me there and ambush me in my office."

Greene's harsh young face rose. He stared at me tensely. "I was wrong about you, Wilde," he said. "I can see that now. I did try to make you quit investigating the case, but I didn't hire anyone to help me. I was in the house when The Prince was killed and I saw the old man cleaning up the room. I'd been working in the library and everyone had forgotten I was there. When the old man collapsed, I wiped off the gun. I was going to move him back to his room, but I heard someone coming and I had to get out. I really thought he had killed him."

I nodded slowly. It all made a crazy-quilt pattern. I figured the short gunman who visited me was probably one of Hollie Gray's hired hands, since he didn't belong to Greene. That was something I'd have to look into later on.

I turned the burning paper as the flame reached my fingers. The final triangle I dropped. We watched it burn on its way to the floor. Only a whisper of warm ash hit the pale gray tiles. I stepped on the ash.

"You're a fool, Greene," I said slowly. "You damned near ruined these people with your games."

"He was my friend," Greene said fiercely. "He's a nigger, Mr. Wilde. How much chance would *any* nigger get?"

I rubbed my eyes wearily. "The Prince was Negro, too." I said heavily. "He never tried to hide behind it."

I let it go at that. Greene was in no condition for listening and I didn't want to try to break through his bitterness.

"Now what?" he asked tightly.

"Now nothing," I said evenly. "It's over. Throw away that gun and forget about it. Forget about all of it."

He agreed soberly. His eyes were bewildered. For

that moment he was young again. The dark bitter tension left his face. "You're all right, Wilde," he said tonelessly. "I suppose I owe you an apology."

"I'm not the one you should apologize to," I said bluntly. I shoved him aside and walked toward the french windows. I pushed down a catch, opened the glass door and stepped out into the snow-packed driveway. I walked to the street without looking back. I heard the window close with a brittle sound.

I got into my car, started it as quickly as I could and drove away from there.

The early winter darkness was working slowly along the streets, lighting everything with a green-tinged air of decay. I drove slowly on the icy pavement, trying not to think of a dying old man who had seen his son die.

It was an accident, the old man said. I didn't argue about it when he told me and I didn't have any real reason to question it now. But the questions that hang on in the back of your brain don't depend upon reason. The Prince had been a very sick man for years. His father could see the change in him and guess what would happen to his son's work if it went on much longer. The old man's pride wouldn't let him watch his son gradually slipping away from his peak. Maybe the old man didn't mean to kill his son. I wouldn't want to guess about it. But I've heard of "accident-prone" people, the ones who crack a bone every time they slip on the sidewalk. The psychiatric wizards say those people have a compulsion toward accidents, something that resembles the death wish that everyone has felt at some time or other. I wouldn't say The Prince's father fitted into that sort of picture. Not exactly. All I could really be sure of was that the old man had pulled the trigger. He was the only man who could explain his action.

The law could require a due penalty. If the law wanted to, that was up to the law. I knew something of what had happened. I also knew that I couldn't prove a word of it and no policeman was likely to be interested in another version of a case that he considered solved.

As for me, I was sure that no decision, no action from society could punish the old man more than he had been punished. The law requires death, sometimes, when a man has been killed. But death would come quite soon enough for old Mr. Prince, much sooner than the law could bring it. The only difference was that he would die in a huge carved ebony bed that had been designed for a nobleman. He would die with no happiness, but a fierce and determined pride. His son had been The Prince.

There is an extensive list of NO EXIT PRESS crime titles to choose from. All the books can be obtained from Oldcastle Books Ltd, 18 Coleswood Road, Harpenden, Herts AL5 1EQ by sending a cheque/P.O. (or quoting your credit card number and expiry date) for the appropriate amount + 10% as a contribution to Postage & Packing.

Alternatively, you can send for FREE details of the NO EXIT PRESS CRIME BOOK CLUB, which includes many special offers on NO EXIT PRESS titles and full information on forthcoming books. Please write clearly stating your full name and address.

NO EXIT PRESS Vintage Crime

Classic crime novels by the contemporaries of Chandler & Hammett that typify the hard-boiled heyday of American crime fiction.

FAST ONE — Paul Cain £3.95pb, £9.95hb

Possibly the toughest, tough-guy story ever written. Set in depression Los Angeles, it has a surreal quality that is positively hypnotic. It is the saga of gunman-gambler Gerry Kells and his dipsomaniacal lover, S Granquist (she has no first name), who rearrange the L.A. underworld and disappear in an explosive climax that matches their first appearance. The pace is incredible and the complex plot, with its twists and turns, defies summary.

SEVEN SLAYERS — Paul Cain £3.99pb, £9.95hb

A superb collection of seven stories about seven star crossed killers and the sole follow up to the very successful Fast One. Peopled by racketeers, con men, dope pushers, private detectives, cops, newspapermen and women of some virtue or none at all. Seven Slayers is as intense a 'noir' portrait of depression era America as those painted by Horace McCoy and James M Cain.

THE DEAD DON'T CARE — Jonathan Latimer £3.95pb, £9.95hb

Meet Bill Crane, the hard-boiled P.I., and his two sidekicks, O'Malley and Doc Williams. The locale of the cyclonic action is a large Florida estate near Miami. A varied cast includes a former tragic actress turned dipso, a gigolo, a 'Babe' from Minsky's, a broken down welterweight and an exotic Mayan dancer. Kidnapping and murder give the final shake to the cocktail and provide an explosive and shocking climax.

THE LADY IN THE MORGUE — Jonathan Latimer £3.99pb, £9.95hb

Crime was on the up. People sang of Ding-Dong Daddy, skirts were long and lives were short, violin cases mostly sported machine guns. Bill Crane thought it was a pretty wonderful time. He was in the Chicago morgue at the height of summer, trying to cool off and learn the identity of its most beautiful inmate. So-called Alice Ross had been found hanging, absolutely naked, in the room of a honky tonk hotel. His orders were to find out who she really was. Alice was stolen from her slab that night! Thus began the crazy hunt for a body and a name, through lousy hotels, dancehalls and penthouses, with occasional side trips to bed to bar to blonde and back again.

MURDER IN THE MADHOUSE — Jonathan Latimer £3.99pb, £9.95hb

Hard drinking, hard living Bill Crane in his first case has himself committed incognito to a private sanitarium for the mentally insane to protect rich, little Ms Van Camp. Terror, violence and sudden death follow when a patient is found strangled with a bathrobe cord. The murderer strikes again but makes a fatal error in killing pleasant little mute, Mr Penny. The local police doubt Crane is a bonafide detective and believe he is suffering from delusions, the non-alcoholic kind. Despite all this, Crane breaks the case in a final scene of real dramatic fury.

HEADED FOR A HEARSE — Jonathan Latimer £3.99pb, £9.95hb

Death row, Chicago county jail. Robert Westland, convicted of his wife's murder, is six days from the 'chair'. What seems an iron clad case against Westland begins to fall apart as Bill Crane races against time to investigate the background of the major players and prove Westland's innocence. Westland's two brokerage partners; his hard drinking, hard riding cousin; enigmatic and exotic Ms Brentino; the amiable Ms Hogan; a secretive clerk; a tight-lipped valet and a dipso widow all have plenty to explain. Aided by a lime squeezer, a quart of whisky, a monkey wrench, a taxi cab, a stop watch and a deep sea diver, Crane cracks the case in this locked room classic.

NO EXIT PRESS Contemporary Crime

A companion to Vintage Crime in the popular pocket book format that highlights both the classic and exciting new books from the past twenty years of American Crime Fiction. Contemporary Crime will feature in 1989 such titles as Day of the Ram by William Campbell Gault, Ask the Right Question by Michael Z Lewin, Act of Fear by Michael Collins, Dead Ringer and Castles Burning by Arthur Lyons all costing just £2.99.

HARD TRADE — Arthur Lyons £2.99pb

LA's most renowned detective, Jacob Asch is on the street once more in a startling tale of Californian political corruption. A troubled woman hires Asch to uncover the truth about the man she is to marry. When Asch discovers the man is gay and the woman is run down on her way to a hastily called meeting with Asch, it becomes clear something big is at stake. Serious money real estate schemes, the seamy side of LA gay life and a murder frame involve Asch in a major political scandal that costs him his licence and nearly his life.

THE KILLING FLOOR — Arthur Lyons £2.99pb

David Fein, owner of Supreme Packing, a slaughterhouse in a grimy little Californian town had a problem . . . he was a compulsive gambler. First he couldn't cover his losses from the takings so he got a loan and went into debt. By the time he took in Tortorello, a clean cut Harvard type but with 'Family' connections he was in big trouble. Now he had been missing for 4 days and his wife was frantic. Jake Bloom, old family friend puts her in touch with Jacob Asch, who figures Fein is on a bender or in the sack with another woman — he's heard and seen it all before. But that's before he finds a body on the killing floor.

NO EXIT PRESS Contemporary Crime